CW00537655

Praise for Jane Lovering's *Slightly Foxed*

"[A] plus for me is [Alys]... it's nice to read about a heroine of [36] who's still attracting attention from men... I like that she faces some harsh truths about herself and goes into the final relationship with open eyes. ...I love Grainger, the grouchy curmudgeon in fur, and Casper the kitten stand-in for tissues... The humor had me in stitches... [and] I delighted in the sharp descriptions."

~ *Jayne, Dear Author*

Look for these titles by
Jane Lovering

Now Available:

Reversing Over Liberace

Slightly Foxed

Jane Lovering

A SAMHAIN PUBLISHING, LTD. publication.

Samhain Publishing, Ltd.
577 Mulberry Street, Suite 1520
Macon, GA 31201
www.samhainpublishing.com

Slightly Foxed
Copyright © 2009 by Jane Lovering
Print ISBN: 978-1-60504-309-8
Digital ISBN: 1-60504-129-7

Editing by Anne Scott
Cover by Natalie Winters

This book is a work of fiction. The names, characters, places, and incidents are products of the writer's imagination or have been used fictitiously and are not to be construed as real. Any resemblance to persons, living or dead, actual events, locale or organizations is entirely coincidental.

All Rights Are Reserved. No part of this book may be used or reproduced in any manner whatsoever without written permission, except in the case of brief quotations embodied in critical articles and reviews.

First Samhain Publishing, Ltd. electronic publication: August 2008
First Samhain Publishing, Ltd. print publication: June 2009

Dedication

To my father, James Playle Lovering, 1928-2008.

A man who loved books.

Chapter One

I fell in love, in the bath, with a man who had been dead for a century.

Typical for me, this inclination towards unsuitable men. This particular one was the author of a poetry collection, a faded dowager of a paperback grown floppy with mildew and bent-paged with waiting to be read. How much more unsuitable could you get, I mean—dead? Even for me, that was a first.

I let the book drop across my chest and stared up at the damp patch on the wall of the tiny, unventilated bathroom, which formed the exact shape of the land mass of Sweden. Or, to the more uncultured eye, a limp willy. I could measure the length of time I had been wallowing in the scummy water by the increasingly priapic nature of that spreading stain, which was presently set to annex Finland. Or star on Channel Five.

"Mum!" A shoulder banged against the door which was only held shut by the weight of the laundry basket propped against it. The lock had been wrenched from the woodwork by Grainger in his one evening of frenzied kittenhood, and never replaced. "What are you doing in there? On second thoughts, don't tell me, I've just eaten."

Slowly I rose from the grimy depths. "Sorry, Florence, did you want the bathroom?" A sixteen-year-old girl with a healthy social life? Does, as the saying went in our literary household, toyevsky?

"Nah. I'm just telling you I'm off to Dad's." A small silence. "Okay?"

I bit my lip. "I wish you'd told me earlier that you were going over there."

"Well I've told you now. I'm staying over. I'll get Piers to drop me at school in the morning, right?"

My fingers tightened on the bath's crumbling enamel edge, but the wetness of my palm made it slither with a sound identical to a tremendous fart.

"I'll take that as a 'yes' then."

I sighed, more deeply than I had meant to. In consequence, the waters lapped at the edges of my new love, who lay upon my bosom like a suitor to whose charms the lady has finally succumbed. "Do you have money for..." slam went the front door, "...the bus?" Duty bound as a parent to finish my sentence so that at least I could say, "I told you so," even though she might not have been listening at the time. Or, even, present.

I stared down the length of my body at the too-white flesh. I was still reasonably trim "for my age", as Florence would no doubt have pointed out. Thirty-six isn't old, is it? Not these days anyway. But it *is* old enough for outlying regions to start bearing a slight resemblance to mascarpone cheese and having a distressing tendency to go their own way, i.e. downwards. To distract myself from the uncomfortable thought that my daughter would, as soon as she arrived at her father's house, be comparing my loose shape to her stepmother's expense-account-gym-membership litheness, I unpeeled the book from my chest and flipped it open again.

The new object of my affection (I wondered how he would have felt, coming runner-up to such luminaries as Florence, our psychotic cat, Grainger, and Johnny Depp) was a man called Theo Wood. Underneath the mould and the water creasing, his pages were virginal and the spine was uncracked as though the book had never been opened. I could imagine him, all those years ago, crouched over candlelight, pouring his never-to-be-read soul out onto the pages of a notebook. Dark eyes fixed on the page, (he'd have deep, poetic eyes of course) hand rubbing uneven stubble in an attempt to conjure the words onto the paper. But despite its historical nature, this book was reasonably new, privately published two years previously. Had someone discovered the poems lying in a dust-haunted attic and decided to make a few quid out of the current vogue for arrhythmic autobiographia?

At the back of the book, almost as though unimportant, came the picture. Black and white, befitting a man born, the biography informed me, in 1850. I shifted my weight to allow the spindly light from the forty-watt bulb access to the pages and was confronted by a thin face, high-cheekboned, with eyes of such depth and substance that I felt exposed being naked in front of his gaze. Dark rumpled attractiveness mingled with a distant stare, making him look almost suicidally creative and also slightly short sighted. He also seemed to be wearing a Marks and Spencer pullover, which was impossible.

I laid the book face down on a towel so as not to cause further damage to the already leprous pages. After all, I had only started reading it in order to find out where best to shelve it. I suspected that Florence would have credited my work with far more dignity had I worked in WH Smith. But it paid the bills and the rent on our dingy little flat in an area which was up and coming in much the same way as an exploding muckheap. I got myself out of the bath, careful not to drip on Theo, and had scuffled my way into the kitchen, when there was a knock at the door.

"Alys?" There in the hallway stood Simon, blond and aristocratic to the point of looking as though he'd been built out of teeth. "I wasn't sure of the address."

In the five years I'd worked for him, Simon had never shown any desire to take our employer/employee relationship further than the local book auction. He also suffered from borderline agoraphobia, which meant that on unfamiliar territory he was liable to collapse hyperventilating. I was therefore so astonished to see him on my doorstep that I nearly dropped my towel.

"Come in. I was just..."

"Having a bath?" Simon's expression was gradually returning to its usual resting state of benevolent arrogance. "I'm sorry to have to come over like this on your day off and everything but—we've got a problem."

We were only "we" when there was a problem. When things went well, Webbe's was a very them-and-us establishment, with Simon being the us, and myself and my coworker Jacinta being the opposition. We didn't really mind and got our revenge in subtle ways, quite a few of them revolving around Simon's HobNobs.

"It must be a big problem, to bring you all the way out here." I readjusted the towel to cover as much of me as possible. Although I'd spent the better part of the last five years trying to determine in which direction his sexual proclivities lay, now was not the time to discover Simon's compass definitely pointed north. "Sit down a moment while I get dressed."

I left him staring at the only chair in the room still decently covered in its original upholstery rather than shrouded in a dubious throw. The reason he was staring rather than sitting was that this chair was occupied by Grainger, a cat whose reputation spread further than his discarded coat, and stuck every bit as hard. He was the only cat I'd ever met who slept with a snarl on his face to avoid having to change his expression on waking. By the time I returned, dressed and— Simon's sexual leanings notwithstanding—heavily coated in mascara, Simon was resting one buttock carefully along the edge of the chair and trying to look comfortable.

"Right. What is this problem we have?" I cleared a pile of Florence's schoolbooks off the sofa to enable me to sit opposite Simon.

"Do you remember my buying in a stack from an auction down in Exeter?"

I nodded. The wondrous Theo had been one of them.

"Well, I had a call this morning from a lady who'd traced us through the auction records. Apparently they belonged to some uncle who died and the books had been promised to her."

"So? Send them to her." I coughed to cover the sound of the rustling as I kicked Theo underneath Florence's essays.

"Ah. You see, there's the problem. You've already shelved most of them and...ah...I..." Simon was not a man to come out and admit that he didn't know how his own shelving system worked. He leaned forward earnestly and his unsupported buttock trembled with tension. I knew because I was watching. Okay I may not currently be a player, but I can still appreciate good action on the field. "It's quite urgent actually, Alys. She wants to pick the books up in the morning. Is there any chance you could come in today and search them out for me?"

"Double time," I said firmly, as though I'd been planning an evening filled with debauched delights instead of *Stargate SG-1* and a Walnut Whip.

"Time and a half."

"Give me a lift?"

"And I'll run you back."

I was about to agree, as long as he threw in lunch, when the telephone rang making all of us jump, including Grainger.

"Alys? It's Piers." Familiar, slightly American vowels, burnished with the sandpaper of good education, as the voice of my ex-husband's stepson drifted down the telephone line. "Has

Florrie left yet?"

"About twenty minutes ago. Why?"

"Alasdair and Ma wanted me to pick her up and bring her over to Richmond. We're going out to lunch with some friends. Thought it would be better if she came straight there."

"She's got her mobile with her, why don't you give her a call?"

There was a bit of a pause. "I kinda thought she might still be home."

"Sorry, no. Goodbye. Oh, and Piers, please don't let her be late for school tomorrow, she's got an exam," I finished lamely, suddenly realising that Florence's GCSE textbooks were spread over the floor in front of me.

"Sure." There was another long pause, as though Piers wanted to say something else but wasn't certain how, which was most unlike him. At twenty-one he already possessed more than his fair share of self-confidence, good looks and credit cards. "Well. Okay, yeah. Bye."

"Goodbye," I said again. "Sorry, Simon. Family stuff."

"Shall we go then?" Simon sounded slightly breathless, and when he turned politely to open the door for me, I saw why. Grainger had stapled himself to the back of Simon's Paul Smith shirt and was hanging between his shoulder blades like an ill-tempered rucksack with halitosis.

Chapter Two

Webbe's stood at the tail end of one of York's most popular tourist streets, where all the shops were so old and bent together that they looked like a pensioner's outing. The bookshop's walls hung unwillingly towards its next-door neighbour, an antique shop which sold overpolished copper warming pans, and with whose owner Simon carried on a viciously polite war of attrition over pavement space. The entire area was so self-consciously historic that I felt I should tint myself sepia just to work there.

As soon as he had unlocked the door, Simon retired to his cubbyhole at the back of the shop. I used his ducking out to hasten my way through the shelves and pick out all the books from the list. They were a diverse bunch, a couple of very nice illustrated Dickens, two books of collected maps, a biography of Margaret Thatcher and a very dog-eared copy of a Jilly Cooper novel minus the back cover. Theo Wood remained securely underneath my sofa. I planned to send him on in a couple of days, once I'd fully appreciated him. With apologies, of course.

Finding the books took me about ten minutes. When I put my head around the edge of the cubbyhole, Simon was sitting cross legged in his armchair, engrossed in the Classic Serial, and waved me away peremptorily with one finger. Whilst I would quite like to have been invited into the inner sanctum with its own kettle and seemingly endless supply of chocolate

HobNobs to listen to *The Mill on the Floss*, part of me was glad of the fully paid chance to ring Florence to check whether or not Piers had caught up with her.

Florence answered, breathless.

"Hello, darling. Did Piers manage to intercept you all right?"

"Yeah, sure. We're in Richmond having lunch by the river, looking at a car that Piers wants to buy."

Bloody Piers, I thought, teeth gritted ever so slightly. "Is it a nice car?"

"Not bad. Porsche 911. Horrible colour though."

"Oh," I said inadequately. "Oh dear. So"—desperate to keep any kind of dialogue going with my daughter—"he might not buy it then?"

Florence broke into hysterical giggles. "Yeah, right! Like there's any such thing as a bad Porsche. He'll have it resprayed. What did you call me for? Only Dad wants me to give a hand with the drinks."

"Just to check whether you wanted to come back and pick up your revision stuff?" I tried to keep it light, only a question, but Florence had the teenage ability to pick an insult out of a shopping list.

"For God's sake. Let me enjoy my Sunday in peace for once without nagging on about those bloody exams!" She turned off her phone abruptly. I could just imagine her nail digging into the rubberised button, wishing it was my neck.

"Children. Such a joy," I muttered.

"Florence is not being loveable today?"

I jumped. "God, Jace. How do you manage to creep up on me in those shoes?" Jacinta simply looked smug. "Why are you here? Does no one ever take a day off except for me?"

"I was coming past and I saw that lights are on. I am bored so in I come."

"Well, come in, don't stand in the doorway. It's like a total eclipse." Jace beamed at me again and sashayed into the shop. Despite standing six foot two in her sheer black stockings, Jacinta always wore stilettos and her well-padded frame draped with tie-dye garments. The ensemble was completed, as ever, with a selection of dangling silver jewellery of various ethnicities. The overall effect was that of Glastonbury on the move. "Your hair looks nice."

"You think?" She reached up and patted at where her long, jet-black hair lay newly coiled around her head. Jacinta had a thing for hairdressers and regularly spent large portions of her (pitiful) salary on them. She'd come from South America three years ago where I assumed she'd lived under an oppressive regime where all hairdressers were locked up for the common good.

"It's lovely." I stacked my selected pile of books against the till. "If you want our esteemed boss, he's in the back room."

"I go have words with him. He owes me moneys from last week and I want to go buy a new dress."

She shimmied her way through the curtain into Simon's space. I suppressed the urge to tiptoe after her and listen in on their conversation. There always seemed to be some kind of unspoken acknowledgement between them, a shared secret. Nothing ever happened to give a clue to the nature of this relationship; it was more a feeling of things unsaid which hung in the air when the two of them were together which made me wonder if they shared more than the occasional HobNob in the back room.

While they were closeted, I served a couple of casual Sunday customers and was mooching around searching the shelves, when Simon reappeared and told me it was time to go home. Jacinta was just behind him, with the sleek satisfaction of a woman on a frock-buying mission. "I go now," she announced from the doorway, "to buy wonderful new clothe. I

17

see you tomorrow, Alys."

I examined both their faces for any traces of residual postcoital contentment, then berated myself. Unless there had been a major change of taste on her part, and his indeterminate sexuality and overwhelming diffidence had been won over by the sight of Jacinta in a bustier and garter belt, I didn't seriously think that any rumpy-pumpy action had been on the cards. "See you, Jace."

"You be nice to Florence." Jacinta wagged a finger at me, leaning against the frame. "She is a very nice girl."

"Yeah, as long as you're not her mother."

Simon politely ushered me out of the shop towards his car where we both paused for a moment, enjoying the seismic sight of Jace rolling her way down the street. "So Florence is over with Alasdair today?" he asked. "I must say, she's turning out to be a very pretty young woman. Beautiful big eyes she has. Must take after Alasdair's family, does she?"

I narrowed my own, by extrapolation, piggily unattractive eyes. "Mmm. I suppose so."

My tone must have penetrated Simon's general abstraction and he turned to me. "Oh, I didn't mean... You mustn't think... It's not... I mean, you're a very...ahhh...umm...yourself, Alys."

I think I might have glared at him at this point.

I was feeling distinctly jaded when I let myself into the flat. Grainger lay curled reproachfully on the sofa, one eye wedged open for my return, the other eye sleeping the peaceful sleep of a blameless cat.

"I'm back," I said unnecessarily to the smell, the silence and the cat. "Now, where's Theo?" He was finally retrieved from beneath the sofa where he had been attracting enough fur to knit another cat. I tucked my feet up under myself, bit the end off a coffee Walnut Whip and opened his pages at a poem called "Distorted Vision", when there was a sharp tap on the front door.

"Oh bugger." I laid Theo down and answered it.

Standing there, and causing almost as much astonishment as Simon's earlier visit, was a man I hardly recognised. I'd known Piers since Alasdair and Tamar had married four years ago, was used to speaking to him on the phone, but I'd not seen him for a while. When last sighted he had been a pretty but unremarkable looking boy, but standing on my threshold he seemed to have a broader chest than I'd remembered. He'd lost the startled-in-a-glue-factory spiky hair in favour of shoulder-length, expensively unkempt shagginess. A smattering of proud stubble adorned sharp, pale cheekbones, his pallid skin contrasting with his shadow-dark hair as though he was trading on what Florence called his "Orlando Bloom with edges" look. He'd completed the show with a pair of D&G sunglasses. This and the black designer jeans, black T-shirt, black leather jacket apparel made him look as though he were on the run from a Transylvanian boy-band.

"Hello, Piers," I said, when he didn't say anything following my opening of the door. I hoped I hadn't been staring at him in silence for too long.

"Hey. Alys." He was gazing past me, into the flat. "I thought, I mean, I heard Florence left her revision stuff here. Thought I'd come by and pick it up."

Maybe Florence had changed her mind about revision. Maybe she'd decided to spend the rest of Sunday rereading her notes. Oh yeah, and maybe I was going to be the next face of L'Oreal. "Did Florence ask you to come?" I was still not opening the door wide enough to let him in, and he was still not meeting my eye.

"Not exactly. I just bought this car—wanted to give it a try-out, found myself over this way. I thought, well, okay, two birds with one stone kinda thing. You know."

"Out *this way?* From *Richmond?*" Richmond was about fifty miles north. Not exactly popping next door.

"Yeah." He took his sunglasses off and began twiddling them between his fingers. "A19." Now he looked at me and I was taken aback by the expression in his dark eyes. He looked almost—nervous?

"Piers." I stood back now to let him come in. "Is everything all right?"

"I'm..." Again, that look of, not panic exactly, but something twitchily close, then it was gone. "Yeah. I'm cool. How about you, Alys, you okay?"

Gosh. It was a long time since anyone had asked that. "Look, Piers, it's really very kind of you to come all this way, but Florrie's already decided she's done enough revision. Do you want a drink or something before you head back? Coffee, tea? Lemonade?" I could have bitten my tongue off. He was twenty-one, for God's sake, not nine. "Whisky? Oh, but you're driving—"

"Nah. Like I said, I'm cool." He looked it, cucumber cool in all that black whilst I felt unnaturally hot and oppressed by the air in the flat.

I followed him into the living room where, to my surprise, Grainger was submitting to a head scratching. It could only be a matter of time before fingers were lost. "How's the new car?"

"Pure kick-ass." Piers left Grainger and whirled to the window, all long-limbed animation like a Quentin Blake cartoon come to life. "There, see? The yellow Porsche? Hey, why don't you come for a drive, Alys? We could shoot through to the coast, top down, catch some sea air?" He was talking without looking at me, couldn't take his eyes off the car.

"Oh." I hesitated, a quick *Thelma and Louise* moment flashing before my eyes as I saw myself zipping along a coast road next to Piers, top off. Off the car, obviously, not off Piers.

"Better not. I've got stuff to do. And there's a book I want to read." I glanced apologetically towards Theo. Grainger was stomping across his cover trying to attract Piers's attention again by chewing the cushions, mugging like Jack Nicholson in a small fur coat.

"Well, okay. But, look." He'd dropped his gaze again, hands in the pockets of his jacket, awkward as a teenager. "I really need to talk to you sometime. It's just family stuff, but I don't know who else I can go to with this shit."

"Really? But I don't know anything about your family." I felt a bit strange having this conversation. A bit wrong footed. My memory had Piers down as a teenager, but here he was, very obviously an adult. Making adult conversation.

"It's Ma and Alasdair. It's getting kinda heavy." Once more he met my eyes, and I found myself wondering, not for the first time, how blue-eyed, epitome-of-WASPness Tamar had managed to produce such a sultry-eyed son. "Please, Alys. I've always been able to talk to you."

"It's—"

"Please." This time soft, fractured. The faint twang of his American parentage crept in around the vowels, made him sound vulnerable.

"Oh, all right." Aware that I'd sounded ungracious, and he really did look unsettled, I added, "If there's anything I can help with."

"How about tomorrow? I told Florence I'd bring her back here after school."

"Um. Tomorrow might be tricky. I have my book group on a Monday night." Because something about his straight stare made me feel like filling in uncalled-for detail I began to gabble. "It was my turn to choose, you see, and I gave them *Dead Air*. I really want to know what they think."

"Your book group." Piers gave a tiny grin. "Is that the one

21

where everyone's over eighty?"

"No, Mrs. Treadgold's only seventy-three. And I'm"—well, thirty-six actually, but damned if I'd admit it—"not eighty either."

"And you gave them *Dead Air*? Shit, Alys, they've probably all had coronaries. Do you know how many fucks there are in that book?"

"Never counted. So, anyway, tomorrow would be tricky."

He gave me an odd sideways smile and pushed pale silver-ringed fingers through his unAryan hair. "I'll give you a lift. Pick you up at eight."

And he was gone in a blur of blackness, flinging himself out of the front door and down the stairs with an energy which almost crackled. Despite myself, I found I was watching from the window as the Porsche roared away down the street. A momentary pang—a drive to the coast would have been nice—then I shook my head and settled myself back down with Theo.

Chapter Three

Jacinta was unlocking the door when I arrived at Webbe's next morning. "Simon says he is not coming in today. He is 'busy'." She stooped to pick up the post. I gave a deep sigh. "You need new clothe," Jace diagnosed as we went round flipping switches. "Several new clothes. Always make me feel better when I am depressing. Without nice clothe, you never find a man."

This morning Jace was wearing a purple blouse and a multicoloured, tiered skirt dotted with tiny mirrors and with a row of little bells sewn around the hem. I wouldn't have been surprised if she'd been pecked to death on her way to work by a flock of disenfranchised budgies.

"No point in buying new clothe...clothes. Florence wouldn't care and there's no one else to notice." I turned on the cash register. "I'm not depressed anyway. And I don't want a man. I've given up men. Three-dimensional ones, anyway."

Jace looked dubious. "You are not saying that when you are meeting that person with the hair. Who is coming to play with his instrument in the shop last year."

"Yeah, well. Look what happened that time." Leonard "Waspy" Binns—what a mistake. "In fact, I think I'm about this far"—I held my hands apart a few inches—"from taking Holy Orders."

"You would make terrible nun." Jace began tidying, her

skirts whirling, chiming and creating fractured reflections as she went. "You have too-pretty face to be under a Mr. Whippy hat."

"I think I just changed my mind," I surprised myself by saying. "How about we pop out at lunchtime?" Maybe some of Piers's devil-may-care attitude had rubbed off on me. It was certainly unlike me to be this spontaneous.

Jacinta nearly fell off the stool she was standing on to flick dust from the top of a cupboard. "Alys! You taking advice from me? I am astonished." She lowered her voice. "Is this meaning there is a man you are deciding upon?"

"Good God, no. Well, there was a man last night that I thought was particularly gorgeous, but seeing that he's unsuitable on account of being dead, then, no. I just feel like buying something."

"We shall buy you something," Jace said, decidedly. "Green. You must be wearing green, Alys. It go with your hair and your skin."

Before you conjure a vision of me as some kind of sickly-hued subsea monster, I should mention that I'm a redhead. Not flaming red, but kind of dark auburn with the associated pale skin which makes hot sun a factor-50-coated ordeal.

"It will depend on what the charity shops of York have to offer us, won't it?"

Jace's face settled into lines of disappointment. "Can we not be buying something really new?" she asked forlornly. "You deserve a dress with still the real price label on, which does not smell of some other hot persons."

"Just paid the Council Tax," I said with the briskness I'd spent years cultivating in a way only the truly broke can master. The bell twitched its nerve-jangling message that a customer had arrived, and I walked through to see a woman standing at the desk, jittering as though she badly needed either the toilet or some Valium. I sized her up as I approached. About my age, tall, well turned out. Good hairstyle, graded bob, but not the cutting edge of the city. Looked like the classic "out of towner". Was she a guilty secret of Simon's?

"Good morning," I announced brightly and she stopped jigging, turning nervous dark eyes in my direction.

"Er. Are you—I mean—is Mr. Webbe available?" The woman had an accent, definitely not local. "I've come to pick up the books that were mistakenly sold at the auction last week," she went on. "Only I spoke to Mr. Webbe and he said I could collect them today?"

Her voice was only a little less diffident than Simon's. If the two of them *had* been a couple, their combined hesitancy would have meant that the relationship would die of reticence before they ever got their clothes off. "Simon's away at a book sale, I'm afraid." I picked up the heap of books I'd arranged yesterday. "But the books are here." I'd piled the books carefully, sure that the early-edition Dickens would be the ones she really wanted. They weren't particularly valuable, but I couldn't see that she'd come all this way for the return of half a Jilly Cooper and a second-rate biography of the Iron Lady. She riffled through them almost nervously. The sight of the Dickens didn't dispel her anxiety and I felt my stomach lurch with foreboding.

"I'm sure—" she began, and flipped through the books again. She seemed almost embarrassed. "There must be another one. Wasn't there? A book of poetry? By"—she hesitated, seemed to be about to say another name then corrected herself—"Theo Wood?"

"Oh, I'm sorry. These were the only books Simon brought over."

The woman's nervousness seemed to step up a notch. "Oh! No, that can't be right. The book must be here somewhere." She spun on a flat-loafered heel as though the 360-degree turn would enable her to spot Theo flashing guiltily from a high

25

shelf. "It—he—I mean, Theo Wood was—is—he was a relative, you see. The book, it's quite important to me."

Oh God, now I felt guilty. But there wasn't time to rush back home and get it. Hell, I'd post it to her tomorrow—after I'd photocopied Theo's picture. "I'm really sorry. I'll have another look around tonight, after we've closed."

The woman handed me a small square of card. "This is my address and number and everything," she almost whispered. "Please, if you could. Only it really is terribly important, you see, that I get this book back."

Isabelle Logan her name was, apparently. The address I only glanced at, Charlton Hawsell, a village with an Exeter postcode. "It's probably just got mixed in with books from somewhere else. It'll turn up." Okay, I'd post it this evening. The library did photocopies and they didn't shut til six.

She smiled tightly. "Maybe you're right, Mrs...er."

"Ms.," I said firmly. "Ms. Hunter. Alys. With a 'y'."

Mrs. Logan gave a deep sigh, reminiscent of mine earlier that morning, and I saw Jace throw a black-eyed glance of concern across at us. I half expected her to come over and recommend "new clothe", but she carried on shelving until Mrs. Logan took her leave.

"Now, why," I asked Jace, "do you think she put that book in an auction, if she was going to miss it so desperately?"

"Perhaps it have secret message in code." Jace leaned against the counter, despite the ominous creaking it immediately set up. "She needs it to find family treasure."

"Have you been dusting the Conan Doyle section again?"

The rest of the day dragged itself past like a hypochondriac relative. At lunchtime Jace and I walked the streets of York and I bought a green dress from a tiny branch of Help the Aged I'd never noticed before. It bore a well-known designer's label and had hardly ever been worn. To Jace's slight jealousy, it fitted me perfectly. She came away with three duvet covers and a CD rack.

Maybe Jace was right and there was some direct inverse proportion between the feeling of happiness and the amount of money one had in the bank, I thought as I climbed the two flights of stairs to the flat that evening. But no, that couldn't be right, otherwise I'd be perpetually ecstatic. Perhaps it was just having something new that made me so cheerful at finding Florence lounging on the sofa and Piers draped picturesquely in Grainger's favourite chair. They were listening to something which sounded like drum 'n' bass recorded in an abattoir marshalling yard.

"What've you bought, Mum?" Florence raised her head half an inch from the sofa, a cross between ethereal as a ghost and a right little madam. "Is it for me?"

"No. It's for me." Piers was grinning rather inanely and there was a slight tinge of blush receding from his skin. I hoped I hadn't caught them out in some illegal activity. "How long have you been in?"

"Not long. Is it something I can borrow?"

"No." I sniffed suspiciously but could only catch the fleeting aroma of eau de Grainger.

"I don't smoke, if that's what you're thinking," Florence said officiously. "It's a filthy habit." Piers said nothing, but his smile went a bit lopsided. "Let's see what you bought." Reluctantly needing her approval, I unfolded the dress and found myself the centre of silent attention from the pair of them. "Wow, Mum!" Florence had got up off the sofa in admiration. "This is just so cool." She pulled the dress from my arm and held it up against herself. "What d'you reckon, Piers?"

Piers swung himself upright in the chair and cleared his

throat. "Yeah, that is pretty cool. It's designer, right, Alys?"

I nodded, watching the feline figure of my daughter whisking around the room, making the flared skirt of the dress dance out behind her. Half of me was proud of her looks, athletically slim with skin that had gone the shade of heather honey in the summer sun, hair so unlike mine or Alasdair's. People often commented on her moonsilver blondeness, how it contrasted with the perpetually tawny skin.

The other half of me was plain jealous. Young and everything to live for. I'd been like that, once, before I'd screwed up so royally. Still. Never mind, no point dwelling. Must get on, be practical, things to do—

Piers was unexpectedly my ally. "It'd look crap on you, Flo. You're the wrong colouring."

Florence dropped the dress on the table. "Oh yeah?" She rounded on Piers. "I wouldn't wear it anyway, piece of second-hand shit," and marched off to her bedroom, slamming the door to leave neither of us in any doubt over what she thought about her stepbrother's opinions.

Piers and I regarded each other in solemn silence for a second, then we both grinned. "Christ, d'you think I was like that at sixteen?" he asked.

"Probably."

"Shit." Piers shook his head. "Madness. Why do people have kids anyway?"

"Good idea at the time," I said briskly. "Most of them would be better off getting a Labrador." I began tidying up the detritus of their residency. Biscuit wrappers littered the floor and there was a jam sandwich on top of the CD player. Grainger was under the table in a tabby ruckus of newspaper and old socks, with Theo forming a good solid base to it all.

"Can you see my ma with a dog?" Piers had got to his feet. Crouched under the table trying to extricate Theo without waking Grainger, I could only see his lower half. "Mud and hair and stuff? I mean, what the hell did she do with me when I was a baby—put me in some kinda crate or something?" I refused to be drawn into speculation on this subject and crawled out, tugging Theo out of the Grainger-nest as I came. I flipped a few pages in hopes that a piece of paper might drift free and solve the "Isabelle Logan Mystery", but nothing happened other than a bit of stray fur floating to the carpet. "So, you ready to face the grey brigade? I can drop you off, wait if you want, you might need backup. I mean, *Dead Air*—what you gonna give them next, *Trainspotting*?"

"I didn't realise you were so literary," I said slightly sharply.

"Yeah. Gorgeous *and* I read. You wearing the green dress?"

I sighed. His self-confidence was tiring. "I suppose. Might give them a bit of a shock though, finding out I've got legs. I think they assume I'm rolling around on castors, like a Dalek."

Piers glanced down at my workday jeans, a little tight around the bum. "Reckon they'll already suspect about the legs." He blew and his hair flipped. "Yeah. Then maybe after we could go get a drink or something? Run down to Opus or one of the bars?"

"You just want an excuse to drive that car."

"You need an excuse to wear that dress. Sounds like a fair trade to me."

"I am not dressing up to have a drink with you, Piers," I said, half-laughing until I saw the quick look of hurt which crossed his face. "Oh, all right. It'll be good for my ego, anyway, having a drink with such a dazzling couple."

"I'm not coming!" Florence shouted from her bedroom.

"Didn't invite you!" shouted back Piers.

"But—" I stopped on my way to my room, dress over my arm. "I thought—"

"You know Flo, Alys. She'd spend the whole evening sulking because she'd rather go clubbing."

There really should be some kind of law that forces guilt to be finite. Because, right now, what with the Theo theft, the frivolity of dressing up to go out to meet a bunch of near octogenarians and leaving Florence so that I could have a drink with a male-model look-alike, I was in danger of creasing up under the weight of my own remorse. But only a bit.

Chapter Four

My book group, ironically enough since I'd joined it to meet like-minded men, comprised Mrs. Treadgold, Mrs. Munroe, Mrs. James and Mrs. Searle, four ladies past pensionable age, and Mr. Mansell, an elderly man so frail I worried that if someone turned a page too quickly he'd blow over. The one male member under forty had left three months ago to live with his partner Malcolm in Derbyshire. Despite this, I'd stayed on and now considered everyone in the group as good friends.

Mrs. Treadgold ushered me to the empty seat next to her and whispered confidentially, "I *enjoyed* the book. It was refreshing." Across the table Mr. Mansell dropped me an extraordinarily ribald wink and Mrs. Munroe, who had a Mastermind-level knowledge of the early works of Dick Francis, gave me a grin so broad that her ill-fitting top set almost came over to thank me personally. I felt ridiculously proud of their broadmindedness.

We broke later for coffee and some of Mrs. James's flapjacks. Mrs. Treadgold sidled over to me as I tried to avoid having my bottom pinched by Mr. Mansell, which was tragically like a Benny Hill sketch in very, very slow motion. "I saw you, you know," she said, in a half-whisper, "being dropped off tonight."

"Oh, right." I took another bite of flapjack.

Her carefully coiffed grey bob bobbed. "I'm just *so* pleased for you."

"Well, yes, it's nice not to have to get the bus."

"I meant your young man. He looks nice. Very"—she rolled her eyes and the hair, which wasn't her own, tootled about independently—"*shaggable.*"

I nearly inhaled my flapjack. I wasn't sure which shocked me most, the fact she thought Piers was my boyfriend or the fact *Dead Air* had obviously corrupted her vocabulary. "Er, actually that was my ex's stepson."

We were interrupted at that point by Mrs. Searle, who was nominally in charge, calling us to the table. But Mrs. Treadgold had time to whisper, "Your young man is your *stepson?* Ooh, Alys, you're so *naughty.*" Then, lowering her voice even more, "I really admire you, you know. You don't have much, but"—she stared down at the impressive cleavage the green dress gave me—"you certainly make the best of what you have."

Maybe I should have explained and told her that Piers was only after my advice rather than my body. But then I saw her whispering to Mrs. Munroe and decided to float on my laurels a little longer. Maybe I should choose *The Female Eunuch* as my next book.

The five of them stood at my back like a parental multiplicity when Piers came to pick me up, shuffling each other aside for better views. Although I suspected Mr. Mansell just wanted a close-up of my legs as I clambered into the yellow Porsche, with Piers obviously trying not to laugh.

"What?"

"Nothing. Where d'you want to go? For a drink? I thought maybe that little winebar in Coppergate? They do great food too, if you're hungry."

"I'm fine."

"Alys." He turned to me, sluicing his hair off his face with long fingers. "You didn't eat when you got in. You must be starved and I'm offering you food, what's with turning it down?"

"Yes, you're right. I'm sorry. It's—never mind." I couldn't really explain that being bought a meal made me feel uncomfortably beholden. Anyway, this was Piers. I was supposed to be doing *him* a favour, wasn't I?

It was five miles to the bar in Coppergate. I know this, because I stared at the speedometer all the way, counting down every two-wheeled curve, every airborne bump and had very nearly converted to any religion that would have me by the time we arrived.

"Okay, Alys? You went a little quiet back there."

"When I get my nails out of your upholstery, I'll let you know." Carefully I climbed out of the low door and tried to adjust the skirt of my dress so that it wasn't showing my knickers.

"I'll drive slower on the way back." Piers locked the car with a flourish of a remote device. "I wouldn't want you not to enjoy the experience."

I suddenly felt rather warm. "You mean you wouldn't want me to have an 'experience' all over the inside of your car."

"You get sick in cars?"

"Never, before tonight."

"Riiiight." Piers led the way. The bar was filled with a weeknight crowd of hardened drinkers all trying to pretend that Monday was the new Saturday.

Piers sat down, then ordered wine. He looked a bit twitchy, distracted. Nervous.

"So. Are you going to tell me what your problem is? Apart from that truly nasty shirt you've got on."

"I—what's wrong with it?" He opened the bottle of wine and slopped a major portion of the contents into two glasses, catching my eye and grinning wildly. Almost every pair of female eyes in the place was swivelling towards him, although that could have been the car-crash fascination of the skintight Liberty print shirt.

"Okay," he said carefully. "Here's the thing." He stopped and began twisting the glass between his hands, slopping the greenish-yellow liquid around the sides. "Nah. It'll be cool. No need to stress you with all the crap that's going down."

"But—" I looked across the table at him, the outline of his face seemed to waver, all eyes and hair.

"I guess I thought I wanted to talk about it. Now I'm not so sure. Do you want to order food?"

Oh, what the hell, I thought, swigging down wine. Good food, good wine and the company of a beautiful man. I mean, how serious could any problem suffered by a man with a platinum Am-Ex card actually *be*? "All right. If it's not that important."

"I didn't say it wasn't important. I only said I didn't want to talk about it right now, okay? Let's just eat. Relax. You know, have fun. Talk. Know something, Alys? You never talk about yourself."

"Er, maybe because I like my friends and don't want to bore them into insensibility." I helped myself to some more wine. It was rather nice, and getting nicer with each glassful.

"That is *so* not what I mean." Piers leaned forward across the table. "I think—"

However, whatever it was he thought, he never got to tell me. A crowd of young, pretty people arrived at our table, friends of Piers, overanimated and dramatic. To his credit he tried to keep talking to me but two of the girls insinuated themselves between us. One of them sat on his lap and played with his hair while the other stroked his leg and drank from his glass. "This your mum, Piers?"

"No. This is Alys."

"Oh, right." The hair stroking went on until I began to feel uncomfortable and drank even more of the wine, without tasting it. The leg stroker turned her back, effectively blocking Piers from me and began slipping fingers between the buttons of his shirt.

He bent forward, looked around her chest at me and winked. "Hey, Alys. D'you want me to take you home?"

"Oooooh," chorused the two girls. They gave me a kind of sneer-appraisal. "Sounds like your lucky night, Doris."

"Alys."

But they'd collapsed into giggles at the obvious ridiculousness of their suggestion and weren't even looking at me any more. Piers was. And not even smiling. Just looking.

"Er, no, I'm fine here." I pretended to toast him with my glass. No girls who looked younger than my own daughter and wore less clothes than the average domestic pet were going to drive me away from the first evening out I'd had in ages. "Maybe later."

Later, and after many more glasses of wine, drunk to spite the girls who'd obviously wanted rid of me, I forced entry into my hallway. With the kind of thuggish enthusiasm typical to those who've had a night out which has proved a little too much for their systems to cope with, I collapsed through doorways. I ended up facedown on my bed.

"That was fun," I said to the pillow. "Piers is nice to be seen out with." A moment's contemplation later I mitigated this with, "Bloody annoying person though. Buying all that wine. Making me drink it. And his friends are so *rude.*"

The pillow turned a cold, glittering eye on me. Grainger was drawing my attention to the fact that he was currently occupying this pillowcase and would I mind buggering off to be maudlin elsewhere because he had some serious bits of sleeping he wanted to catch up on.

Chapter Five

"You are looking very white still, Alys." Jacinta's voice boomed around inside my head as I attempted to sort books without bending down. "You must get in bed early tonight." The shop bell jangled like tinfoil across my nerve endings and she looked at me expectantly. "Is your turn."

"Oh, have pity on me, Jace, please." I groaned, resting my forehead against the undisturbed coolness of the Jane Austen section. "I couldn't sell anything if it was 'Buy a Book or Die' day."

"Hmm." Jacinta, decidedly lacking in sympathy, muttered, "It not pity you need, it man with big muscle."

Honestly. First all I needed was "new clothe", now it was "man with big muscle". What was she going to prescribe next? Liechtenstein?

My stomach gave a small lurch and I hastily started pulling books from the shelf to distract myself. A rogue *Northanger Abbey* needed a swift sort out before it tried to infiltrate Iain Banks on the rack below.

"It is a man." Jacinta's voice from the other side of the shelf made me jump, as did the sight of her face peering through the recently made gap. She looked disturbingly like a bird of prey when all her features were squeezed into the book-sized space. "He wants you."

"Oh, if only." I sighed. "Why does he want me?"

"He is not saying. I say you are not feeling bright today and that you have brought back your tea."

"More information, Jacinta, than I think *anyone* needs. So he didn't say who he was, or anything useful like that?"

"No. He is very pretty, you go see."

"But I don't know any...oh. Hello, Piers." I tried to become unaware of Jace's looming, pouting presence as I confronted Piers in front of the till. The thumping in my temples had worsened suddenly, but he looked perfectly cool. "Um. Do you want to buy a book?"

By now Jace had walked completely around Piers, giving him the benefit of her Alpine-level cleavage and, for such a large woman, her absurdly pert bottom. Over his shoulder she was making lip-smacking faces in my direction.

"No, I wanted—just making sure you were okay. You seemed kinda tanked last night and we didn't get to talk a whole lot on the way back. Worried that my friends might have, ah, upset you."

Jacinta was now giving me thumbs-up signs with both hands and winking like a pantomime dame behind Piers's back. "Well, as you can see"—I waved my arms in what was meant to be a look-how-fine-I-am gesture, but came across as though I was struggling to keep my balance—"I'm completely all right. Super, in fact."

"Yeah, okay. Sure. Just thought I'd, well, you know." Piers turned and almost collided with Jacinta who managed to wobble most of her assets in her attempt to get out of his way. "See ya."

As soon as the door had shut behind him, Jacinta was in front of me, grasping me by both shoulders and squeezing until my clavicles squeaked. "Alys, you have a man! And such a man. So—*lindo*." She burst into a torrent of Spanish, punctuated with occasional shakings of my limp form which might, in my fragile state, have proved fatal if Simon hadn't walked in at that moment.

"Now, now girls," he said evenly. "No need to fight."

"She has a man." Jacinta managed to make it sound accusing and her eyebrows, usually neatly pencilled arches on her brow line, became two brackets containing an outraged frown. "She did not tell me of any man."

"It was Piers," I said wearily. "He's got some family crisis and I offered to help, that's all. Nothing else."

"Piers? Alasdair's wife's boy?" Simon looked puzzled. "But he's about twelve, isn't he?"

"Something like that." My head was banging now, my brain felt like the last biscuit in the tin. "Look, sorry, Simon, but I think I've got to go home. I feel absolutely rubbish at the moment. Jace can cope, can't you?"

"If you say." Jacinta helped me find my jacket and held open the shop door for me. "He is very big boy for twelve," she muttered in my ear as I left.

Chapter Six

I awoke some time later, in bed with a migranous headache and Theo Wood looming pixelatedly in front of my left eyeball. *Shit.* I'd meant to post him off to Isabelle Logan last night. I hadn't accounted for getting rolling drunk and forgetting. I'd already admitted his presence to Simon, pretending that I'd taken him home by mistake, and had to face Simon's upper-class tut at my carelessness. If things had gone to plan, Theo would have plopped through Isabelle's letterbox by now.

I unstuck Theo from my cheek and wiped as much drool off his face as I could, before I groaned my way into a more comfortable position. Why on earth had I drunk so much last night? I turned onto my side and felt the bed dip as Grainger landed alongside me. He walked the length of my body to *gurn* toothlessly into my face before settling himself against my chest with a small purr of self-satisfaction and a smell like old anchovies.

I closed my eyes and let myself drift off into a pleasing half dream about Theo Wood in which he was reciting poetry to me in a breathless, love-struck voice, but woke again with a start of recognition at the sound of a key turning in the front door. Theo's gentle exhalations of desire turned into Grainger's fishy snores and the background sounds became voices. Florence and one other, male and young.

"Mum's at work, so we've got hours," and his reply, "Great!

So, d'you want to do it in here then?"

I lay, frozen, somewhere between embarrassment and outrage. Okay, so Florence was sixteen, legally overage, but even so. I really didn't think I could lie here and listen. But how could I reveal my presence and ever be able to look my daughter in the face again?

"I'll get my equipment unpacked." I heard the sound of a lot of zipping and lifting, before some heavy items thunked onto the living-room floor.

"Jesus, do you carry *all* those lenses all the time?" Oh, thank God and the patron saint of mothers everywhere. "Shall I sit over here? Is the light good enough?"

"Yeah, it's fine. I'll get the meter on you, just in case. D'you want to change?"

"Nah, this'll be cool. Do a couple of shots, full length and a portrait, that'll be fine."

I held my hand against my heart which was beginning to slow down and tried to stifle a giggle of relief. Florence was having her picture taken. She must have persuaded one of the school camera club to do the honours. It was my birthday in three weeks, so maybe this was intended to be my present. Well, it would make a change from the usual half a pound of Dairy Milk and a card bearing a joke which I didn't understand.

He did seem to know his business, asking her to toss her hair back off her face and pretend to be looking out of the window. I wished I dared peep out at my daughter, posing and teasing yet with such innocence in her laughter and delight in her voice. It reminded me of listening to her playing with Alasdair when she was much smaller. I couldn't wait to see the finished results.

When I heard her close the front door, I relaxed and picked Theo back up off the covers. His face looked a little bleary from my sleeping on him, but he still retained that saturnine expression which hinted at dark passion, proved by the words of his poetry. I plunged into his metaphors with gusto—this was a man who had known *exactly* where to put his alliteration for maximum effect.

I read on for a couple of hours, finishing the book, and stared at the face of the poet as dusk seeped into the room. Why couldn't I meet men like this? Where were they all, the sensitive, artistic types with eyes which could pull the soul from your body? How come the only men I met thought that buying you two egg sandwiches and a Mars Bar made them irresistible? Next door the telephone rang, I heard Florrie answer and could only hope that she would have better luck in her relationships than I had. *Hold out for one who's out of the ordinary*, I breathed in a silent wish for her. *A man who wants to be your friend first and your lover second. Someone who knows you.*

Florence came in, flooding the room with bright light and energy. "It's Simon on the phone for you," she said, then, "What? Why are you looking at me like that?"

"No reason." I wobbled to my feet, jet-lagged after an unaccustomed afternoon away from the vertical. "Just wondering what kind of man you'll end up with."

"Oh, that's easy." She danced into the kitchen and closed the door, shouting "RICH" as she did so.

"Hello, Simon."

"Alys. How are you feeling? Are you recovering?"

"I'm fine."

"Good. Good. Ah. So you'll be able to come back to work? Only, I need a favour."

Florence had re-emerged from the kitchen and sprawled herself across the sofa with a magazine, obviously listening. "Simon, I'm not running any more consignments of crack across town," I said, deadpan.

She simply raised an eyebrow and mouthed, "Oh, *Mother.*"

"I'm sorry?" Poor Simon was baffled.

"Never mind. What can I do for you?"

He had only assured Mrs. Logan that I would personally deliver her book into her hands within the week. I breathed a sigh of relief that I hadn't already posted it. Simon really went for the personal touch.

"You know I can't travel, Alys," Simon said reasonably. "I'd be having panic attacks before the train left the station. And sending Jacinta wouldn't be fair."

"But what do I do about Florence? I can't just hop off for a couple of days and leave her alone. She's got school. Exams, that sort of thing. She needs me."

"No I bloody don't," came the loving reply from the sofa. "I'll go and stay at Dad's."

"It's only for a couple of days. Train down, taxi to Mrs. Logan's house, hand over the book. I'll pay your expenses. Come on, Alys." He took a noticeably wheedling tone. "You went to university in Devon, didn't you? Wouldn't you like to go back and have a look round?"

"I was at Exeter, yes. Briefly." I tried not to look at Florence when I said this, but failed. She was sitting very still, carefully not reacting. "Oh all right. I'll go."

"Thank you. I'm sorry to be asking, but it *is* due to your carelessness that the book is at your flat."

"Yes, yes, all right, I get that. I did apologise. It must have fallen into my bag from the pile on your table. I was going to post it to her, but—"

Thankfully Simon's insuck of air prevented me from having to admit that I'd been out on the lam with Piers. "*Post it?* A valuable book like that? I'm surprised at you."

You'd have been a lot more surprised if you'd seen me last

night, I thought.

Chapter Seven

All the taxis at the rank outside Exeter station told me that they only did trips into the town and Charlton Hawsell might have been Ulan Bator as far as they were concerned. So farther onward travel was provided by a single-decker bus which smelled of damp paper towels.

I sat behind the driver, trying not to catch his eye in the mirror, and stared out of the window as the bus ground its way out of Exeter towards the countryside, passing places I'd known so well seventeen years ago. The seedy newsagent's shop was still there, on the corner by the roundabout, where I'd first met Alasdair. Over there was the restaurant he'd taken me to on our first date. He'd walked me back to my tiny room, tried to kiss me goodnight and I'd got the impression that my response had somewhat taken him by surprise. He hadn't left until the next morning. From the continued apologising, I gathered that nicely brought up, young Scots boys didn't do what we'd spent the night doing without some kind of formal agreement signed in triplicate.

I deliberately turned my head away and focussed on the image of the bus driver's reflection. He had a bead of dried snot stuck to the edge of one nostril and the disgust which this engendered in me managed to carry me past most of my one-time haunts, past all the memories which I so reluctantly bore. There was only one time I looked. Deliberately I forced my eyes across the crowded buildings towards the site which, in my time, had been a rough plot of land, vaguely green with nettles and goose grass and strewn with various impermanent forms of dwelling. These, and the scabby thorny hedging, had now been replaced by an expanse of tarmac ramping into a multistorey car park.

I knew I shouldn't have come back. Some memories were too fragile, too delicate, for return visits. My remembrance of the last night I'd spent here was gone, crushed beneath a casually parked black Mercedes.

As we got farther out of town, the memories dried up. Down lanes which grew narrower and narrower, we chugged, like that last drop of cholesterol down a clogged artery, until we pulled up finally in a tiny hamlet. "This is you, love." The bus driver flicked his head at me and I disembarked, pleased to note that this civic act had finally dislodged the excrescence from his nose.

I slumped down on a convenient bank beside the road and rummaged through my bag, unearthing Theo in the process. I resisted the urge to clasp him to my sweaty bosom, laying him down on the grass instead. As I did so I noticed a protruding edge of card which I'd been using as a bookmark. It was Isabelle Logan's card, the one she'd handed me back in Webbe's. I grovelled once more in my bag and found Simon's mobile, which he'd lent me under protest, and dialled Isabelle Logan.

"I think you're about a mile and a half from Charlton. If you walk on into the town, I can pick you up from there. There's a little tea shop in the marketplace, if you go in I'll come and find you. Oh, and Mrs. Hunter—"

"Ms.," I said wearily.

"Thank you *so* much for bringing the book. You could have posted it."

"Don't mention it." I resolved to hide Simon's HobNobs

when I got back.

"Well, you must come for dinner. I would invite you to stay overnight but we've a full house at the moment."

"It's okay. I'll stay in town. Don't worry." I hung up and hauled myself to my feet, feeling unpleasantly clammy.

Charlton Hawsell was surprisingly pleasant. In the marketplace, the one tea shop was easy to find. I sat down at a window seat with a cup of coffee and a scone, and wondered how Florence was getting on. It was the French exam this afternoon. I hoped she'd revised. Apart from singing *Frère Jacques* at primary school, I'd never heard Florrie utter a word of the language.

The street was busy. As I stared aimlessly ahead, a maroon Land Rover jerked to a halt in front of the tea shop and a man got out, leaping lightly down onto the cobbles before dashing across the road into a shop opposite.

I nearly dropped my cup, all thoughts of exams gone. Surely...

Leaving my scone untouched, I hastily shoved a fiver under my saucer and fled for the door. I would probably have been more circumspect if the fiver hadn't been part of my expenses. Once out on the pavement, I pretended to look in shop windows, keeping the reflection of the Land Rover in sight until I saw the man returning, carrying a heavy sack hoisted up on one shoulder. I watched as he opened the back of the Land Rover and threw the sack inside.

I moved in, turning so that I could see him properly as he got into the driver's seat. His eyes travelled around, checking the road behind him. Then, with the merest flick of his indicator, he was gone, leaving me standing breathless, pink in the face again.

Theo Wood.

No, of *course* it wasn't, not Theo Wood, but someone who

looked very, very much like him. Raggier haired and more stubbled than Theo, and wearing glasses, but still very, *very* much like him. So much like him that my heart had risen into my throat. Perhaps this was one of those places where incest and inbreeding meant that the locals only had three faces to go around. I hazarded a quick look up and down the street to check, but there seemed to be the normal mix of dumpy and dull, hawk nosed and handsome. Then—he must be some kind of throwback, great-grandson or some such?

I couldn't remember the last time I'd felt so reckless. Sweeping my rucksack off my back, I galloped across the road and dived through the dark, narrow doorway he'd entered without even noticing the kind of merchandise on display.

"Can I help you, m'dear?" A friendly voice in the gloom, and a man popped up from behind a counter, carrying what appeared to be a saddle. In fact, my surroundings indicated that this was a shop which sold saddles. They festooned the walls like large fungi, assorted leather straps hung from brackets and large paper sacks of horse feed were piled high in all visible corners. The shopkeeper turned and hung his burden up on another wall-mounting.

"The man who came in here just now. He bought a big sack of something."

"Oh ah." Unmoved the man polished idly at some leather with his sleeve.

"Do you know who he is?"

"Ah."

"Well, could you tell me?" Strain made my voice a little shrill. The man looked at me suspiciously.

"Ah. That's Mr. Forrester. Charlton Hawsell stud."

Well, I knew he was good looking but— "*Is* he?"

"No, m'dear. He *owns* Charlton Hawsell Stud. Got the best Welsh stallions this side of the Brecon Beacons, so they say."

Horses. I might have known there would be horses involved somewhere. Ever since Florrie had learned to ride aged seven, my life had been blighted by the damn things. Then Alasdair had bought her a pony of her own, a terrifying orange thing which hurtled around seemingly uncontrollably. Happily, since she'd outgrown Dylan and sold him to a friend's younger sister, she had discovered the delights of manipulating boys instead. My weekends had been a lot more peaceful as a result. Or at least, differently worrying.

"Ms. Hunter! Alys!" It was Isabelle Logan, waving at me from the driver's seat of a Volvo Estate.

Chapter Eight

Beercroft Farmhouse proved rather disappointing. No whitewashed cob walls, no roses around doors overlooking a yard full of cackling hens, just a concrete cube at the end of a muddy lane. It looked like a council house on an exchange visit. The kitchen in which we sat contained not much more than a balding carpet, an enormous Aga which made curious bubbling sounds, and a bench table and chairs which seemed to have been appropriated from a local picnic spot.

"Would you like some tea?"

"No thanks. To tell you the truth, Mrs. Logan, I could have handed you the book and gone, you really didn't have to give me dinner." To tell even more of the truth, I would rather have stayed in Charlton Hawsell and tried to catch another glimpse of the Stallion Man.

"No, I wouldn't hear of it! You've come all this way, the least I can do is feed you. I'll run you back to your hotel later. Have you booked in anywhere yet?"

"No. Didn't have time."

"Well. The Star should have a room. I'll give them a ring in a bit, if you like."

The door opened and two men came in, identical except for years. Both square, sandy and freckled, both similarly booted and both smelling like pickled manure. They stumped across the kitchen without acknowledging either Isabelle or me and vanished through the opposite door, muttering darkly about "the AI man". It was like living through an episode of *League of Gentlemen.*

"My husband and son," Isabelle explained.

I refrained from saying, "Who's the other man?" because I was afraid she wouldn't see the joke. "Here. Before I forget." I held Theo out. "It must be awful to find you've inherited something and then find it's been sold by mistake."

"Inherited?" she said. Simultaneously the door opened again, and the man I'd seen that afternoon walked into the kitchen. He muttered, "Little buggers jumped out," and walked through, taking the same path as the other two men.

I stared after him, mouth open.

"Ah," said Isabelle Logan, the woman with the corridor house. "Um."

"That's—" I started, still staring at the far door. "It is, isn't it? He's considerably less dead than he should be."

"Oh dear." She dropped her head into her hands. "Oh God. Come into the study." Isabelle opened another door and led me into a tiny book-lined room. "I don't want him to overhear us. He gets very sensitive about things." Sensitive? Looking like that *and* sensitive? Bloody hell. She poured two glasses of whisky and handed me one. "That man—Theo Wood. His name is really Leo. He's my brother. Are you sure you want to hear this?"

It was a little like being told that Johnny Depp was moving in next door and was notorious for running out of sugar. My dream man was no longer a dream but a real, striding-about-in-my-vicinity human being. "Yes please." I took a mouthful of alcohol against it being a story I wasn't going to like.

"It was Leo's thirty-fifth. He'd had a rough year, what with his wife..." She tailed off.

Of course there'd have to be a bloody wife in there somewhere.

"...and he's just so *frustrating*. Always scribble scribble at those damn poems, never letting anyone see or read them. Always like it, even as a child. He's got books full of them at home you know. So, I sort of *crept* into his attic and chose a selection, and got them privately published at a little place in Exeter. Of course, knowing how shy Leo is, I thought if I made up this dead poet and pretended that *he'd* written the poems only his family would know who he really was, you see."

Leo Forrester. Theo Wood. Dear God, did this woman have no imagination?

"I gave one copy to our parents, and one to our uncle who lived over in Topsham, then one copy to Leo for his birthday. Well, he—"

I had a brief, scary flash into the mind of a shy, poetic type forced to face the realities of his words becoming public property. "He wasn't very happy?"

"Er. No. He didn't mind *too* much about the copies I'd given away, but he made me give him the other hundred. I was going to give them to the bookshop in Charlton, but Leo didn't want— anyway. Our uncle died six months ago. I just didn't think, got a house-clearance firm in to get rid of everything, but Leo asked me what had happened to the book. He made such a fuss, I *had* to get it back."

"Okay." I slowly drained my glass. "So I guess it's probably best if I don't mention that I've read it."

Isabelle's eyes widened. "Hell, I'd never thought of that. Look, if he asks, well, not that he's likely to but, you know. Can we say you're an old schoolfriend who's popped in on her way past?"

Past? From where to where? On a tour of obscure backwaters which haven't featured anywhere since the

Domesday Book writers rode through and thought, *Oh, go on then, might as well use up this ink?*

"How are you going to explain the return of the book?" She'd got up and was heading back into the kitchen. I followed, my Sex God readiness switched up to red alert just in case he turned out to be spread-eagled over the table, panting with insatiable lust.

"Oh, I'd already told him I'd got it back, said that I'd destroyed it, so—" As she spoke she thrust the book into the Aga and slammed the door on it; I shivered as though watching my best friend burn. "Leo's not had an easy time." The door opposite opened and she smoothly changed tack. "But farming in general is having a really bad few years." I nodded slowly, trying to keep my eyes from shooting to the doorway, but anyway my nose had let me know who the incomers were. "Josh, Ivan, this is Alys. She's come by to visit me, we were at school together, you know."

"Oh, aye." The two men nodded in my general direction, then leaned their ample bottoms against the Aga rail. "Leo having his dinner with us? We could have a word with him about those fences."

"Yes, what a good idea," Isabelle said brightly. "Go and ask him, Josh. We can introduce him to Alys."

Oh God. Here I was wearing my least flattering jeans, the ones that made my bum jut out sideways. I was caught between desperately wanting to meet my idol and not wanting to be seen looking like a shelving unit. "Isabelle, is there anywhere I could change? Maybe get a wash?" I asked.

I was directed to an upstairs room, where I waited until she'd shown me how to work the shower and gone back downstairs, then hoiked the mobile out of my bag.

"Jace? It's me," I hissed into it.

"Of course it's you." Jacinta's reply was loud and clear.

"Who else would be ringing me?"

"I need help. I've got to have dinner with this gorgeous man, and I've only got my jeans and that white T-shirt to change into."

"Hmm. Which jeans? The ones that are making your bottom veeeeerrrry wide?"

"No, those others, the pale blue ones."

"You have no worry. They is good. Anyways, men are never seeing what women is wearing, they are too busy thinking what she is looking like *not* wearing clothes."

"I don't think this man is quite like that, Jace." I heard her snort of disbelief. "But how do I look alluring, sexy and available yet classy, in jeans and T-shirt?"

"You must make shorter the straps on your bra. Is simple. Lift up your bosom further and make it look out."

I peered down my front. "Hair up or down?"

"You have hair on your bosom?" Jacinta sounded confused and I could hear Simon's voice asking if there was a problem.

"On my head! Up or down?"

"Up. But not too far, you are not wanting to look like a dog. I must go now, Simon is fitting with me."

"Having a fit," I corrected, but she'd already gone.

I washed and changed, pausing midway to ring Florence. "Hello, darling. How did the exam go?"

Florence grunted. "Okay, I suppose."

"Was it easy or hard, or what?"

Another grunt. "Okay. Look, I've got to go. Piers is taking me out."

"Out? You've got Maths tomorrow!" But I was talking to myself and I felt the tiny sting of memory, how she'd wanted to tell me everything about the SAT exams she'd taken, aged ten.

Now I was lucky if she'd tell me it was raining.

I made the necessary adjustments to my undergarments, then went downstairs. Approximately halfway it occurred to me that I'd shortened my straps too far. Although this gave me a cleavage which looked as though I was peering out from behind a couple of boulders, it meant that if I raised my arms higher than my waist, my bra would forcibly propel itself upwards and out through my neckline.

"Go and sit in the dining room, Alys. Help yourself to some wine, we won't be long." I went through the indicated door and found myself in what would have been a nice room if every wall hadn't been groaning under the weight of photographs, each one featuring a small, fat pony.

I poured myself some wine from the open bottle on the table. A reflection caught my eye in the glass frame of one of the photographs. I'd not quite got my hair right and without thinking I raised my hands to the back of my head to tweak down some curling tendrils around my face. My bra was thereby freed from its supporting position at the top of my rib cage and relocated halfway up my chest. "Oh shit!" Crouching to see my reflection more clearly, I shoved my hand up my T-shirt and tried to yank my underwear into a more serviceable position.

"Charlton Thistle."

I froze guiltily. "I beg your pardon?"

"Charlton Thistle. The stallion in the picture you're looking at. He was my first success."

I forced my eyes to refocus, away from my reflection and onto the picture itself whilst furtively tugging under my shirt. "He's very handsome."

Bugger me, you can say that again, I thought as I turned around and saw Theo Wood—Leo Forrester, glass of wine in hand, only inches away from me. Close enough for me to see that his eyes weren't the deep brown I'd assumed, but a clear green, and that he had a tiny scar running from his nose to the corner of his mouth. It made his face slightly flawed, more perfect.

"Mmmm. He was a little long in the back for me, but the judges seemed to like him."

A pause followed. He carried on scrutinising the photographs while I tried to think of something intelligent to say, staring at him fixedly all the time. Without the flattening effect of the camera lens, his face was thinner, bones more prominent. The whole thing added up to a look which could have made a career out of fronting aftershave adverts. The pair of rimless, angular glasses he wore only added to the lust factor, emphasising those green eyes.

Come on, Alys, make a move. I'd confronted him so many times in fantasies over the past couple of weeks that I should have a line ready. But that had been when I thought he was dead. Safe. "I'm..." I started, but he'd already begun to speak.

"He only died last year you know. Thirty-three, bloody good age for a stallion. Mind you, his dam lived to be twenty-eight."

Now I'd have to wind my introduction back up again. "Yes," I agreed without having much of an idea what I was agreeing to. "By the way..."

"Leo. Leo Forrester." He whipped around suddenly and grabbed my hand. "Izzie's brother. You're Alys, I understand? At Blandburgh with Izzie?"

Isabelle entered carrying a huge casserole dish and took in the scene with wide eyes. Her brother appeared to be holding my hand, whilst my underclothing was heaving-to at an angle previously only seen on a post-iceberg Titanic.

"I see you've introduced yourselves," she said indistinctly. "Leo, could you go and shout for Ivan?"

Leo let go of my hand, leaving it tingling slightly and went out.

Isabelle looked sideways at me. "It's nice to see Leo talking to someone he doesn't know." She distributed stew onto plates around the table. "He's usually terribly shy."

I turned away and gave one last hoik under my T-shirt. My cleavage subsided somewhat, but at least everything was now tucked back where it should be. "He seems very sweet," I said, understating.

"Oh, he is. He's a lovely man, he's just..." At that point we were interrupted by the entrance of Ivan, Josh, Leo and a small dark girl who was introduced as "my daughter Emma". We sat down to eat, leaving me fretting about the potential end of Isabelle's sentence. *He's just...* Just what? Just psychotic? Just got a half-inch willy? Just gay?

The conversation went on around Leo and me. We were seated opposite one another which gave me the maximum of opportunities to stare at him. Although a carelessly placed jug of water cut off most of my view from midchest down, I'd already noted that he was wearing a black T-shirt and close-fitting black jeans. His dark hair was long in an I've-been-too-busy-to-get-to-the-barber's way, curling around the back of his neck and wisping down over his forehead. He had short nails, slightly bitten, and his face was stubbled with a couple of days' growth. All in all, desirable.

"It's bad news about The Star, Alys, I'm afraid." Isabelle ladled me another helping of stew. "Fully booked."

"Oh." Damn, blast and bugger. "Well, if you can give me a lift to somewhere, I can get the bus. I'll find somewhere to stay in Exeter. Or go back tonight."

Everyone exchanged a smile. Even Leo. Perhaps this was the moment that someone said, "Oh, you can't go out after dark. Not round these parts."

"There won't be a bus back to Exeter until tomorrow

morning," Josh explained. "Trains up to York stop running at eleven. It's nearly nine now."

There was a short pause then Leo, with his eyes fixed firmly on his stew, mumbled something.

"Oh that would be wonderful," Isabelle said. "That will save Alys a lot of bother."

I smiled brightly. Leo looked up and caught my eye. Although he seemed a bit panicked, he managed to give me a small grin. I wondered what he'd suggested. I drained my glass of wine and hoped he hadn't offered to post me home in a Jiffy bag.

Chapter Nine

The evening petered slowly to a close, helped to its conclusion by a steamed treacle pudding which Isabelle bore triumphantly from the kitchen accompanied by a jug of custard. I hadn't seen so many calories on display since I caught sight of some illustrations in *The Lard Modellers Handbook*. Eventually everyone pushed back chairs and emptied glasses, looking at watches and making noises about how late it was getting.

I helped Isabelle clear the table in the hope that she'd drop some hints about what Leo had suggested for me.

"Um. Alys. Later. Well, it's not that we're not delighted that he's taken to you but—if you could be a *little* bit careful about what you mention. Only, there's the poetry, *obviously*, and it might be best if you didn't mention his wife either. Still a bit of a sore spot. If he asks anything about school just bluff it. I said that you left after a year to go and live in South Africa, so he shouldn't."

"What if he asks something about South Africa?"

Isabelle slammed the dishwasher shut. "Oh. I never thought of that. What do you know about South Africa?"

"Um. Apartheid. Nelson Mandela. That's it, I'm afraid."

Leo walked into the kitchen and stood by the Aga, his arms full of lengths of rope. He was tying and untying knots in them, but every now and again his eyes would flicker up and rest on me for a moment. I pretended to be busy swilling out some pots and not noticing, but I could feel it each time his gaze landed on me almost as though it had physical weight. Once I turned and looked over my shoulder, addressing a remark to Isabelle, and his eyes caught mine. He looked away after a second but—had I imagined it?—a blush crossed his face as he glanced back down at the twisted rope in his hands.

When the kitchen was tidy, I stood awkwardly. Leo bid his sister goodnight and the pair of them looked at me. "Er," I began, but Isabelle cut me short by wrapping her arms around me and giving me a huge hug.

"Well, Alys, it's been lovely seeing you *after all this time*. Thank you for coming all this way."

Leo seemed to be waiting for me. Cautiously I followed him to the door. "Goodbye," I said, somewhat quietly, in case I wasn't going. "Thank you for dinner."

Leo was standing outside the door with a torch in his hand. I picked up my rucksack and Isabelle closed the door behind us with a resounding and somewhat thankful thud. So. Let me recap. I was standing in the dark, with a man I desired marginally less than I liked breathing, and that man showed every sign of *wanting* to be there. I let out a silent murmur of thanks that I'd been keeping my karma shiny and bright. I must have been very, *very* good, probably in quite a lot of former lives, to have deserved this.

"So," I said, as we began to pick our way by the narrow torch beam up a dusty track.

"I hope you don't think I normally do this." He spoke without looking at me. "Taking women home when I've just met them. But, I don't know, there seemed to be some sort of *connection* between us, when I saw you standing there in front of the photos of Thistle...and...you seemed...it was almost as though you *knew* me when you looked at me. Like a flicker of recognition. I'm sorry. That sounds really pathetic, doesn't it?

But I knew that I didn't want you to disappear off to wherever it is that you come from. Not without my at least having the chance to talk to you."

My foot chose that particular moment to shoot into a rut. My leg gave way. I stumbled and lurched forward a couple of strides before I pitched to my knees in the dust. Great. I wanted to come over suave and sophisticated and here I was impersonating Frankenstein's monster's trial run. But there was an advantage. Leo lifted me to my feet by my upper arms. He was much more muscular than he looked, that black T-shirt must contain a decent body. As he placed me back upright, his hands lingered for a moment, and I felt the hairs along my forearms react. He was so close I could smell the scent of hay and horses from him, also something spicy and definitely sexy. I was feeling quite ridiculously hot and wondered how I was going to talk myself out of this.

"Oh, look." His voice had the breathless, dreamy quality that I normally associated with men when they were about to suggest that I might like to dress up in a rubber catsuit. "That's Sophia."

"Who?" We'd emerged from the lane and now the trackway was crossing an open field, well moonlit, but I couldn't see any sign of anyone else. "Where?"

"There. Isn't she beautiful?"

I looked where he pointed. "What? Behind the horse?"

"Pony. Sophia is my champion Section A mare. In foal to Cleavers, if everything works out right." We continued walking, uphill now, past the grazing pony, towards a stupendously lovely house which was gleaming yellow in the moonlight. "I'm sorry. I get a little bit carried away about my animals, sometimes. They've been everything to me since—well, for a long while now." We walked on, around to the front of the house, which made me stop for a second and catch my breath. It was a large Elizabethan building with high mullioned windows and arched doorways. A proper gravelled driveway led off between neatly clipped lawns into the distance.

"Gosh. The last time I saw anything like this, it was a recreation on *Time Team*."

"It is rather lovely." Leo pushed open a door which bore more metal decoration than your average body-piercing enthusiast and led me into an enormous hallway. I followed him through into a kitchen. A large range took up most of one wall and a huge butler's sink occupied a greater portion of the other. A scrubbed table stood in the middle and the corners were occupied by dogs' beds, horse rugs, saddlery and assorted piles of papers, boxes and bottles. It was a mess. But, I was pleased to note, there were absolutely no feminine touches around the place, not even so much as a rag rug to warm the chilly stone flag floor. If he *did* have a wife, she was a complete domestic slob.

Leo glanced around at the empty dog beds. "I wonder where the terriers have got to?" He opened a door. I admired his back view as he took a few steps out of the kitchen. My subconscious checklist of desirable male features was sagging under the weight of ticks—the way his hair curled slightly over his collar, the broad line of his shoulders, the neatness of his buttocks. All this and the sensual frisson which had definitely slithered between us when he'd helped me upright. He was, without a doubt, what Florence would call *fit*.

Florence. She'd be back from wherever-it-was that Piers was taking her by now, surely? Especially with an exam to sit tomorrow.

"Hey, Mum!"

For once she sounded pleased to hear from me. "Is everything okay, darling? Are you back at Dad's?"

"Yeah, everything's cool this end. What're you up to?"

"Well, I'm sitting in an Elizabethan mansion chatting to a

rather nice man."

A snorty kind of laugh. "Yeah, right. And I just pulled the Arctic Monkeys."

"No, I am. Honestly."

A pause. "What, a man? A real one?" There was a sudden, frantic amount of whispering off-mouthpiece as Florence relayed this piece of information to someone else.

I heard Piers say, "Is she all right?"

Piers obviously thought the only way I'd ever be in contact with a man would be for one to have abducted me. "It's all fine. Look, I'll be back tomorrow. Ask Piers to bring you home in the evening, if he doesn't mind."

There was a lot of rustling at the other end, then Piers's voice. "That'll be okay, Alys. I'll bring her back around nine. Will you be in?"

"If I'm not I won't be too late. Thank you for running her around, Piers. I hope it's not interfering with your life too much."

"Well, you know, things are kinda quiet at the moment."

We were silent at each other. I heard Florrie say, "Let me talk to her again," petulantly, as though Piers had been withholding the handset. "Mum, you don't have to come back on my account, you know. It will be fine for me to stay with Dad a bit longer."

"No, I'll come back tomorrow. I've got to work. Bye darling!"

Florence muttered me a goodbye, another set of plans obviously thwarted by her evil mother, and I laid the phone down. Leo was standing just inside the door.

"I'm sorry," he said. "I should have realised."

"Realised what?"

"I...umm..." His eyes headed for the ceiling and began following the contours of the walls. "I'm afraid...I'm...oh bugger it. I should have realised that you weren't available. My fault. Sorry." His eyes continued to roam somewhere above head height, but the rest of his face assumed a wry expression. "I hope I haven't compromised our...friendship by saying that." He'd obviously heard the tail end of my conversation, all *Piers* and *darling*.

"Oh, but I am," I said. "Available, that is." Aware that this made me sound like Tart of the Century, I hastened in with, "I was talking to my daughter. I'd promised I'd ring. But apart from her—oh, and Grainger, he's our cat—well, there's nobody." Then, because that gave the impression that I was Billy No-Mates, "Nobody special, that is. I mean, I see people, of course I do, doesn't everyone, but not men. Well, some of them are men, obviously, at least half, but I don't see them, I mean, I *see* them, otherwise I'd fall over them all the time, but not in that way. If you see what I mean." It had finally dawned on me that I was gabbling.

"In other words, you don't have a significant other?"

"I don't have any kind of other." And forgetting everything Isabelle had told me, "What about you? Married?"

Leo sank suddenly into a chair. "I hope you'll excuse me." He put his head in his hands for a moment as though he was very tired. "I *like* you Alys, but there are things I find quite difficult to talk about. I'm not naturally a very open person."

"I think most poets aren't," I said without thinking, then blushed a bright and unflattering shade of cerise.

"How...?"

"Isabelle." I dropped his sister firmly into the cesspit of fraternal relations. "She mentioned that you wrote poetry sometimes. A lot of poets aren't good at verbalising relationships and things. They put everything into words in a different way." Because I was panicking slightly and his expression was a bit blank, I added, "W.H. Auden was exactly the same!"

"Ah. Was he?" Leo got up and went to a cupboard, which turned out to be rather satisfyingly full of wine. "Drink?"

We drank. Talked. Leo seemed to talk a lot but without giving much away. He told me about the stud, his five champion stallions and the mares. I tried to ask intelligent, nonprobing questions but it was really awkward. Curiously, this made him more exciting, more inscrutable, like a wrapped parcel under the Christmas tree.

Eventually we both sat back and yawned in tandem. "Do you realise it's nearly three o'clock?" He rubbed his hands over his cheeks. "I need a shave. And a haircut. I do apologise, Alys, for being such a scruffbag. You deserve better and next time we meet I shall try to be a little more presentable."

"I think you look"—I couldn't meet his eye—"great." Understatement of the year. "You don't need to do anything on my account."

"But I'd like to." Leo leaned across the table, put a finger under my chin and gently tilted my head so that I had to look at him. "May I, Alys? May I see you again? I admit, I've got no idea how, but all I know is that I'd like to, very much."

"Yes," I almost whispered and hoped that he'd take the pleading expression in my eyes as an invitation to kiss me. Whatever he took it as, he didn't kiss me. Didn't even close the gap between us, just let go of my chin and sighed.

"It's late. I'll show you to the Green Room, I think you'll like it. I'll run you through to Exeter tomorrow to get the train, but I'm afraid I'll probably not see very much of you before that. I'm up at six to start on morning stables."

I followed him up the most stunning flight of stairs ever seen outside a forties Hollywood musical, and along a twisted tangle of corridors and landings. At last Leo stopped in front of a door. "This is the Green Room. Bathroom is down the corridor there. Good night, Alys. Sleep well."

I half pursed my lips in expectation of a kiss, but he was gone, striding away into the darkness. I went into the bedroom and undressed, then lay and cursed. Maybe I should have asked Leo where his room was? Maybe he'd appreciate being swept off his feet, maybe he didn't know *how* to make the first move. But Leo struck me as a man who liked to do the gentlemanly thing and, let's face it, sleeping with a woman you've only just met who's largely off her face on white wine is hardly gentlemanly. I didn't really know *how* to make the first move—not these days. Anyway, hadn't I secretly preferred him as a dead man?

If only he wasn't so *damn sexy.*

Chapter Ten

"And this," Leo continued, as I gritted my teeth to stifle a tiny bubble of yawn, "is Charlton Persephone." He leaned over yet another stable door and rubbed the neck of yet another small grey pony. "All my mares have women's names and the stallions are all named after plants, as you might have noticed."

I had noticed. I had also noticed that Leo was clean shaven this morning, was wearing a black hooded sweatshirt and a worn pair of denims and that he smelled of Aramis. He leaned companionably close over the half-door, and I became very aware that his shoulder was touching mine. I turned around to hold my face up to the sun, letting the urgent light burn away some of the heavy-lidded desire for more sleep. To my gratification he turned too, then stood in front of me forming a shadow which blocked almost all the rays. Enough light was getting past him, however, to mean that I could only look at him through half-closed lids.

There was a moment of silence. The blinding light meant I couldn't see his expression, only the outline of his head. "Excuse me," he said softly. "Do you mind if I just—" His head came forward, a hand reached out and cupped the back of my head. I closed my eyes waiting for lip impact. Instead I felt a brief fiddle at the front of my hair, and he pulled away again causing the sunlight to strobe across my face. "You had a piece of hay caught."

My lips slammed together. "We'd better get going," I said rather tersely. "I don't want to miss my train."

"Plenty of time." Leo moved on to the next stable. "Come in here a second."

He unlocked the door and I followed, into a loose box full of straw but no pony. "What?"

"Oh. Only this." He grabbed me very firmly by both shoulders and kissed me deeply. I'd got used to being kissed by men who made the event feel as though my face was being attacked by half a pound of raw liver, but Leo—well, let's just say he was *hot*. He didn't attempt to explore the contents of my T-shirt, but a definitely not-disinterested hand roamed about between my shoulder blades and there was a distinct pressure against my hip. Finally he let go and stood away, shaking his hair off his face and holding his watch up in front of his eyes. "Hmmm, better get off to the station."

"Oh." I found myself slightly embarrassed. "Yes. Yes, I suppose so."

"You don't mind? That I kissed you?" Leo opened the stable door and ushered me out as though we'd done nothing more meaningful than examine some paintwork. "I felt that it was something I wanted to do."

"No!" I said abruptly, then feeling this could be open to misconstruction added, "I liked it, Leo. It was good. Lovely, in fact. I'd like to do it again sometime."

"You're the first woman I've...since... It's come as a bit of a shock to me. Finding you attractive. Must admit, I feel a bit guilty about the whole thing."

Now he was going to come out as married. Or, I supposed, to top it all, a married Catholic.

"My wife—" He stopped again, went very quiet until he'd unlocked the doors to the Land Rover and we were both sitting inside.

In the heat, it smelled strongly of baked dog and I wound the window down to avoid suffocating. Leo's knee hovered very close to mine and I wondered what he'd do if I touched his leg. Did I mind that he was married? Did *he?* Was it worth the risk? Was he inwardly quivering, poised and waiting for some sign that I wanted to take things further? Was this respectable behaviour for a mother-of-one?

The big engine shuddered into life and I watched him drive for a while. Capable hands, lean, long legs, a body like an action-packed adventure and the face of a thriller. He looked like a poster boy for Poetry Please. "Sorry, what was I saying?" he seemed to come to, to remember I was there in the car with him.

"You were telling me about your wife." I decided to be brave and upfront about it. "How long have you been married?" Maybe it was seven years. Maybe I was the loofah to scratch the itch. Did I care?

"Sabine was killed. Drunk driver. Paris, two years ago. We'd been married for eight years." Totally factual, totally emotionless.

"Oh. God, I'm sorry, Leo."

Two years ago. And Isabelle had printed his poems. His wife had just died and she thought it would make him feel better to have his love for her nailed down in words on paper? The woman was barking.

"It... There were things... It wasn't like...oh *bugger!*" The Land Rover twitched to one side, pulling towards the verge with a dragging sound. Leo stood hard on the brake but forward momentum carried us until, with a lurch and a bang, we came to rest in the hedge. "Sod. Puncture. You all right, Alys? You sure?"

"Fine."

I was glad that Leo was happy to do the macho thing with

jacks and wheelbraces while I sat on the verge. I'd *thought* he was too good to be true. He'd not shown any of the signs that men who wanted to date me normally displayed, i.e., travelling everywhere by bus with a stolen pensioner's pass. Now he was, whoa, taking his *shirt off.* There was a sudden, almost reverential, lapse in my thinking ability while I watched a Diet Coke ad come to life in front of me. He didn't even have the decency to have a hairy back or a disgusting tattoo emblazoned across his torso. When he turned around to tell me the wheel was fixed, I could feel my eyes getting sucked down from his face towards his navel, registering the tidy whorl of hair which encircled it, fighting with myself not to let my stare go any lower.

"Alys?" He was coming at me out of the sun again. "Are you really sure you're all right?"

"I'm fine." I managed to roll my tongue back into my mouth. "Got a bit of a headache, that's all."

So there I sat, next to Mr. Perfect-except-for-a-dead-and-adored-wife, for the rest of the run into Exeter. I tried a few times to reinitiate the conversation we'd been having, but he would change the subject immediately, almost as though ashamed of having said as much as he had. Unfortunately the only other topic available to him at short notice was the stud and by the time we reached Exeter station, I had more knowledge about stallion management than I suspect anyone who works in a bookshop could have found a use for.

"Well. Goodbye, Alys." There was a brief, awkward hug exchanged, as though the kisses of the morning had been an aberration on his part. "Could I have your telephone number?"

I wanted to have the mental strength to tell him that I didn't think that was such a good idea, unless he could manage not to be gorgeous when we next met. Oh, and if he could have some kind of electric-shock treatment which caused him to totally forget his deceased and no-doubt-also-gorgeous wife. But

I didn't. I had no mental strength at all as I wrote my home number on a slip of paper provided by the man in the booking office.

My train pulled slowly into the station, and Leo looked down at his feet. "I will call you," he said as I pushed through the crowd to get on board. "I will call you!" he raised his voice to shout.

"Yes. Please."

As the train jerked out of Exeter, I could see Leo standing and watching it go, one hand raised in a salute of goodbye as I wibbled my way down the aisle to my reserved seat. *Reserved* was a good way of describing Leo, I thought. But stonkingly beddable was better.

I'd meant to spend the time reading, catching up on Mrs. Munroe's brave book-group submission of *The Lovely Bones* but the daydreams I fell into became dreaming for real. York station caught me unawares so I felt greasily sticky and disgruntled when I disembarked and entirely justified in using some of Simon's cash to get a taxi back to the flat. The streets were crowded with summer's night visitors taking horse-drawn tours around the minster or just wandering about. Bunches of foreign-language students formed little clique-knots outside pubs, like the United Nations going clubbing.

The windows of the flat shone yellow and welcoming as I paid the taxi driver and added a generous tip. Florence must be home.

"Hello, darling." I greeted the flat with blanket coverage but there was no response, so I trailed through to the living room and tried again. "Hello, dar..."

"Hiya, sweetie," Piers drawled back. "Good trip?" He was sitting cross legged on the floor reading a newspaper.

"Very clever. Where's Florrie? And why are you here again? You're becoming ubiquitous, aren't you?"

"Yeah. Totally. In fact, I'm going for omnipresence next." Piers stretched out his legs to reveal that he was wearing striped jeans and an equally stripy shirt. "Flo's run down to the pizza place on the corner, we were both kinda hungry."

Grainger appeared out of my bedroom, treating me with the disdain he reserved for anyone who'd been missing for more than a couple of hours and cheap cat food. I stroked his sticky fur and realised I could feel his backbone. "Grainger? Are you okay?" I watched him sway towards the kitchen. "Do you think Grainger could have worms?"

"Nah. He's all right, aren't you?" To my horror, Piers swept Grainger up off the floor and contained him against his chest.

"Piers, be careful. He…" But Grainger just let out a throaty kind of grumble and submitted to the petting with the embarrassed air of someone trying on a new suit that they secretly think makes them look *really* good. "…he actually likes you," I finished, slightly puzzled.

"Yeah. Seems to." Piers let Grainger jump to the floor. "But you're right, he does look a bit…"

"Manky. He looks manky." I glanced up at the sound of the front door opening and Florence entering, rustling plastic bags. "Don't you think he looks a bit manky, Florrie?"

"Oh, hi, Mum. Yeah, completely. It's a shit outfit, Piers."

"Not Piers, Grainger. Although you're right, it is a horrible combination. What happened, did you get dressed under the influence?"

"Hey, no ganging up on me, girls." Piers backed away, hands held in an attitude of surrender, but he looked furtively rather pleased. Florence went to put the pizzas onto plates in the kitchen and Piers followed me back through, helping me to pull the table out so we could all sit round it. "It's not that bad, is it, Alys?"

"I can't honestly tell, Piers. I can't focus on it for long

enough."

"Ah well. At least it gets me noticed."

"Lucky it doesn't get you arrested."

Florence came back with slices of pizza arranged haphazardly on too-small plates. I was hungry. Leo hadn't provided any breakfast and anyway, he was so gorgeous that my appetite knew when it was beaten. All three of us ate in a companionable silence.

"Mum..." Florence eventually broke the chewing silence. "I've got something to ask you."

"Yeeeeeessss?" I said, dubiously. She was being way too nice for this to be good.

"Do you promise you're not going to be mad?"

I became motherish. "I think you mean angry not mad. You're getting influenced by Piers and his dreadful mid-Atlantic phraseology."

"I'm American! I can't help that," Piers joined in, less indignant than he sounded; instead he looked sparky, animated. "And I think you mean being influenced not getting influenced. I might be American, but I can still do grammar."

"Shame you can't do dress-sense," I said waspishly but he laughed.

"Oh, Alys, I am wounded." He held a hand to his chest, rings gleaming. "To think I don't appeal to you because I have no sense of style. You shallow, shallow woman."

Florence was watching this exchange with a baffled expression, obviously desperate to say *yes, enough of this, now let's talk about me*, but intrigued enough not to.

"I didn't say you didn't appeal to me," I said without thinking, laughing despite myself at his ridiculousness. "I just said—" But Piers had leaped up and was grabbing his leather jacket from the back of his chair.

"No more! I am deeply offended, and I'm going. Leave you two females to your heavy talking. Oh, and Alys." He leaned forward and almost breathed in my ear. "Next time I'll try and wear something that *does* appeal to you, yeah?"

Both Florence and I were giggling helplessly as he walked out, but I managed to control myself enough to shout, "That's try *to*, not try *and*. Bloody Yank!" and heard an offended *huh* in reply as the front door closed. "Piers is growing into a really nice lad." I picked up the last slice of pizza. "Funny too."

"Yeah, yeah, a real stand-up, our Piers." Florence watched me eat. "Look, Mum. I want to go to London. It's okay, not on my own or anything. Oh, and not with boys either, if that's what you're thinking. My friend Keisha, you know Keisha, from school? Her sister lives in Highgate, and she's asked Keish to visit and bring a friend and Keish asked me—and I'd really, *really* like to go!"

"Oh." I was taken aback. "When would this be?"

Florence seemed encouraged by my not immediately shooting her down in flames. "Not for nearly two weeks, after the exams are over. But Lex, that's Keisha's sister, she's said she'll take us to the Tower of London and on the London Eye and stuff like that and I've never even *been* to London before, have I, Mum? It would be fantastic. So, what do you think?"

"Welllll, as long as I can speak to Keisha's mum first, to check things out. Not that I don't trust you, darling, it's just to make sure that it's all right with Lex." I knew Keisha and her sister, two improbably beautiful girls. Florence would have a whale of a time with them. "Then yes. Of course you can go." Bonus, I'd have a couple of weeks to myself, maybe get to see Leo. I mean, I liked spending time with Florence—when Alasdair and I had parted, we'd become a tight little unit she and I. But since she'd hit her teens, she'd become so worldly-wise it sometimes felt as though she were the adult and I were the child. A little time to be me would be welcome.

"Wow." Florence looked stunned. She'd obviously thought she'd have to put up more of an argument than that. "That's great! Thanks, Mum. Oh and you don't have to worry about spending money, 'cause Dad's already said he'll let me have a grand. For clothes and stuff."

Florence skipped out of the room, leaving her dirty plate on the table and me with a flare of resentment firing off in my chest. Maybe I was wrong, telling Alasdair that I wanted no money from him, and if he wanted to give Florence something that was between them. Okay, so it ensured that she never went without school uniform or riding lessons or anything else it entered her head to ask for, but was it giving her a sense of values? A thousand pounds, just for a couple of weeks in London? I swallowed the knot of bitterness in my throat.

Perhaps she could lend me a tenner.

Chapter Eleven

I went back to work, and Jace and I settled back into our usual pattern of bitching about Simon during his absences and working conspicuously hard when he was present. The book group met, Mrs. Searle's book choice proving to be a romantic novel which Simon refused to stock and I'd had to borrow from the library where they'd only had the large-print version. I'd read it in one evening and it was like being shouted at by Barbara Cartland.

Leo hadn't rung. Maybe it had been one of those Brief Encounter things.

"What I am not understanding is"—Jacinta heaved a huge box of books across the floor—"why you are not asking him about his wife?" She slit the cardboard side of the box and books spilled out. "Maybe he is hating her and is hiring a missionary to kill her."

"Mercenary." I sorted through the tumbled books which lay like stunned pigeons over the matting. "And it's not really the sort of thing you can come out with, is it? 'Oh, sorry your wife was tragically killed, did you love her at all? And, by the way, how would you say I compare in the looks stakes?' Urgh, no. After all, what would I have done if he'd spent the next hour telling me how gorgeous and wonderful she was and how much he missed her?"

"Helped him to miss her a little less?"

"He's not really like that, Jace." I clasped a rather dog-eared Keats to my sweater. "He's shy and kind of hidden. Keeps everything under cover. If I hadn't read his poetry I'd probably think he was a bit cold, but he's so much more than that underneath."

"Then you must get underneath him." Jace started ticking books off the packing list.

"If only it was that easy," I began, but she looked at me sternly.

"Alys, I know a lot about men, and this I know, they do not tell you things that you *need* to know, they tell you that which they are *wishing to say*. And if you are being serious over this man, you are needing to be talking much with him over things which are not said. They are the important things, Alys, the things which are in the head."

"But he hasn't rung me, so how can I talk to him? Maybe he wasn't really that keen on me." I remembered the kiss in the stable. "Or at least, maybe he didn't feel the same way after I'd left."

"Are you thinking seriously about him?" Jace handed me the book list.

"I'm not sure."

"What he looks like?"

"Oh, about six foot, dark hair, needs a good cut, green eyes. Nice face, he's got the whole cheekbones thing going on. Long legs, good body, I mean—whew, yes, good body. He looks a bit unkempt, a bit slept in. Oh, and he bites his nails."

"Alys, if you want this man you must show him that you are wanting him! If you *really* want him then you will find a way."

All the way home on the bus, I thought about Jacinta's words and by the time I'd arrived I was determined. Okay, so I didn't have his number, but he ran a commercial business. He wasn't going to be Mr. Elusive, was he? It was obvious—he doesn't ring me, so I ring him. Would he think I was chasing him? But, did it matter? *If you* really *want him*, Jacinta had said, and I did really want him, didn't I?

As I went through the front door, I became aware that the flat smelled strange. But I ignored it, desperate to carry out my plan before Florence got home and started asking awkward questions. I found a directory service, got the number for Charlton Hawsell Stud, and was halfway through dialling when my foot found the source of the odd smell.

"Grainger!" I bellowed, my toes squishing about in a puddle of semisolid coldness. "You complete *bastard*." Grainger half raised a bleary eyelid as he lay in his current comatosery, a basket of clean but unironed washing. "What do you think your litter tray is *for*?" I hopped off across the floor, berating the cat all the while, although he had long since furled his eyelid back down like a blind, proclaiming him to be a cat Seriously Asleep.

While I was standing poised on one leg with the other foot in the sink like an inferior Degas painting, Florence came bustling through. She was laden with bags and carrying a bunch of flowers which had definitely gone past their best. She poked them individually into the tops of the glass jars and bottles awaiting their visit to the recycling bin.

"I'm not even going to ask," she said, watching me perched less-than-athletically, sponging off my offending foot under the tap.

"Well, I am. What on earth are you doing with those flowers?"

A superannuated lupin drooped pathetically from the neck of a milk bottle and Florence dreamily tried to re-erect it. "They'd been left next door with Mr. Roberts last week. But he had to go down to Sheffield because his mother had had another fall, and he completely forgot that he'd got them. When he saw me coming up the stairs he gave them to me. There's a card."

I found it, sticking wetly to the stem of a white carnation. *Looking forward to seeing you again. Regards, Leo.* I grasped the damp square of cardboard as though it was a message from the gods. He'd sent me flowers! But—I regarded the senior citizens of the bouquet world slumped in the assorted glassware—that had been last week and he still hadn't rung. I mean, he'd had his chance, hadn't he?

Oh, what the hell. I could at least ring to say thank-you for the flowers.

"Charlton Hawsell Stud, Leo Forrester speaking."

"Horny. I mean, hello. Hello, Leo, it's Alys. Alys Hunter?"

"Yes, Alys, I know who you are. It's so lovely to hear from you."

Well, he sounded genuinely pleased. I thanked him for the flowers and he apologised for not having rung me yet, but explained that, "I've been blue-arsed fly busy here." There was a bit of a pause after that, long enough for me to think that he didn't really want to speak to me at all. Then he cleared his throat. "Um, Alys, look." Here it came, the big brush-off speech. "I'm really crappy on the phone. I can come up to York, leave my stud manager in charge of the place for a couple of days. I wondered, would next Tuesday be all right?"

"Oh! Next Tuesday is my birthday."

"Sorry, is that a problem?"

So, did I come out and admit that I was such a miserable old sod that my birthday evening was to have been spent admiring Johnny Depp's very *particular* walk in *Pirates of the Caribbean*, possibly after a swift gin and tonic in the Ha-Ha bar with Jace? And Mrs. Treadgold had made me a cake. Coffee Victoria sponge, my favourite. "Well, I had been intending to catch a gig at the jazz club, but I can easily give that a miss. Maybe we could go for dinner."

"Meet you at the station at eightish? The best train for me to catch is due in York at seven forty-five. Look, sorry Alys, but I really have to rush off now."

"I'll see you next Tuesday." But I was talking to a dead line, he'd already gone. I hugged myself in an over-rush of silent glee, seizing a senile gypsophilia stem and whirling it over my head. "She shoots, she scores. And the crowd goes mad!"

"They're not the only ones. Have you gone completely off your elderly trolley, Mother?" Florence had her entire wardrobe spread over the floor in the living room and was piecing together outfits which looked more like piece than outfit.

"Oh Lord. You're off tomorrow, aren't you? Piers not here, helping you to pack?"

"Nah, he's busy looking at flats."

Piers currently lived in a self-contained flat attached to Alasdair and Tamar's house. I wasn't surprised he wanted to move. It must be tricky having a constant procession of girlfriends pass by right under your mother's eye. It would be like permanently having sex in public. Unless that was what turned him on. Eww, I did *not* want that thought. "You'll miss him when he's not there every time you go over."

Florence stuffed another pair of micro-knickers into her bag. "Yeah. Piers is cool. Oh, by the way Mum, before I forget." She pulled a long, heavy-looking parcel from underneath the bag. "Happy birthday for next Tuesday. You can open it now, if you want."

"Oh, thank you, darling." I tried to pretend surprise but I could feel the glass weight in my hand. It felt as though she'd already framed the photographs. "Oh. What a lovely—chopping board."

"Yeah, well, I noticed the worktop's getting a bit scratched. Oh, and there's a card."

This one bore a joke at which I guffawed appreciatively and

silently swore to get Jacinta to explain to me. Maybe the photographs hadn't come out as well as Florrie had hoped. She was self-indulgently vain, in the way that only a beautiful sixteen-year-old girl could be.

I went to bed and left her to her packing, so that I could lie under the deep gaze of Theo Wood. Better take that down before next Tuesday, I thought to myself. Not many men like having an oversized version of their own faces criticising their seduction techniques.

Chapter Twelve

Next morning I waved Florence off on the early London train, in company with Tina, Keisha's mother, both of us looking as though we were sending a couple of five-year-olds off on their first day of school. "They'll be fine," Tina reassured me. "Lex has turned into a sensible girl now she's got the baby and Stevie to look after. What's Florence most keen to do down in London?"

"She wants to spend loads of cash, obviously, and her Dad's decided to indulge that particular whim so…"

Tina sighed in sympathy, having brought up her three girls with the minimum of paternal contribution, although hers had been the result of a decamping husband rather than a moral stand. "You're from London, right, Alys? Is she going to visit any relatives while she's there?"

Now it was my turn to sigh. "No. My parents died when I was at university, I've no relatives there any more. She'll be quite happy to go along with whatever Keisha wants to do, I should think."

Tina and I glanced at each other nervously, full of memories of what we had wanted to do when we were sixteen, and imaginings of what we would have done if let loose with pockets full of money and only a twenty-two-year-old sister in charge. "They're sensible girls," Tina said hopefully. "They'll have fun."

Yeah, I thought miserably as I caught the bus to take me from the station to Webbe's. They'll have fun and sex and booze and dancing and boys and wild nights, and it's not fair! I was going to miss having Florence and, by extension, Piers around the flat. She might be a grumpy, uncommunicative devourer of all the biscuits, but she was *my* grumpy, uncommunicative devourer.

"Wish I was going to London with not a care in the world," I muttered to Jace as I slumped over the till.

"But then you would not be seeing your lovely man," she pointed out. "You cannot have everybody's life, Alys."

"I know, I know. Take no notice of me, I'm just feeling peevish." Also depressed at the awfulness of my flat. Even if Leo did seem to run his own home in a cross between junkie-chic and Oxfam, it was still furnished in the eccentric way of someone who could buy better, but wasn't bothered. My place was furnished but only just. I couldn't afford a lifestyle. I couldn't even afford lifestyle magazines.

"I go make tea. I must adjust my makeup." Jace shimmied off towards the cubbyhole, leaving me making faces at myself in the shiny surface of the desk.

There was a pile of literary magazines propped up to display their artfully designed covers next to the till and I glanced over them. "*Slightly Foxed.* That's me to a tee that is. More than *slightly,* more like bloody *completely* foxed. Probably hedgehogged as well. Wouldn't be surprised." I pulled another series of huffy faces. When the bell clattered, I hardly even bothered to look up.

"Wind'll change y'know."

I glanced in the direction of the doorway. It was the postman, bearing our usual bundle of mail and a large wrapped parcel.

"That looks exciting," I said, in an ironic way.

"Now, now. It's not for you anyway. It's for Jacinta. She about?"

Curiosity overcame me. "No, sorry, she's"—I lowered my voice, although I knew Jace couldn't hear anything behind the curtain—"gone home. Women's troubles, you know."

"'Nuff said." He handed me the wedge of brown and buff envelopes in one hand, and I signed for the parcel with the other.

I waited until he'd stepped back into the street before I gave the package a good scrutinising. Okay, it was wrong of me but, well. I spilled the beans to Jace about every detail of *my* life whilst she didn't seem to see anything wrong in keeping secrets from me.

The parcel was soft. Squashy. I turned it every which way, but there was no clue to the contents. It was addressed by hand in bold biro and covered in what looked like enough stamps to mail an elephant. I shook it and was just about to "accidentally" tear one corner when Jace emerged, newly made-up.

"This is for you."

Her eyes went round and she let out a little squeal. "Oh, this is very *very* good. In time for my weekend too!"

I waited expectantly for her to tear off the wrapping. Instead she shoved the whole thing into her capacious bag. I opened my mouth to ask but closed it again. If she'd wanted me to know she'd have told me, wouldn't she? I huffed off into the darkest reaches of Biography where I sat on Stephen Fry. Jace obviously thought this all stemmed from my morning whinge and left me to get on with it. Although, to her credit, occasional emergency cups of tea were left at the entrance next to consolatory piles of biscuits for the rest of the day, as if she were feeding the Minotaur in its lair.

I began cleaning and tidying the flat. At least with Florence away, areas that I tidied stayed more or less that way. The bathroom I couldn't do much about. Cracked tiles and damp walls were still very much in evidence. I went shopping and laid in supplies from the discounted shelves where they sold those items nearly out of date, what Florence always referred to as the "botulism counter". Dips and mousses, finger foods which would taste their best eaten in bed. Oh dreadful thought, perhaps he wouldn't want to come back here at all. But, that kiss—that had promised such a lot.

I bought a new duvet set for the bed, crisp Egyptian cotton in classy off-white. Calm tranquillity in my bed was not quite what I was aiming for though. How did I conjure up torrid sex with a tiny hint of long-lasting passion? Unfortunately the years of single parenthood had given me such a complex about spending money on myself that I was almost overcome with guilt at the whole expense. I had to bite my fingers to prevent myself from taking the bed set back to the shop. In the end I bought (in the charity shop, to assuage my mother-guilt) a throw in glowing red velvet and made some scatter cushions from some old curtains, although my sewing technique was not the best and the stitches were so large that the cushions looked like accident victims. With the hint-of-yellow walls and light blue woodwork, the pine dressing table and bedhead, the throw made the bed stand out throbbingly, like a boil on a suntanned bum. It was, to put it mildly, *obvious*.

Ah well, I thought, standing back to admire my efforts, *better obvious than diffident*. I mean, look at Simon. I bet he hadn't had sex since 1989. With anyone. Of either gender. I bet *his* bedroom was wall-to-wall beige and he could only find the bed by running his hands over the carpet.

Urgh. I shook myself out of this unhealthy preoccupation with my boss's sleeping arrangements. (Maybe he didn't have a bed at all. Maybe he rolled himself in sacking and lay on a stone floor. He looked the type.)

"You come to my home on Tuesday," Jacinta advised on Monday. "Before you go to the station, I will make you up."

Which certainly made sense since Jace lived midway between Webbe's and the station. So after work on Tuesday the two of us made our rather giggly way to Jace's tiny house. It was a one-bedroomed terrace, so tall and thin that on first seeing Jacinta at home, I'd assumed that she could only turn round by going outside. Jacinta opened a bottle of wine. "How many birthday cards are you getting today?" she asked while I struggled into the green dress.

"Um. Well. Simon's never remembered my birthday, Florence has already given me my card, the book group gave me a joint card yesterday, so did Piers, oddly enough. So—one."

"One? And what about the card I am giving you?"

"That was the one."

"Ah, Alys." Jace sighed and drained her glass in one mouthful. "You need a good man."

"Perhaps today I'll actually go about getting one." Another spark of anticipation fizzed inside me and I gave a beaming smile.

"Well." She looked me over appreciatively and smoothed some wrinkles out of the dress as she did so. "You are certainly going to grab some eyes. You are lovely woman, Alys. Lovely." Jacinta gave a small sniff and wiped her eyes with the back of her hand. "Now, are we going to make you a face?"

By the time the wine was finished, we had indeed made me a face. I barely recognised myself in the mirror. "Good God," I said, impressed. She had been spending so long over applying my makeup that I had begun to wonder if I would emerge looking like a drag queen. But, in the best traditions of makeup artists everywhere, Jace had made me look as though I were wearing none at all. "I look—pretty."

"Stand up and go around," she ordered and I obliged,

feeling the green skirt flare away from my thighs as I twirled. My hair, which Jace had pinned into a casually tumbled style, flowed around my face. I was impressed. My hair normally made me look somewhere between an auburn poodle and a seventies footballer, but right now it was coming in just to the left of Nicole Kidman. "Beautiful." Jace quickly sliced away another tear. "You look so certain of yourself."

"Right now," I said, pouting at myself in the mirror, "I could proposition Johnny Depp."

"Then let us hope he is not at the station. You would not be wishing for punching and fighting."

I felt out of place standing on York station at seven thirty. Around me milled a crowd of returning commuters, all wearing workaday suits and office-dishevelled hair, whilst I stood like a misplaced ageing ingenue, overglamorous and hyped to distraction. I watched the Arrivals board, the seven forty-five which Leo would be on was running ten minutes late, so I bought myself a coffee. I had to ditch most of it on account of my bladder being overwrought with nerves. In the Ladies, I sprayed on more perfume, then worried I would smell too pungent.

As I crouched at the sink trying to wash off the worst of the excess, the creeping self-doubt began. Was I cut out to be a girlfriend anyway? Shouldn't I be at home, baking cakes for my daughter, whilst she crayoned in the next room? All right, maybe sixteen was bit old for crayoning—perhaps I could bake while she revised, calling out the odd question about the causes of the First World War, or the structure of the ear?

I fished a handful of paper towels from the dispenser and dabbed at myself where the water had splashed over my dress, and thought of Florence's reaction the only time I'd tried to help her with her homework. She'd fixed me with a baleful glance from an overmascaraed eye, corrected my Latin pronunciation and told me she was going round to a friend's house to revise.

Where it was quieter, apparently.

By the time I emerged, the Exeter train was being announced on Platform Three. I placed myself casually, but with my heart thundering, against a pillar. It would give me maximum time to make an impact particularly if he thought I wasn't there.

In the event, it was he who wasn't there. I watched every passenger from the seven forty-five off the train, and every passenger from the eight twenty-nine, and from the nine oh-six. Leo was none of them. By twenty past nine I was so blasted with misery that I got a taxi home and as soon as the front door enclosed me into the safety of my flat, I started to weep.

When the phone rang I wanted to ignore it. But eventually maternal instinct took over. What if it was Florrie? It was Leo.

"Alys! Thank God you're there at last."

"Mmmm. I am," I said, somewhat coolly.

"Only I've been trying to get you since ten o'clock this morning. I'm so, so sorry I couldn't make it. Believe me, I would have if I could, but I've had a mare go into premature labour here. The vet's just left, poor old girl's absolutely exhausted. I really cannot apologise enough, Alys."

"I'm sorry you couldn't come too." I tried not to sound forlorn. "But I know how animals are. Unpredictable."

"Yeah, so, look. Um. I know this might be difficult for you and everything." To his credit he really did sound quite distraught. "Happy birthday by the way. There's an all-day screening of *The Lord of the Rings* trilogy at the Odeon in Exeter on Friday and I wondered—if you could get here and everything—if you'd like to go. With me, obviously. We could have dinner afterwards and…"

Oh, please Leo, don't bother with the "and". My imagination was already working on *that*.

"I'd love to," I said, now enormously cheered. He hadn't

rejected me. We parted telephonic company after an exchange of pleasantries and normal small talk, and I put his picture back up on the bedroom wall; it was only slightly creased from where I'd jumped on his face.

Chapter Thirteen

When I walked into Webbe's next morning, Simon was pricing up some new books and placing them on a stand. "Good morning." He put down his pencil and looked at me critically. "And how are you feeling today?"

For one horrible second I thought he was making some kind of ironic reference to his having overworked Jace and I chronically over the last few days. Then she appeared over his left shoulder and started making boggle-eye faces at me.

"Oh, I'm fine."

"Only Jacinta said that you might not be in today. Says that you were feeling really rough yesterday."

"I..." I hesitated, uncertain as to the nature of my supposed complaint, until I saw Jace making hand cupped to mouth and heaving gestures. "It was something I ate. Much better now. Up all night though. Terrible. And once I stopped being sick, it started coming out the other end," I added smoothly so as not to waste his sympathy just in case I felt like sloping off work early.

Simon's face registered a mixture of concern and repulsion. He began to back away. "Well, if you feel at all—you know—today, you get off home." Jacinta was making obscene gestures and rolling her eyes towards the door, and it dawned on me what this was all about. She thought I'd have such a sex-soaked night I'd be unable to get in to work. "No, it's fine. All over now."

As soon as Simon was safely away in the cubbyhole, Jace marched me into the cover of Biography. "Well? Is he coming passionately at you?"

I wrinkled my nose. "He wasn't coming in any sense whatever." I gave her the details of the attempted telephone calls.

"Hmm." Jace looked critically into my face. "He is sounding like an unreliable man. Does he have nobody to be petting his horses if he is not there?"

"He did try. Anyway, it doesn't matter, I'm going down tomorrow for the weekend."

"I am thinking that it matters very much, if he cannot leave his horses to come and see his woman." Jace turned away. "I hopes you are taking some care, Alys. Hearts should be given to those who earn them." I would have credited this with more philosophical depth if I hadn't noticed the Mills and Boon she'd shoved under the counter, bookmarked halfway through. She and Mrs. Searle were obviously kindred spirits.

I began dusting Queen Victoria since no one seemed to have taken any interest in her for quite some time. This meant lying along the floor to blow dust off the angled edge of the bookcase. I was thusly prone when a shadow fell over me and a voice said, "It's okay, Alys, you can worship me later."

"Piers!" I tried to jack-knife to my feet but ended up on all fours performing a sort of press-up manoeuvre with my duster in my hand. "How are you?"

"I'm cool. Listen, when is Florence due back?"

I hauled myself to my feet with judicious use of the shelving. "Not for another week, did she not tell you? She's having far too good a time, if you ask me." Out of the corner of my eye, I saw Jace lurking in Poetry, wiggling her eyebrows, and I made shooing motions. She just winked broadly and lasciviously, and pretended to be rearranging books in order to earwig our conversation.

"She may have said, can't remember. I wanted her to—hey, perhaps you can help instead."

"As long as you didn't require her to do anything gyratory in very small trousers, I shall do my best to replace her," I said solemnly. Piers did the thing where he combed his hair back off his face. It drew his tight T-shirt close around his body and Jacinta nearly poked her eye out with Ted Hughes.

"I've found this flat, need a female perspective kinda thing. It's very central, very open. But I dunno if it's really, like, *me*, you know?"

"I'm not sure I'd be any use, Piers. I know nothing about property buying and anyway, you've *seen* my place. Would you trust the opinion of anyone who lives in a shoebox?"

"Yeah. I would." Piers noticed Jacinta. It wasn't difficult since she was hanging from the far edge of Biography like a cross-dressing mountaineer. "You reckon I can trust Alys's sense?"

Jace realised he was talking to her and quit her pretence of tidying, dropping neatly to the floor alongside us. "I think she has much sense. In some things." She threw me a glance which was probably meant to be meaningful. "Anyway, if she cannot help you, *I* am very good indoors."

I gave in and introduced them, and to Jace's great gratification, Piers did the slow look up and down that men reserve for women whose charms have not totally passed them by. But then, Jace's charms took quite a long time to travel past anyone. "Hi, Jacinta. I've heard a lot about you."

You liar, I thought, but it was nice of him to make the effort.

Jace almost broke into a purr. "But you. Alys is not telling us of *you*."

"Yeah, well, Alys likes to keep me under wraps, you know?" Piers dropped his voice to a loud whisper. "I don't think she wants people to know that she's got this crazy young guy who can do real *amazing* things to women with a tub of ice cream and a feather."

Jacinta's eyes went very round and she stared at both of us for a second, until I gave her a poke on the arm. "Jace, he's winding you up. He has a very peculiar sense of humour." In explanation, "He's American, he can't help it."

"So, meet you back here at, what, five o'clock? You finished by five, Alys?" Piers consulted his watch which caused the T-shirt-stretching thing to happen again, pulling the fabric close to his rib cage until even *I* could see that Piers had the makings of a very nice six-pack. Jace could probably have described his underwear.

"Yes, of course, but—Piers, don't you have any girlfriends you could take to look at this place? Or your mother? I mean Florrie would be next door to useless unless you wanted an opinion on the coolness of the location."

"It'll be good that you're coming instead then, won't it?"

"Does no one do any work around here except me?" Simon's slightly cantankerous tones broke in. "There's a lady here who would like to buy a book and I can't get the till open because *someone* has got the key."

I went to his rescue, leaving Piers to wink goodbye to Jace, who had to sit down rather heavily on the library steps as soon as he'd gone.

"Why can I not find a man like that?" She fanned herself with Mary Astor, her chest heaving with the exertion.

"You could always make a play for him," I said. "I don't think Piers would be averse to an experienced woman."

She seemed for a second to consider it, the fanning stopped anyway. "No, I think he is interested elsewhere. But I would like to be seen with such a man. It will make other men curious to be knowing what I can be doing so good."

I went back to sorting shelves. About half an hour later, I was summoned to the cubbyhole by Simon who stood holding a bouquet of deep red carnations like a man holding an unaccustomed small child. "These just arrived for you. I'm beginning to feel more like a dating agency than a bookshop."

I flipped the card open. *Incredibly sorry about yesterday*, it read. *Can't believe how much I was looking forward to it. Can we try again on Friday? Leo* and three *x*'s. By now Simon was tutting so hard he sounded like an unexploded bomb. "Sorry, Simon. These are a one-off. And it was only Piers again."

"Still wanting your help with a 'family matter'?" Simon sounded sarcastic, which was not like him at all. I spent the rest of the day incarcerated in the back room, which was Simon's equivalent of the Punishment Cell, sorting a heap of dusty old volumes that he'd bought in from another sale. At five o'clock, Jace had to beat me clean with a damp rag before I could meet up with Piers, who'd been hovering outside in the Porsche since four thirty.

The flat turned out to be the whole top floor of a Bonded Warehouse right on the river. Huge metal pillars supported the roof, but apart from that it was one long, empty space with the bathroom a very visible corner behind stylish glass bricks.

"Well?" Piers stood in the middle of the room, hands in pockets. "What do you think?"

"I think it would make a great rollerblading rink. But a flat? I don't know. It is very *you* though, Piers."

"How, me?" He rocked back on his heels watching me intently. I wasn't quite sure why.

"Very cool, very trendy. Very exhibitionist. I mean, if there was anyone here with you, you wouldn't even be able to scratch yourself without them seeing."

"So, you reckon I'm a cool, trendy exhibitionist?" His eyes were glittering.

"No, you're—" But I stopped myself.

"What *do* you think of me, Alys?" He came a little closer. "I mean, am I a nice guy or a psycho, or what? Y'see, you never say what you think, you keep it all locked away, up here—" He reached out to touch my forehead but, disturbed for no reason I could think of, I shied away and waved a hand to indicate the bare brick walls.

"Can you imagine curling up in here with a video and a pizza and listening to the rain outside?"

"Er...Alys..." Piers held his hands out in front of him. "Twenty-one. Male. Too fucking cool to live. I do *not* sit in with pizza."

I had a sudden flashback to last night, my birthday night, sitting in front of the TV, cheese stringily dripping onto my lap whilst Mr. Depp strutted his sizeable funky thing for my delectation. My sole conversation had been with Mrs. Treadgold who'd rung to make sure I'd enjoyed the cake. "If all you want is a sexy address, this will do you fine. But if you want a *home*—this will never be a home, Piers."

"That was straight from the heart anyway." Piers looked the place over, with a sigh. "But I guess you're right. It's a little municipal."

I instantly felt contrite. "But the view, the view is lovely." Bobbing away down the Ouse were the houseboats and the tourist craft. On the far bank were the riverside pubs and clubs. "Very urban."

"Noisy, at night."

"Yes, but lively. And handy for the station and the shops."

Piers just looked at me, steadily. "You hate it."

"Well, yes, but it's not *for* me, is it? Do you like it, that's the question. What about your girlfriend, does she like it?"

Piers turned away abruptly and leaned on one of the windowsills, gazing out across the rooftops of York. "I'm—kinda between women at the moment." There was a peculiar tone in his voice and I wondered if I'd put my foot in a monumental great hole.

"Are you gay?" The question came out rather faster, and more breathlessly, than I'd meant. I'd heard all about his penchant for young girl model-types who left not one inch of him uncovered with lipstick praise, mostly in scathing terms from Florence. But maybe they'd been symptomatic of a struggle with sexuality.

Piers seemed unoffended. I suppose, looking the way he did, all hair and rings and androgynously sexy, it must be something he got asked a lot. "No. I'm not. There *is* someone, but it's all kinda difficult at the moment, you know?"

I stood beside him and together we looked out of the window. "Life, eh?" But I had to admit that he made me feel a tiny bit better; he might be beautiful and well connected, but he still wasn't happy. *I* could manage to be miserable without any of those advantages. "Better get home. Grainger's been a bit off-colour lately and he's not too hot with the litter tray, so I don't like to be late."

"You won't come for a drink, then? Maybe some food, say thanks for coming to look at this place?"

"Wellll, all right, Grainger can cross his little furry legs for a bit longer. But you are absolutely not to order any wine, okay?"

"Yes, *ma'am*." Piers executed a very smart salute. His mood seemed to have switched from forlorn to cheerful in nanoseconds.

"And we can only go somewhere that won't mind my jeans, I haven't got anything to change into. Oh, and Piers, have you got anything to put on over that T-shirt?"

"Yes, ma'am, sure thing, ma'am. Why?"

"Oh, nothing, it's just that every time you move it's distracting."

"Yeah?" Slowly and deliberately Piers stretched his arms upwards, straightening out his spine and rolling his shoulders backwards, until his T-shirt moved up his torso, over the waistband of his jeans revealing, inch by inch, bare flesh studded with dark hair.

"Piers, you are *such* a poser." I turned away quickly so he wouldn't see that I was enjoying the show. "Come on, stop flaunting yourself and let's go."

"Sure thing." Bouncing on the balls of his feet, Piers led the way out of the flat. We ate in an Italian restaurant and chatted until they closed the place around us. I was surprised by just how much I enjoyed myself.

Next morning I woke up with the feeling that I'd done something I ought to regret. I padded out of the bedroom with my towel, heading for the bathroom. At least it was early enough that I could have a shower before work.

As I passed Florrie's bedroom door, I heard Grainger give one of his plaintive *murp*'s on the far side of it. Somehow, and I could be almost *positive* I'd left the door open, Grainger had become shut in.

I flicked the door and Grainger ran through my legs. To check that he hadn't already downloaded last night's Whiskas onto Florrie's duvet, I put my head around the door, only to pull it back so fast that I nearly got friction burns from the air molecules.

Piers. His T-shirt and jeans were neatly folded on the floor, the boots he'd worn were propped up near the door. He was sprawled face down, and very obviously naked, across Florence's bed.

Oh bloody hell. Now I remembered what I'd done. Piers and I had been laughing hysterically coming up the stairs, recreating a scene from an old TV sketch show that we'd both treasured. He'd asked if he could stay over to save himself the drive home, and I, desperate for the loo and the comfort of my duvet, had agreed.

I peered cautiously into the bedroom again. I was so used to seeing Florrie, duvet tucked up to her chin, that seeing Piers angled, arms above his head, one leg bent and the duvet—well, it certainly wasn't covering much of his body, put it that way— was very strange. As I watched he stirred, one hand twitched and he made to roll over, at which I withdrew very smartly and went and had a very noisy shower. With singing. There was going to be absolutely *no chance* of him still being spread-eagled nude when I came out of that bathroom.

Chapter Fourteen

I sat on the Exeter train opposite a man who was clearly very fond of cheese and onion crisps, and next to a woman who seemed to be going for the world record in marathon mobile conversations. I really hoped that both of them were only going as far as Bristol, because I'd rather be left alone to imagine Leo with his shirt off. But my mind was being squeezed into far more workaday lines. Such as—Jacinta's face when Piers had dropped me off at work that morning, and her comical outrage when I insisted there was absolutely nothing going on between us, other than his staying over so as not to have to drive all the way to Thirsk very late and ever-so-slightly over the limit.

"He stay in your home and you are not even *kissing*?" Jace had shaken her head. "Alys, you are disgracing women."

"Look, for the last time, it's *Piers*, he's so much too young for me that he might as well be in playgroup, he is not interested in me nor I in him. And anyway, how come you're always in so early? If you came in at the proper time, you wouldn't even have seen him drop me off."

"I am aroused at six by my alarm."

I'd gone "hur hur" in a childish way. Jacinta had given me a very arch look and I'd been quite glad when five o'clock came and I had been able to head home and pack far too many clothes for my weekend away.

It *had* been quite nice though, I had to admit, having Piers over. When I'd finished my entire repertoire of shower songs and emerged fully dressed, he'd been sitting at the table drinking tea, eating toast and reading Florence's *Cosmo Girl*. We'd indulged in a brief exchange on not taking Agony Aunt's advice too seriously, I'd pinched a piece of his toast and he'd given me a lift to work. All in all it had been a lot nicer start to the day than my accustomed grunt from Florrie. No wonder I'd arrived at Webbe's with a grin on my face and, I suppose, no wonder Jacinta had misinterpreted said grin.

Exeter station was sweltering under a copper-gold sky when I disembarked. This came as a shock to the system. In York the weather had broken, grey rain was tipping out of bleak chilly skies, and I was dressed accordingly in a sweater and long skirt. Once I'd steamed onto the platform, it was obvious I was as ridiculously overdressed as a pantomime horse at a lap-dancing club. I was wondering if I'd have time to sneak into the Ladies and change, when Leo came charging onto Platform One, leaving assorted stunned-looking women staring over their shoulders, as though the Milk Tray Man had gone Express Delivery. "Alys! God, I was afraid I'd missed you."

He looked both better, and worse, than last time I'd seen him. Better in that he'd had a haircut and a decent shave. Worse in that he was wearing a T-shirt stained with what looked like creosote, the most horrific pair of shorts outside an Eric Morecambe tribute show and a pair of rubber ankle boots which made him look a bit like a kinky pixie. "Sorry about the get-up. I was down on the yard, completely lost track of time— had to come blasting over without changing."

"It's good to see you again." Inadequate maybe, but what else can you say when you're only on your second meeting? So much hung on this.

"And you, Alys." I found myself enfolded in a tentative hug which gave me the maximum opportunity to ascertain that, yes, the substance on his T-shirt *was* creosote. "Gosh. You've certainly come well wrapped-up."

"Well, it's grim up north." It was a bit tricky to balance in the top-only hug, and my legs were beginning to give out. I performed a little shuffle and Leo took this as a hint to let go and step back.

"Let's go, shall we?" He picked up my bag, gave a tiny grimace at the weight, and we went outside to where the Land Rover was triple-parked on a taxi rank. "If you like you can come and take a look at the new arrivals. Would you like to?"

As opposed to, say, shagging you senseless round the back of the feed bins? "Mmmmm," I said, with what I hoped was the right note of enthusiasm.

He started the engine, shot me a look over his glasses and gave a little half-grin. "I didn't tell Isabelle that you were coming down again." He hauled the big vehicle out into the traffic. "I wanted to keep you a secret, just for now. Since Sabine died, there hasn't been anyone, because I couldn't *let* there be anyone, if you understand. And now, well, I'm not sure that I know how it all works any more, the whole relationship thing. I'm terribly out of practice, Alys, and really rather scared you see." He was keeping his eyes on the road.

I looked at him. A sudden line of poetry came into my head and I muttered it, without realising. *"All my life, a wrapping round the gift."*

Green, green eyes met mine. Unblinking. "That is so like something I wrote once. I don't remember exactly how it went, but it was along those lines."

I was proud of myself, I didn't flinch or look away, just looked into those jaded pools. "Spooky."

"Yes. Uncanny. Perhaps that's why I feel this—attraction to you, because we have a similar outlook on things."

Damn, and I was hoping it was my sexy smile and my delicious bottom that had won the day. "Maybe."

He focussed on the road with a fierce kind of expression, his thoughts clearly a million miles away from the automatic act of driving. I found it strangely attractive to watch. He was here and yet not here—physically present but his soul was sunk somewhere in the poetic depths which held him. I wanted to ask him what he was thinking, but that seemed a little presumptuous. After all we really didn't know each other that well.

"Better get some Stud Nuts."

"I'm sorry?"

"Oh. Sorry, Alys, I forgot it was you there for a minute. Usually the only person I'm driving is Jay."

"Your stud manager, yes?"

He beamed a brilliant smile at me. "Yes. Jay is, well, she's my right-hand man."

She? This *I've been on my own and unsullied since my wife died*, and all the time he'd been knocking around on a day-to-day basis with a *woman*?

"Couldn't get by without her, she's a wonder with the ponies."

We drove towards Charlton Hawsell, down the narrow, banked lanes. The air smelled of singed dust, but the heat had lifted as darkness sank over us. A pleasant stroke of anticipation passed down my spine as I looked at the man driving next to me. In this half-light, he was even more attractive. Blurred edges made him a silhouette of perfection, with his glasses gleaming now and then in the headlights of passing cars. I wanted to reach out and touch him but didn't dare.

"Here we go." The Land Rover bucked and rolled as we turned up the driveway and I saw the chiselled angles of Charlton Hawsell House in front of us. Its chiselled owner swung the wheel to the right and we passed by the house proper and down the gravelled pathway which led to the stable yard. My heart sank somewhat. I was tired, grubby and hungry after my journey, sweat was still trickling down my back under the jumper and I was developing the bumps of prickly heat. If Leo decided to take the plunge and sweep me off to bed tonight, it would be like sleeping with a newly plucked turkey. One which smelled of grimly hard-working twenty-four-hour deodorant at that. But I remembered from Florrie's days of pony owning, horses seemingly required more care and attention than your average newborn.

The yard was full of activity and completely floodlit. What was going on, it appeared, was horse care on an industrial scale. It was Teenage Girl Central. I could feel the angst and acne from here.

"Some of the girls come up from town, especially in the school holidays to help around the place." Leo killed the engine outside the gate.

Some of the girls? It looked to me like the whole of the underage female contingent of Charlton Hawsell. The teenage boys round here probably had to date each other.

"Hi, Leo." As soon as we walked within range of the floodlights the greetings went off.

"Hello, girls." Leo seemed oblivious to the hero worship which crackled in the air. "Alys and I are just going to take a look at the foals, then I'll give you a hand." I felt every pair of eyes swivel away from the four-legged beasties and towards me. The air thickened like hormone soup. If Leo left me alone for a second, I'd probably be bludgeoned to death with cherry lip gloss and copies of *Mizz*. "Through here, Alys."

The foaling boxes were in blessed semidarkness. Two mares were quietly eating hay in a determined way, one had a foal suckling beneath her and the other foal was lying by its mother, sprawled untidily in the careless way of the very young. He indicated the shape like a badly made sock puppet spread over the straw in front of us. "I thought we might call her Alys. Would you mind?"

Charlton Alys. *Sounds a bit like a football team.* But I was absurdly touched. "I wouldn't mind at all." I watched my namesake wave a dreaming leg briefly.

"Good." Slowly Leo turned me around until I was facing him, lowered his face to mine and gave me a kiss, a brief stroke of the lips. I was glad he hadn't gone for the full face-eating scenario, what with all the rampant adolescence going on outside. Puberty might not be fatal, but being submerged under a jealous heap of it could be. "Why don't you go on up to the house and make yourself at home. I'll lend a hand here then come and join you. You know where the wine is. Leave your bag in the wagon, I'll bring it on with me."

I wandered on up and into the dark hallway where I found some light switches. These lights revealed that I was at the front of the house, in a wooden-floored area with doors leading off to left and right, and the big staircase I had ascended on my previous visit behind me. I opened a door at random, it gave onto a huge room with a moulded ceiling and an impressive array of mismatched armchairs. Another door led into a room lined with bookshelves, and another into what seemed to be an office with a computer screen eerily lighting a semicircle around itself.

I giggled to myself, but the giggle was magnified, thrown along distant corridors, rattling off into the shrinking distance, growing more and more indistinct as it vanished around unseen corners. No wonder people who lived in houses like this tended towards keeping mad women in attics as a recreational activity.

"Alys?" Leo was calling me from somewhere, it sounded like several corridors away.

"I'm here!" I called back.

"I've got your bag! Do you want to come to the kitchen and

I'll find us some supper?"

"That would be lovely!" I yelled. Courtship by megaphone. "Where *is* the kitchen?"

"Hold on, I'll come and get you."

It must be nice to be able to walk around your house without having to sidle past the furniture. And to have rooms large enough for two people to be in without having to stand buttock to buttock. Although I could probably spend all night happily buttock to buttock with Leo, I thought, as he rounded a corner and came towards me, swinging my bag casually from a slender wrist and whistling under his breath. Even the shorts had a new charm from a perspective where I didn't have to be seen out with them.

"Hi there. Stables go all right?"

"Oh yes, fine thanks. We did think Felicity had a touch of colic, so we've brought her up onto the yard, but apart from that—" He advanced towards me and put my bag on the floor at my feet. "And how about you?"

I smiled. "Can I go grab a quick shower and get changed? I'm feeling terribly overdressed here."

He backed away a few steps, his eyes glimmering with something like panic. "Oh, um. Well, yes...um...of course...but..." He obviously thought that I was going to slip into a wisp of lace and two nipple clamps. "Wouldn't you rather we have a bite to eat first?"

God, what was it with me? I didn't exactly want to meet a man who'd rip all my clothes off with his teeth and a bullwhip, but I seemed to find myself attracted without exception to men who'd bought their sexual personas from Reticence R Us. But then, Leo's shyness was part of his charm, wasn't it?

"I'd like to change first, if that's okay." I undid the zip on my bag. "I'll wear these"—I grabbed jeans and a long-sleeved T—"if you show me where."

"Oh I see. Changed, yes." Leo reached out an arm and flipped open a door, pulling a cord to flood a tiled room with halogen lights. "In here. Just come on through to the kitchen when you've...well, yes."

I went inside and he pulled the door shut behind me as though relieved that I had, indeed, chosen to take my clothes off behind a door. I glanced around at a room which was completely tiled, with a central drain and several nozzles jutting out of one wall. It looked either like a cubicle in a slaughterhouse or a luxurious urinal.

After about a minute's showering, and while I still had some skin left, I turned the water off and stood dripping, realising with a nasty sinking in my stomach, that there were no towels in here with me. Woollen jumpers, I found, are not as absorbent as they look or feel. When rubbed over a wet body they slide over water droplets with the ease of a cabinet minister avoiding an awkward question. So, still slightly moister than I usually liked, I went in search of Leo.

Chapter Fifteen

"You must be starved."

When I found the kitchen again, after a couple of false starts, it was filled with an appetising smell. "I am rather, yes."

Leo looked a bit embarrassed. "It's nothing very special, I'm afraid." He bent to the door in a gigantic iron range which would invoke sleepless nights for any wicked witches with a gingerbread inclination. He straightened up bearing a baking sheet and flourished it onto the table in front of me. "Pizza."

"It looks delicious." In reality it had a kind of second-hand quality to it.

"I did think about taking you out to eat." Leo began slicing the pizza in an inept way, causing the base to split and drag the topping from one slice to another. "But I thought it would be better if we could stay here and talk. There wasn't anything much in the freezer apart from pizza so I hope you like pepperoni."

Leo sat opposite me and we chewed at each other for a few moments. Eventually he sighed and rested back in his chair. "You really can't buy this feeling."

I didn't know how to answer. I knew offhand of three places where you could purchase the makings of chronic indigestion, but didn't think that was what he meant. "Mmmm," I said, noncommittally.

He put his elbows on the table and leaned forward, cupping his chin in his hands and looking at me intently. "You've brought out feelings in me, Alys, feelings I thought I'd buried with Sabine. Do you realise what that means to me?"

I shook my head. There was blood pounding in my head, echoing my heartbeat.

"When I saw you in Izzie's dining room, looking at the photographs with such—such *fierceness*, such concentration—for the first time in these two years, I felt that I could relate to another person, that I wasn't totally alone." He reached out a hand and loosely clasped fingers around my wrist. "I'm sorry if this is all a little fast for you. Believe me I can't really get my head around it either. But—I'm hoping—well, actually I'm praying, Alys, that you feel the same way."

I turned my hand over and let my fingers tangle with his. "I think so," I said through dry lips. His fingers felt hot and my pulse was booming against the veins in my wrist like an insistent incoming tide. We were lit only by a small table lamp with a lopsided lampshade. I could see his glasses gleaming, the soft fall of hair across his forehead, but the rest of his face was vestigial, features drifting in and out of focus in a surreal way as he moved slightly and the light twisted against his skin.

"I—" he began, when a strident beeping broke out of nowhere, crashing into our little idyll, making me jump and jerk out of his grasp. "Oh *bugger.* This is just—" He was thrusting his hands into pockets in a desperate search for the source of the beep. "Bloody *typical.*" Finally he withdrew his mobile, still squealing its message-received tone to the world, and glanced at it. "Sod. It's Jay. Says Felicity is down in agony, do I want to phone the vet?"

He stared at the text as though it might spring into life and wrench him out of the kitchen. He was so clearly torn that it seemed the only kind thing to do was to help out.

"Why don't you go on down to the yard and do what needs

doing. I'll clear up in here, pour a couple of glasses of wine and we can carry on talking when you get back?" Given that two minutes ago, I'd been half a dozen heartbeats from flinging myself across the table at him, I thought this was particularly decent of me.

"Well, I—look, are you sure you'll be all right?" He was running his hands through his hair, and hayseeds were falling like bucolic dandruff onto the table. "This is particularly unfair, but I should really—"

"Go. I'll be fine." Then to make sure, "I'm a big girl, I can cope."

"I could take you down with me." He was already halfway to the door. "But if we get the vet out, it could be a long wait and you'd, well, you might..."

"I'd only be in the way." I gave him a cheery little wave and didn't add that I really didn't like horses that much. "I'll just mooch about, read, have a drink. You go deal with your emergency. Go on. Go."

When he'd gone, I managed not to give in to the urge to fling his mobile repeatedly against the wall until it broke. Instead, I picked up the pizza plates, put them in the sink and switched on the main lights. Romantic illumination was all very well when things were going romantically, but when they weren't going at all, fluorescent glare was the thing. This room really was grotty and in need of a female touch—hell, in need of any touch at all. It was tinsel-chained with cobwebs, the flagstones were patterned with random muddy paw prints and an examination of the greaseproof-wrapped butter on the middle of the table showed the unmistakeable marks of tongue raspings. But, if tonight was anything to go by, Leo clearly didn't have a second to call his own. It wouldn't be reasonable to expect him to spend his spare time cleaning every inch of the house.

Another ten minutes passed. I made myself tea in a mug

which necessitated dispossessing several woodlice of an apparently ancestral home. I'd even begun to leaf through a copy of *Horse and Hound* when the mobile on the table buzzed into life, urgent and unignorable as an alarm clock. I leaped for it and picked it up.

"*Alys. Very sorry, looks like I'll be late. The Green Room is yours again, see you in the morning. Leo.*"

Right. Well I might as well go to bed. I switched off the lights and groped my way along the hall towards the main staircase. At the base of the stairs a telephone squatting on a wisp of a table cast a mighty shadow on the wall behind.

I dropped my bag and lifted the receiver. The thought of calling a taxi crossed my mind, but stomping off in a huff was a bit juvenile.

I took a deep breath, overwhelmed with a longing to be home. Back in the flat, with Florrie's music thrumming from her room and a pile of Book Club selections beside the bed. A bar of chocolate, a cup of tea, and possibly Mrs. Treadgold on the phone gossiping about Mrs. Searle and her family. All this buildup, all this longing. Now, here I was. Lonely.

"Jace?" It was twenty past eleven, and her answerphone was picking up? Where the hell was she? Jacinta never went out after dark. She had what I considered to be a totally irrational fear of being attacked. I repeatedly pointed out that she was by far the most scary thing on the streets of York, but she resolutely stayed in and watched videos. I wasn't sure *which* DVDs, her shelves were always bare of the evidence, but I suspected that she was to Benicio del Toro what I was to Johnny Depp. "Jace, if you're there, pick up. It's me. Alys."

Nothing but her pre-recorded message. Anyway, what could I say? "He's left me on my own"? I could almost hear Jacinta's scathing voice as she listened to the tape. *Alys you are a big wimp. Go to bed or you will be baggy in the morning.*

"Sorry Jace, I was—er—ringing up to check everything was okay after I left today. Don't forget that I left Mrs. Winterbourne's order parcelled up on the desk. Okay, thanks, goodbye." Then I dialled my only other friend.

"Hello?" The voice sounded tentative. "Who is it, please?"

"Mrs. Treadgold. It's Alys."

"Alys, is something the matter? It's not that young man of yours, is it? I was saying to Mrs. Munroe only yesterday, Alys'll have to be careful. He's a bit of a looker. She's going to have to keep an eye out for the other girls. But, saying that, he really does seem smitten, doesn't he?"

"Um, no. It's—no. Nothing like that. I was just—I'd forgotten whose turn it was to choose a book this fortnight and I wondered if you knew," I finished, feebly. Here I was, fully paid-up member of the Gloria Gaynor *I Will Survive* club, ringing a seventy-year-old just to hear a reassuring voice. Too much of a chicken to admit I was wondering what the hell I was doing here. I hadn't told the book group about Leo. They were all so convinced I was being naughty, as they would have put it, with a lovestruck Piers. Admitting I was really involved with someone else would be tantamount to pitchforking puppies.

At the far end of the phone, Mrs. Treadgold coughed gently. "Are you sure? If you're in any trouble, I can get Mr. Mansell to ask his niece for the loan of her car. We can come and get you, you know."

"No. No, I'm fine. Sorry to have bothered you."

Having heard a voice apart from my own brought me back to earth. If I'd been Florence, I would have got a good talking-to for being petty and selfish. He wouldn't just shrug his shoulders and leave an animal rolling around a stable in pain, would he? I was tired and grouchy and not in the best frame of mind for seduction anyway. I should go to bed and arise all fresh and dewy eyed, the better to ravage him on the morrow.

I hefted my bag again and set off up the stairs, moonlight shadowing my heels like a ghostly dog. At the top I turned for the Green Room, but halfway down the corridor I stopped. All right, so he might be back late. What was there to stop me from simply being there, in his bed when he came in? Warm and willing and sleepily disarranged. I could feel his fingers against mine even now, as they had been in the kitchen, firm and dry and promising. I felt like Bluebeard's wife, pushing open doors all along the landing as I went, hoping nothing nasty was going to jump out at me. Past two largely empty rooms, another bathroom, and then I hit pay dirt.

It was a big, airy room with the windows thrown wide to catch the cool night breezes. Full-length muslin curtains fluttered like lazy phantoms into the room, almost brushing the items off the top of a dressing table; a silver-framed photograph, some scent bottles which looked empty and a book which, disappointingly, turned out to be on the subject of breeding Welsh ponies.

The bed was enormous, made up with white crisp sheets and a lovely puffy white duvet. The look was slightly spoiled by a pair of Leo's jeans lying on top and two grubby T-shirts crumpled on the floor, but the room was almost obsessively tidy apart from the dropped clothes.

I slipped naked between the refreshing cotton sheets. The photo in the silver frame caught my eye, and I picked it up and held it under the lamp to get a good view. Bloody hellfire. If that was Sabine—and, let's face it, who else was it likely to be, a woman in a wedding dress hanging onto Leo's arm and laughing fit to bust at the camera—she was absolutely frigging *gorgeous*.

Huh. On *my* wedding day I'd been feeling fat and nauseous. Florence had kicked my stomach all through the ceremony. While the registrar had had a kerfuffle with the rings, I had

111

been quietly sick into a decorative urn. This woman looked as though she could have partied all evening, given her new husband the night of his life and still been up at dawn, golden haired, impeccable in a negligee, with breakfast on a tray.

I turned off the light, arranging myself on the pillows in as decorative a manner as I could, fanning my red curls across the white bolsters. I tucked the covers around me in a form-fitting way, suggesting that I was somewhat more shapely than was the case, and allowed myself to sink down into the mattress. It really was comfortable.

Bright. It was very bright. The room was washed with sunshine, heating the waxed pine of the floor and making it smell musty. Despite the fact that the window was still open, the curtains were dangling limp as melted ice cream. I turned to see the unmarked pillow next to mine. Leo had clearly not decided to climb in next to me. I propped myself up on one elbow and nearly fell out of bed with shock as the door flew open and Leo, wearing only a small towel around his waist, barrelled into the room.

His shout of horror was almost equalled by mine. He dropped the towel but that was fine because I'd shot under the duvet, and by the time I resurfaced, he was tucking it very firmly back around his middle. He looked great, by the way, with wet hair, clearly straight from the shower because droplets were running down his back and chest. "What on *earth*—Alys?" He'd retreated to the far side of the room and had one hand on the towel for added security.

Think fast, Alys. "I got lost last night. It was late, and somehow I must have gone wrong at the top of the stairs; I was really, really tired, so I came in here."

"Oh." He looked as though he was considering challenging my story, but no alternative came to him, thank God. "This used to be Sabine's room. Now I use it as a kind of dressing room, keep most of my work gear in the wardrobe. Hence—" He indicated his near nakedness with the hand not holding up the towel.

"Oh. Right." Pressing the duvet against me to prevent anything sagging in an off-putting way, I sat farther up the bed. "Um."

Leo was still adhering to the wall, clearly terrified by the view. "Look, I'll just go and—in another room. Er—I'll meet you in the kitchen?"

"Yes, all right. Shall I cook us some breakfast?" An insubstantial smell of bacon frying was wafting through and making my stomach writhe.

"Oh, I've already had mine. It's nearly nine. I've finished morning stables, came in for a quick clean up, thought we might take a run into Exeter in a minute if you're up for it. I've got to pick up a couple of bridles that are in being mended, and there's the cinema."

"That sounds very nice." Then I remembered last night. "How's Felicity?"

Leo's face darkened and he almost forgot himself enough to let go of the towel. "A bit so-so really. The vet managed to stop the spasms but she's not herself at all yet. Jay's going to keep an eye on her today, maybe walk her around a bit, see how she goes."

He sidled out of the room hell-bent on not letting me get so much as a glimpse of his buttocks. He could have saved his energy, I'd already sussed his gluteus maximus. It was the sort of thing which drew the eye. Particularly in those shorts he'd had on yesterday.

I found the kitchen after only one false start, but Leo had beaten me to it. "Gosh, Alys you look"—I held my breath— "fantastic."

Better or worse than your average horse? I felt like saying, but didn't. "Thanks. So do you." I meant it. His hair was still damp and dripping onto his black T-shirt, his jeans were creased and his jodhpur boots were dusty. But he was wrapped in an aura of careless sexuality, so absolutely the type of man I fancied that he might have been an Identikit-Date. I was about to suggest a cup of tea before we got going, anything to keep my stomach quiet, but at that moment the telephone rang. Leo picked it up and turned to me after a second.

"Alys, it's for you."

"What?" I shook my head. "No one's got the number."

Leo just gave a sideways shrug. "It's a woman. At least, I think it is."

"Ah, Alys, you are there. I was worrying because you were ringing in the night, making a panic of yourself."

"Hi, Jace." Of course, good old 1471. "No, only wanted to check that you knew about Mrs. Winterbourne's parcel."

"She is here now, telling me about her big bottom." I couldn't even begin to interpret this one. Leo was shuffling his feet, obviously impatient to be off. "So you are okay?"

"Fine. No worries. Anyway, Jace, where the hell *were* you last night? Got yourself a hot date, did you?" There was a small pause, and Jacinta giggled. "You didn't? You jammy cow!"

A little unfair, given that I had spent the night in another man's bed, even if the bed in question hadn't, strictly speaking, been *his*. It hadn't been for want of trying.

"It was not a date, Alys, I was just having drinks with Piers. He is very nice boy, you know? Very, very cute."

Obviously Piers had taken to Jace more than I'd thought. My stomach gave a mysterious little wobble. "I bet that was fun."

Jacinta giggled again. "I was learning to drink Snakebite. We were having a competition, and I think he is very poor today."

Behind me Leo had stepped up the shuffle. "Right. Lovely. Well, I'd better go, Jace. I'm off to Exeter. Talk to you later."

"I hope you are being careful of yourself, Alys." Jace's voice was suddenly serious. "Do not let what is in his trousers run away with you."

I kept my face straight. "I shall try to make sure it is well contained. Bye."

I was giggling over Jacinta's warning when I climbed into the Land Rover, Leo looking at me quizzically. There was no way I could have explained Jace's idiosyncratic approach to the English language to him, so I contented myself with saying, "It was Jacinta who I work with, just checking up."

I turned away to look out of the window at passing Devon. Didn't want him to know about last night's little panic. The sun throbbed down, all the vegetation which lined the lanes was smothered in a layer of sandy dust thrown up by the passing wheels. If it rained now, there was going to be eyebrow-level mud.

Rain seemed as far away as Christmas as we drove into Charlton. I was still watching the passing view and Leo hadn't remarked on my silence. Whenever I glanced towards him, he was staring straight ahead at the road, every now and again thumbing his glasses back up towards the bridge of his nose.

"I'll need to pop in and see Alan," Leo said at last, without any reference to the conversational lapse. "He's got a couple of in-hand bridles for me to pick up. Okay?"

"Fine."

"Hey. Alys. Come in with me. I want to introduce you to Alan." He took my hand across the gearstick. I resisted for a fraction of a second's peevishness, then let his fingers fold over mine. "Really I just want to show you off." He lowered his voice. "I can't believe you're real. Introducing you to people makes it all more solid somehow, more *true."*

I thawed faster than a choc-ice in a chip pan. "I'd love to. Do I look all right?"

In the shadow of the Land Rover, Leo pulled me tight against him. "You look absolutely bloody *amazing,"* he said slightly hoarsely.

Now *this* was promising. "So." I leaned into him. "Why don't we go back?" I gave it the full works, hair tossing, lip licking, I even attempted a small, knicker-twisting hip-wiggle.

He let his hands fall away. "Well, it's not often that I get a day off like this, to go and do what I want and we'll have plenty of time, won't we?"

I told myself not to be so childish. "Of course. I'm looking forward to the film." And, hopefully there will be hotdogs, and chocolate. My stomach let out a little groan of anticipation. "Shall we go and meet your Alan?"

"Good idea." Leo took my hand and began to lead me across the road, to my horror into the same saddlery shop that I had rushed to beg information on him. I reared back against the pressure of his fingers. "It's okay," Leo said, misunderstanding. "You don't have to be shy. Alan is a great guy, known him for years."

Inside the shop was as dark as ever, still redolent with the soapy organic smell of leather. My heart rose a little, there didn't seem to be anyone behind the counter. Leo wandered around, lifting and sorting various items as though he did this every day. "Al!" he called, freeing a tangled mass of leatherwork and teasing it out into component items. "I've come for the tack."

"Hello there." The voice came from behind us, forestalling my instinctive idea which was to crouch down behind a feed bin. "'Tis you again, Mr. Forrester." The middle-aged man who I'd encountered last time came into the shop through a side-

116

mounted door which led to a back room.

"It is indeed. I've got a couple of youngsters coming out at the Devon County next week, and I knew you'd finished with the bridles. So I thought, since we were passing—" He looked around for the we part of the equation, but she was currently busying herself with a totally fake interest in a set of luridly coloured nylon head collars hanging conveniently far away. "Alys?"

"Er. Hello." I hoped that enough strange auburn-haired women walked in here that I might be lost in the masses.

Leo introduced us but I didn't hear. I was still pulsating with terror about what Alan was going to say. His eyes registered nothing but a passing interest in Leo's words and a friendly recognition. I held my breath; if Alan told Leo we'd already met, then I'd have to admit to Leo that I'd already known who he was before I met him at Isabelle's.

"So. I see you found 'im." Alan's first words were about as bad as it could get but promptly got worse when he explained, "Your lady friend was in here—oh, few weeks back now, asking after you."

It wasn't malicious, that I was sure. I mean, how could he have known? It was a casual, passing remark, nothing more. I felt my bladder drop to my knees.

"Alys?" Leo was only mildly curious.

"I was on my way up to see Isabelle. I saw you come in here, and I thought—God, this sounds so weird—I thought I recognised you. You must have reminded me of someone, I don't know who."

"Came in wantin' to know who you be." Alan handed over two bridles surely too small to be worn by anything outside of a model farmyard.

"And then we met at Izzie's?" Leo looked stunned. I opened my mouth to leap in with a further explanation and realised I couldn't think of one. "That is *amazing*. What kind of serendipity must have been at work that day, hey? That feeling of *recognition*. You thinking you knew me, and then us meeting and my feeling that you understood me, somehow, like you had some secret knowledge about me...? That is—words can't describe it, can they?"

Well, I could think of a few.

Chapter Sixteen

We had fun that day. A breeze from the river was cooling the Exeter streets, blowing through the disappointing post-war architecture of the city centre like a mud-scented mistral. We wandered the pigeon-haunted close, where kids played on the statues and teenagers lay coiled around one another in the shade of the cathedral. I had another brief stab of missing Florence, part of me hoping she too was wrapped around some beautiful youth on a baked stretch of greenery, but most of me hoping she was sitting indoors reading Ancient Greek and knitting a wimple.

The Lord of the Rings was reassuringly full of carbohydrates and Pepsi. By the time we staggered back out onto the dreaming streets, the air was heavily dark and smelled musky.

"Well," said Leo. "I enjoyed that. Deserved all those Oscars, didn't you think?"

My enthusiasm was slightly less than his because I had spent a considerable portion of the time wondering what Piers and Jacinta had been up to last night. Snakebite? Piers must have lowered himself considerably if *that* had been his drink of choice. What on *earth* had brought that about? Had he been trying to get her drunk?

"Alys?" Leo was scanning my face. "You looked lost there for a minute. Deep in thought?"

"Not really. Nothing important."

We walked on through the cooked air, back to the Land Rover and Leo pulled his mobile from his pocket. "I'd better just drop by the yard on the way back. Jay's had the vet to Felicity again, says she doesn't like the way things are going. I won't be long."

Surely this contravened the Geneva Convention or something? On the one hand, Leo was behaving as though I was the most desirable woman on the continent. On the other, it seemed as though he wanted to put a wall of horseflesh between us. Was I deluding myself into thinking he was attracted to me?

We drove through the darkness back to Charlton, passing occasional comments about the films and the heat, until the Land Rover swung into the drive. "I will honestly only be about ten minutes." Leo spoke to me out of the driver's window as I stood with gravel in my sandals. "Put the kettle on."

I trudged into the house, the kitchen smelled doggy, but again the perpetrators were nowhere in evidence. I wondered where they were. Probably down on the yard with all the other nasty biting objects. Then I wondered whether that description included Jay, and why Leo hadn't introduced us. Had he got something to hide? Was she a gorgeous blonde, with topple-over tits and hips like a python? If she was, *why* was *I* here?

"Alys?" He must have come in another way. I hadn't even heard the car. "Are you all right? You look absolutely miles away again. Is there something worrying you?"

I shook my head. "No. I'm fine. You were quick."

"Well, look, do you mind if we have a drink? I'm a bit, gosh, well I suppose I'm nervous if you want the truth."

"Nervous?" I stared blankly at him. "About Felicity?"

"No, Alys, about you." Leo poured two glasses of wine, although I didn't touch mine. "I know that I'd like to take things further." He swallowed down the contents of his glass. "I just—

and it's been so long since Sabine and I—"

"I think you'll find that you don't forget how. It's like riding a bike," I said, then wished I hadn't. If he was going to compare me to Sabine, there was only going to be disappointment in store.

"Would you like to come upstairs?" Leo took off his glasses and fixed me firmly with his green eyes. The sheer attractiveness of him stopped this from being the most cheesy line I'd ever heard. "It could be a terrible mistake of course, but if you're willing to take that chance?"

My heart was throbbing like a pain. "Yes."

I let him take my hand, his fingers were cold from the glass, slightly moist and his touch was so ethereal it was barely there. It was like holding hands with fog.

"I am"—he advanced slowly—"really, really scared." Chilly fingers brushed my cheek and tipped my face towards his. "Everything seems to be running out of my control." Gentle lips grazed against mine, then came back for a more exploratory kiss. He was pressed full-length against my body, leaving not much of his desire to the imagination, cupping my face between his hands and kissing in an almost exploratory way. If this was the first intimate contact he'd had with a woman since his wife, an experimental approach was probably not surprising. Maybe she was the only woman he'd ever been to bed with.

"You mentioned upstairs?" I whispered into his ear when he broke contact for a moment. "It would be a bit more comfortable."

"I don't know if I can do this," Leo whispered back. "I want to, so badly, but is it all too soon? Am I rushing things?"

"Rushing?" I'd known tectonic plates that moved faster than this. "Well, you mustn't do anything you don't want to." Inwardly I let out a groan. Being understanding was all very well, but I was so turned on by his kissing and his closeness that if he kept this up much longer I wouldn't be able to walk, except possibly like John Wayne.

"Let's go upstairs." He tugged at my wrist.

I let him lead me up the staircase and along the landing, through a door I'd previously not noticed, into his bedroom. There was a saddle on the bed, which he hastily plopped onto the floor, giving me time to glance around and notice there didn't seem to be any pictures of the stupendous Sabine in evidence. There were, however, a couple of TVs mounted high up in one corner. I hoped he wasn't into watching movies. Or making them. "I'm sorry it's a bit untidy." Leo shifted the saddle again, awkwardly. "I wasn't expecting..."

He could obviously carry the reticence on all night. "We could just sleep together," I said. "Without any pressure."

"What, you and I in the same bed? Sleeping? Together?" He looked amazed. "Without—you know—anything happening? I think that sounds—very sensible." He seemed to gain a bit of confidence by having the pressure to seduce me taken off. "We could just lie together."

"Right." I started to unbutton my shirt, very slowly, keeping my eyes fixed on his, and after a moment I was gratified to see his gaze dropping downwards. His mouth opened, a little slackly, his expression glazed, then his eyes came back up to mine and he grinned.

"I don't think I'm scared any more."

Chapter Seventeen

I lay under the weight of the sleeping Leo's arm and stared up at the ceiling. His breath puffed regularly on my skin and I hated myself for wanting some postcoital reassurance that Sabine, despite her earth-stopping appearance, had made love like a woman shoving a supermarket trolley through a muddy gateway.

The sex had been good. In bed Leo's reticence became tenderness, his reserve, restraint. I hated to admit it, but I'd become used to brief sexual encounters to make sure I was still alive. To reassure myself I wasn't just Florence's Mum. But the York dating pool available to penniless single mothers of teenagers seemed, as far as I was concerned, to consist of men who wanted no commitment. So having Leo here, one arm looped about my waist and a long leg inserted between my thighs, was something of a coup.

I tried to move without disturbing him, slipping from his partial embrace slowly and stickily, inching from beneath the covers so as not to cause a great blast of chilly air to go slashing into his sated sleep. He gave a tiny sigh and rolled into the piece of bed I'd been occupying, but didn't wake up. I tried to head for the door but tripped over the saddle which stood on end beside the bed.

"Shit." The leather was cold and slippery and for a moment it felt as though I'd tripped over a dismembered corpse. The saddle fell with me and sprawled out on the mat on its back with its skirts flapping like a disembowelled torso. "*Shit!*"

Leo sat suddenly upright, one smooth fluid movement. "What's happening?"

"I fell down." The way he'd moved was eerie, lying deeply asleep one minute, but managing to be vertical and awake within seconds.

"Thank God. I was dreaming—I thought it was Jay coming to wake me up and get me to give a hand."

"Does Jay often have to come get you out of bed?" I asked carefully, disentangling myself.

"Only when the monitors are off." Leo waved at the TV sets. "And that's hardly ever. Don't worry." He flipped the edge of the covers back. "I've given myself tonight off, Jay can cope on her own. Come back to bed."

I inserted myself under the duvet, curling up against the warmth of him. So, Jay knew where his bedroom was, did she? The thought stayed with me even after he reached out to me again. It was a little off-putting, to say the least. My mind jittered from thought to thought as we rolled together, Leo and Jay, Leo and Sabine, Piers, Piers and Jacinta.

Leo's murmur of triumph whispered into my ear and he collapsed on top of me. "Oh, Alys."

I relaxed under his weight. "This is nice." I meant the closeness, the intimacy rather than the sex.

"Yes." Leo struggled himself up onto his elbows and looked down into my face. "I really didn't think I'd ever have anything like this again."

"Surely you must have had women chasing you?" I waved an arm to indicate the whole of Charlton Stud. "You've got all this—and you're not exactly ugly either."

He sighed and flopped over sideways leaving my body

feeling chilled. "I've never really noticed women. Horses were always my life. I probably wouldn't have noticed Sabine either if she hadn't had Charlton Stud. Oh I know, you thought this was all mine." He pulled a wry face. "The fact is that I inherited it when she died. It belonged to Sabine's father. She took over the stud when her parents died. The huge irony is that we were on the point of divorce when she was killed. I was waiting for her to get back from France so that we could get the papers drawn up to sell this place." There was a curious little smile on his face. "I nearly lost everything."

"I thought Sabine was perfect," I blurted out, thinking of the photograph in the other bedroom.

"Oh, she was. Absolutely. Perfect skin, perfect hair—perfect." Leo sounded very bitter. "Trouble was, I wasn't the only man to think that. Every time she went away to sales or showing, I'd wonder. In the end I had to tell myself I didn't care, that if she came home and said she'd met someone else, it wouldn't hurt." He smoothed my hair off my face. "I'm not very good with people you see. Too shy, too single minded. Whereas with you, Alys"—those green eyes looked down into my face again—"I feel that we share something deeper, something beyond communication."

I lay for a long time in the dark, listening to his breathing become slow and regular, trying to find the sleep which had eluded me all night. Leo had opened up to me! I gave a little shiver of glee, partially occasioned by now knowing that Sabine hadn't been the epitome of perfection I had imagined. Maybe she had liked the admiration, fed on it, encouraged it—perhaps fidelity hadn't meant anything to her?

Nice thought.

I slid into unnoticed sleep and woke with birdsong, the sound of hooves on gravel and an absence of Leo in the bed. I'd left my bag downstairs and my clothes were nowhere to be seen, so I searched for something of Leo's to put on. A quick scout round the room revealed a chest of drawers, under an enormous pile of old horse magazines.

I opened the first drawer, but it contained nothing more than some old show programmes and rosettes. The next drawer seemed to be packed with receipts and invoices, and I began to wonder whether Leo actually *had* any clothes. Then the third and last drawer. Revelations. Poems. Poems that made my heart pinwheel and pushed my breath into my throat, words dragged from the depths of a burning soul. *Such pain. Such dead resignation to fate.* Suddenly ashamed, I closed up the drawer and went to the window to gasp in some air, feeling as though I'd somehow forced reluctant admissions from the lips of a dreamer.

Wrapped in the duvet, I watched the morning coming to life outside. Once again the sun was coating the world with its adhesive rays, beating the brightness out of it and flattening the shadows. Out on the driveway, Leo stood holding a pony by its head collar. I looked at him with new eyes, new insights into the depths of him, watching as he glanced up at the approach of another pony being dragged reluctantly along by a woman.

I peered into the baked morning. Was this the elusive Jay? In my head she had become almost as much of a paragon as Sabine, efficient around the horses and a siren elsewhere. The real Jay looked approachable and more like a best mate than a manager, with a curvy figure and dark brown hair scraped back and tied into a tidy, workmanlike bun.

She tugged her animal to a standstill alongside Leo, letting the rope go slack. The two of them bent, side by side, Leo pulling at the pony's leg, Jay looking down at the hoof. I opened the window and called down a greeting but neither of them seemed to hear, both entranced by equine matters.

There I stood, wearing only the sex-damped duvet, and there was Leo, on his knees. With another woman. Not a beautiful woman, but an ordinary, everyday woman. He'd left his bed with me in it, to go to her and the horses.

I'd rarely felt so bereft. Oh, I'd come close of course, when Alasdair and I had split up, and Florence and I had moved out of the four-bedroomed place in Harrogate and into the little flat in York. But then the only things I'd lost had been material. Now I felt like I'd lost a chance.

Maybe it was the words I'd just read which made me more vulnerable than I would otherwise have been, because I stood glumly contemplating the scene coming to an end as the girl wheeled her pony around and set off back the way she had come.

Everything inside me had sunk. Yesterday I had been so buoyed up with excitement and anticipation culminating in last night's triumphant sexual regatta, complete with flares igniting and waves crashing on the shore. Now I felt like the last voyage of an old dredger.

The dull central core of pain nagged at me like toothache as I retrieved my hairbrush from the table, my yesterday-night shirt-of-passionate-abandon from the chairback and tried to repack them without letting the memories come too. I didn't want to pull these clothes out of my bag to remember the way he'd kissed my shoulder when I undid my buttons, the feel of his fingers tangling in my hair as I'd arched above him. No.

Chapter Eighteen

"...and so I told him I had an urgent phone call from home and had to come back." I sat slumped in Simon's chair behind the curtain, chain-eating HobNobs.

"Alys." Jace shook her head slowly. "You are sometimes a very silly girl."

"What?" I felt as though she had punched me. Surely, unequivocal support was what friends were for? "Why?"

"Because once again you are not talking. You are seeing him with this girl and you are feeling that you are—what?—too old, too used up, too *dry* to be loved? But you are running away instead of standing up and saying 'I am feeling very bad and I wish for you to comfort me'?"

"But he never—" I sniffed back the tears. "He never told me I was beautiful or great in bed or anything. He thinks we've got some sort of recognition-thing going—and *that's* only because I've read his poetry." I flopped back in the chair, my indignation spent. "I feel crap. Used and crap."

"No." Jacinta's voice was very firm. "I am not listening to you any more, Alys. Always you are going round and round with the questions with me, but what can I tell you? Is it that you are *wanting* me to be saying that yes he is *bastardo*? This I cannot say, because I do not know him. And neither more do you. So, no more talking of it, unless you are going to be ringing up this man and having a good talk about how you are feeling.

All right?"

She broke through the curtain, sweeping out of the cubbyhole like the QE2 setting indignant sail. Even though the HobNobs had lost their flavoursome moreishness in the face of her annoyance, I ate a couple anyway, flicking the crumbs sadly onto the carpet.

Okay, so Leo had appeared upset by my precipitate leaving. Not simply upset, but bewildered, baffled. I'd had to concoct a story about Florence arriving back from London to find the flat flooded and the fire brigade on the doorstep before he'd agreed to drive me to the station. He'd even offered to come back with me. I remembered the feel of his farewell hug, how I'd briefly relaxed into the sensation of being wanted, before the mental picture of him and Jay talking came floating back and I stiffened away. I wanted to talk to him—oh, how I wanted to. But I needed the reassurance of home.

"Alys!" Jace called to me from the shop floor. "You are broody like an old hen. Come here and be helping me, I am wanting to finish with these books because Piers he is coming to take me to lunch."

I dragged myself from my weary tangle of thoughts and went through, trailing biscuit crumbs. "You're going out with Piers again?" Even my voice sounded heavy. "Where's he taking you?"

Jace gave me an odd look from under lashes so heavily mascaraed that any single one would constitute an offensive weapon. "I am not knowing. Why, do you wish to come also?"

"I wouldn't want to cramp your style." Although with the way Jace was dressed today, even anthrax would have had a job cramping her style. She looked like a gothic lampshade.

"I am sure Piers will not mind." Jace lifted a pile of books.

Companionably, our slight tiff forgotten, Jace and I carried the priced-up books through, then I left her to get on with

129

shelving so that I could man the till. Shelving was a job Jace was ideally suited for. She could easily reach shelves which had me teetering on a stool. *Perhaps I should wear stilettos.* I looked down at my shoes. I'd worn sexy boots at Leo's, why not at work?

"Do you think I should wear sexier shoes?" I called through.

"I am not hearing you. What did you say?"

"Do you THINK," I bellowed, "that I should wear SEXIER SHOES?"

"Oh yeah, talk dirty to me again."

I jumped, hadn't heard him come in. "Piers!"

"Were you thinking, say, heels? Kinda like—*real high*?"

I couldn't tell if he was winding me up or not. "Um. Jace!" I called. "Piers is here."

"Or suede? I get real hot for suede."

"JACE!"

Piers looked at me sideways. "Hey, what's up with you today? You seem kinda edgy."

"Alys is not liking men right now." Jacinta loomed into vision like a war barge. "I say we are taking her away to eat and she will forget all the bad doings."

Piers frowned. "Bastard stand you up again? Just say the word and I'll punch him out."

I laughed. Piers was an unlikely champion. "My knight in shining cotton." I brushed a casual hand over his arm. "Thanks, Piers. But it wasn't really Leo this time, it was me. I just felt, well, Leo can compartmentalise his life so easily. There's the horses"—*and Jay*, my mind whispered—"and there's me." I made little "boxes" with my hands. "I can't do that. I want a man who can overlap. Who can make me feel like I'm the centre of his world."

Jacinta snorted. "You tell me when you find that man, Alys. I feel you may have long, long wait."

Piers held his hands up. "Hey, you two want to be alone with your bitterness and anger, or we going to lunch?"

We decided to go back to my flat and have lunch there. I tried to step back, to suggest that Jace and Piers go off somewhere alone together, but they were adamant. We arrived at my front door in the Porsche. It was not a stylish arrival.

"I think I'll walk back." I levered myself from the miniscule shelf which passed for a backseat and where I had spent the journey sitting bolt upright between them like a cross between a chaperone and a cocker spaniel. "This is *not* a three-seater."

Jacinta untied her headscarf and forced her hair forward with both hands. "Is a little fast driving for no roof, Piers. You too are looking like you have been very well blown."

"Uh, yeah."

The flat smelled terrible. It had smelled bad last night when I'd arrived. This was worse.

"Foargh," Jace exclaimed. "Alys, it is smelling like you are keeping dead persons. It was not smelling like this when I was coming to feed Grainger." Then her face creased into a frown. "Although I think that Snakebite made my nose not work."

I ran round apologising and opening windows. Then we ate and Jace updated Piers on the latest chapter in the disaster that was my love life.

"So, Alys, why are you thinking he is like this?" Jace asked as I returned to the table after another brief and fruitless hunt for Grainger.

"Hmm—he's not been very well lately, so it's only to be expected that he might not be able to control himself as well as he used to." It was only when I saw their confusion that I realised she had been asking about Leo. "Oh. I don't know. I'm just so confused. Men, huh! Sorry, Piers, present company excepted, of course."

"I'm glad you think so."

"I have been thinking that this is a man who is not having thoughts of you. Is easy with horses, you give them food, you clean up shit and there they are, all happy. I think this man is not good with women. Are you still caring?"

Ah, the inevitable question. Did I care? I collected the soup bowls and ran water into the sink while I thought. Yes, I cared. I cared that I felt stupid—that he'd been more interested in sex than in me. I cared about the way *I* felt. But him? Did I care about him? Enough to swallow my pride and talk to him? I could still feel the burning chill from the power of his words, lying there useless and impotent in a drawer when they should have been etched into a million souls. I thought of his green eyes, his cool, muscular body—

"Hey, Alys." Piers came and stood behind me as I pensively rinsed dishes. "I've been thinking, Florence isn't due back until Wednesday, right? So why don't you come out with me tonight? There's a couple parties on, you know the kinda thing." Jacinta snorted and said something shortly in Spanish. To my surprise Piers replied, also in Spanish then switched languages. "How about it? Cheer you up, guaranteed! Come shake yer funky thang."

The potential of Jace shaking her funky thing made me smile. "I haven't heard you speak Spanish for years." It was all I could think of to say.

"Yeah, well," he said. "Been keeping it up, putting in some practice talking to Jacinta here." Jacinta gave a small smile. "Y'see Pop's from the Argentine. Met Ma when she went down buying polo ponies. He's still there, given up the ponies now, spends his time building boats, so when I call him I speak Spanish. I was bilingual til I was about twelve but—hey, use it or lose it, yeah Alys?"

I wasn't sure about the way he was grinning at me. I was even less sure about the hand on my shoulder. I could feel his rings cool against my skin where my much-washed T-shirt sagged.

"Come out tonight. Show this Leo guy you're not sitting in pining."

"Oh, I don't know. I ought to be here in case he rings again." Leo had rung a few times, but somehow fate had conspired with bad luck to make me miss each call. I'd been going to ring him back this evening, but really, was it worth it? Was *I* worth it? If he started to wonder about my motives, they might not stand up to much investigation. Particularly if he quizzed Isabelle and found out I was not the old schoolfriend I'd pretended to be. Whatever I wanted Leo to think I was, a gold digger definitely wasn't it. "All right I will. Thanks, Piers." Piers and Jace exchanged a look and I could have sworn she winked. "Shall I meet you at your place, Jace?"

She shook her head. "Tonight I have things to do. I am sorry, Piers." Piers gave a mock-formal bow in her direction. "But I am staying in."

"Oh, Jace, isn't coming out with us better than sitting indoors? That's so boring." Besides, I wasn't really sure I wanted to go out on my own with Piers. I had the feeling his idea of partying was a long way from mine. Which, owing to my somewhat limited social circle, had tended until recently to involve small girls in party dresses and hysterical levels of excitement.

Anyway, I had nothing to wear.

Jace gave a huge sigh, her bosom rose and fell like a speeded-up film of the creation of mountain ranges. "No. I am sorry, but I think that now is the time."

"Time for what?" Did I imagine it or was there a glance exchanged between the two of them? Was I missing something essential here? "Jace? Piers?"

A snapping line of Spanish and they both shrugged.

"What, you reckon we can't enjoy, just the two of us?" Piers leaned towards me. "You want that I show you a good time, Alys?"

"I'm not sure that I want you to show me *anything*, Piers," I said, more sharply than I meant to. "You're not actually *afraid* to go out, Jace, are you?"

"Me? Afraid?" Jace drew herself up and looked down at the top of Piers's head. "I think it would be me protecting *you*, but no, this is not the case. I am deciding to stay inside and prepare for next weekend."

"Having Antonio Banderas over are you? Jace—"

Piers shook his head. "Nah. 'Sokay. Don't sweat it. We'll enjoy on your behalf. Right, Alys?"

What else could I do? The pair of them had clearly ganged up on me, so I nodded grudgingly. "Okay. I'll go out. I'll enjoy myself. But I won't *enjoy* it, if you know what I mean."

"Whatever." Piers still had his hand on my shoulder. "Come on, I'll drop you back at work."

So he drove us, more slowly, back to Webbe's, where I continued to hover over the phone in a sweat of indecision for the rest of the afternoon.

Chapter Nineteen

I told myself it was only Piers, and that he was simply being kind. None of this helped. I couldn't make up my mind whether to be totally casual and throw on a pair of jeans (although not the ones which made my bottom an odd shape, I wasn't prepared to be quite *that* casual) or to go the whole set and wear a dress and heels. Would that make me look as though I was expecting everything to be classy and catered?

Most of my wardrobe and several drawers lay on the bed. I'd laddered the only black tights I possessed, and I hadn't found Grainger to put him on his litter tray for the evening. It was six thirty, Piers was picking me up at seven and I was wearing a dressing gown. My fingers itched with the urge to phone Jace, just for advice and reassurance. So she could tell me I wasn't being a total tart for going out partying with my stepson rather than sitting at home worrying about my potential relationship. After all, so what if Leo did have more going on in his life than pining after me? *So bloody what?* He had a business to run. What was I expecting? Breakfast in bed and cuddles? Yes, actually. But—oh, sod it. I'd give myself the night off. A night without thinking about the jealousy I'd felt of the obvious communication Leo and Jay shared, of the feelings I *knew* he kept contained.

Oh bugger, it was quarter to seven. *Come on, Alys, what to wear?* Maybe Florrie had left something in her cupboards which wouldn't make me look like a cross between a teenage street prostitute and an urban mugger? I went into her room and opened her wardrobe doors. The smell which came out was certainly not associated with Florrie's taste in perfume.

"Grainger?" My eyes fell on the curled shape, hidden in the deepest recesses of the jog pants. He didn't move and I felt my whole body stop. "Grainger? Sweetie?" I reached in. Touched the tip of his crumpled tabby ear. It didn't flicker. "Oh, cat." I reached farther, almost reluctantly stroking one hand down his furry flank. This was the cat who'd escaped certain death under the wheels of the Park and Ride bus, emerging in a cloud of blue exhaust fumes as the bus rolled away down the road, with an expression of scorn on his whiskers. This cat had fallen off my bedroom window ledge two stories into the suspect hedging beneath and got away with nothing but a case of chronic embarrassment. Surely he'd go out with a bang, causing a four-car pile-up, not quietly expiring mixed up with Florrie's outgrown clothing and dirty laundry.

"Grainger?" I pushed both arms around his curled body and drew him out towards me. He wasn't totally stiff yet, nor cold and I held him close to my chest, bending my head to kiss his fur. "Oh God." I'd got seven minutes before Piers arrived, I couldn't bury Grainger in seven minutes. But neither could I face leaving him here until I got back from the party. He'd be stiff by then and almost impossible to bury unless I dug a hole that could have interred a Great Dane. Perhaps I could put him in a box?

I sat on the sofa, cradling the soft bundle against me. Florrie had pleaded and pleaded for a pet. When Alasdair had finally admitted that, yes, he'd fallen for another woman, and we had moved into this place, it had seemed the perfect opportunity. So she had, fairly uncomplainingly, exchanged her father for a scruffy half-grown tabby, and we'd settled here together, all three of us.

There was a slamming knock at the door. "Hey! Ready to party?" Piers erupted over the threshold, took one look at my sad little mass and sat down suddenly. "Shit. Is he—y'know—?"

I shrugged, suddenly awkward at being in my dressing gown. "He's not moving," I said, in a ridiculously childish voice.

"Oh, Alys." Voice soft, Piers gently reached out. I thought he was going to touch the cat, but the extended fingertip touched my face instead. "Grainger—"

Deep against me there came a slight tremble, an indistinct thrumming sound, the merest hint of vibration. "He's purring," I almost shouted. "Piers, he's not dead!"

"Steady, Alys." Piers took Grainger from me. "I don't think he's good. Looks kinda like a stroke. You want we should call the vet?"

As usual, the vision of the pathetically small numbers on my bank account crept into view. "I don't—I mean, I'm not sure."

Piers looked up from the cat. His eyes were a very deep brown tonight, I noticed. Not that I should be noticing such things, but I couldn't help it with the way he was looking at me. "Hey, Ally. I'll get the bill."

"You can't."

A mad smile. "Wanna bet?" The smile died as he leaned his head down and brushed the tabby fur with a cheek. "Do the words American Express mean anything to you?"

"I didn't mean you couldn't, I meant—I can't take money from you."

"Because? Hey, I thought we were friends. Or are you gonna pull that 'you're the son of my ex-husband's new wife' shit on me? Friends, Ally, friends help each other out, that's what they're for. Now, you make the call."

As I flipped open the little black book which contained all

the phone numbers Florence or I ever needed, I wondered when Piers got so macho. Maybe it was the Argentinian rancher in him coming out, I thought, as I spoke to the vet's receptionist with one eye on the floppy tabby body he still held close to his chest. "We're to take him in. Now."

"Glad you saw sense. Let's go."

"I'm in my dressing gown."

Piers looked me slowly up and down. "Oh yeah," he said, but I didn't believe for one second that he'd only just noticed. "Come on." He walked through into my bedroom. I think he was trying to distract me, but having him raising his eyebrows at the throbbing red throw was more distracting than I could really cope with. "Okay, this"—he nodded towards a jade green halterback top that I hadn't worn for years—"with this." A pink suede short skirt, which actually was Florrie's. "And"—with a grin—"those real cool boots."

I felt like a lap dancer on her day off when we left for the clinic.

"Definitely a stroke." The vet gave the recumbent Grainger another last look through his bifocals. "At his age it would probably be best if we..."

I clenched Grainger against my chest so hard that he gave a little gasp. "No."

"Ms. Hunter." Wearily the vet pulled his glasses off and rubbed his eyes. "Recovery from a collapse of this kind would be such a long, slow process it might be kinder."

"She said no." Piers put both hands on the examination table and leaned forward. The vet leaned back. I felt sorry for him. He looked as though he hadn't slept in days and his white coat was three sizes too large. Probably the last thing he needed right now was an annoyed American looming at him. "Give the cat a shot, whatever, and we'll take him home."

I dropped my head again and some more tears damped Grainger's fur. My nose was running and all I had to wipe it on, apart from Grainger himself, was my arm. I sniffed instead.

"Look. If you insist on my treating this cat, he'll need to be admitted. Possibly only for a day or two until he starts to respond, *if he does*. But in view of the cost, I really would advise—"

Piers ignored the vet and turned to me. He crouched down in front of where I sat in one of those slightly-too-small plastic chairs that vet's surgeries always have, holding Grainger between my chest and bare knees. "He'll be okay here, Alys. They'll look after him. You want that? Yeah?"

"B-but the cost..."

Piers ignored me. "Keep him here. Do everything you can for him." He gave the poor vet another glare. "And I mean *everything*. I get any whisper that you gave up on this cat and I'll have your badge."

As we walked back to the car, Grainger-less, I gave a snorty, snot-filled kind of laugh. "I don't think vets *have* badges, Piers."

Another manic Piers-grin. "I know that. But, it's all in the tone of voice. He knew I meant what I said, what I *really* said doesn't matter. Would you rather I said I'd have his balls?" He flipped open the door of the Porsche and I tried to get in without flashing him my knickers.

"No, it's just that it's going to be expensive. Are you sure we shouldn't have, well, you know. Made the final decision?"

"You *want* that? Grainger sent on his way? You just say the word, Ally, I'll go back in there and—"

"No!"

"Right. So, shut up about the money, yeah?"

I took a deep breath. "I'll pay you back. Honestly, I will. I don't know how, yet, but—"

Piers looked down at my bare legs and did the grin again. "I'll think of something."

This time I laughed properly and slapped him on the shoulder. "You are such a tart."

"Yeah? I'm not the one in a micro-mini and stilettos, babe."

"Maybe, but you chose this outfit."

His smile died a little. "Glad I did, too. You look great, did I say that already? Come on, the big G's in good hands here, let's go find us a PARTY!" He dropped the clutch on the little yellow car and it jumped forward with a lurch I could feel from my heart down to my stomach.

Chapter Twenty

"My name's Alys. Alys, with a Y," I bellowed at the young man who'd enquired, screaming to be heard over the wailing which permeated the air.

"That's Alicey then, isn'it? So, *Alicey*, what're you doing here? You're not"—the hand which had been hovering on my leg retracted—"you're not Si's mum, are you?"

"No." I edged towards the kitchen, which had been my destination when I'd been accosted by this pink-haired punk-approximate. "Look, excuse me, I want to get another drink."

"Yeah, great idea! Let's go get another drink. C'mon guys, fuck off out of it, Alicey wants another drink." A crude method maybe, but the crowd blocking our way parted, and I reeled through the doorway only to crash my hip against a table which had been formed by standing a board between two beer crates.

At least it was quieter in here. Very, very smoky, but quieter. In fact—I coughed for a second until my lungs caught up—it was so smoky you could probably get high simply by standing in the same post-code. "So, what'ya drinking, Alicey? Look, have some of this. Tastes like piss but—wheeeeewww!"

Oh God, and for this I'd worn suede. "No, thank you. I'll just have some wine."

"Nah." My pink-haired attendant grabbed a bottle of something suspiciously cloudy and upended it over a glass.

"You want some of this. Loosen you up, know what I mean?" He peered into my eyes, which were still red from crying over Grainger.

A hand extended over my shoulder and passed me a glass of white wine. I recognised the scary pattern of the sleeve. "Thanks," I said, with relief.

"Maaaaaaan!" My new friend slammed Piers on the back, missing a couple of times. "Where you been? This"—he gestured more or less in my direction—"is Alicey." He lowered his voice to a subtle shout. "I'm gonna get her upstairs after another couple."

"Oh, sorry, was that your foot? These heels are really quite sharp, aren't they? Whoops, there goes my wine, clumsy me."

"I'd better get you out of here before you kill him," Piers muttered, tugging me by the wrist through the kitchen and out of the back door. I took deep breaths of the clean air, spoilt only by the smoke from the joint which Piers was carrying. "How're you doing?"

"What, apart from being chatted up by men with all the romantic subtlety of Australopithecus? Fine, thanks."

Piers shrugged, tugged at the cuffs of his jacket and took a mighty drag. "Yeah, sorry. I didn't think this place would be quite so uncool. You want we go on somewhere else? Somewhere quieter?"

I sat down on a low wall overlooking a lawn which sloped down to a summerhouse. "No, it's fine. Just what I need really, to stop me sitting at home moping, a spot of culture shock. Another drink and I'll be dancing on the table with my top off like the other girls."

He grinned. "Now, that I'd pay to see." He held the joint out. "You want?"

Motherhood, legality and upbringing came swarming to the surface. "No thanks." I crossed my legs and folded my arms in an attitude of total denial, until I realised that this revealed my knickers and pushed my boobs beyond the help of my strapless bra.

"Hey." Piers leaned down until his face was level with mine. "Live a little, yeah?"

Oh, what the hell, I thought.

We sat on the wall and smoked in a pleasant kind of silence. When we finished, Piers dodged into the house again and emerged carrying two glasses, an untouched bottle of wine and another joint.

"Piers, can I ask you something?"

"Absolutely anything, Alys." He handed me a glass. "So long as it's not the square root of anything. Crap at math, always was."

"Where do you get these *terrible* clothes?" I pulled at his jacket lapel to draw attention to its awfulness. "I mean, how many sofas had to die to make this thing?"

"That bad, eh?"

"Worse. You look"—I indicated the floppy bell-ended sleeves—"like the bastard offspring of Lawrence Llewellyn-Bowen and an Axminster carpet."

"A mating that I would also pay to see." Piers poured himself another glass of wine. It occurred to me at this point that he wasn't going to be fit to drive home, but I'd reached the stage where this was simply a thought, not a practical eventuality. "I dunno. I kinda buy stuff that I like. I prefer to be an individual, you know? I don't follow the crowd."

"I don't think they'd *let* you," I muttered.

"Okay. My turn."

"Turn for what?"

"To ask you something." He lit the second joint but passed it directly to me. "Play fair, now." He wasn't looking at me, I noticed, keeping his eyes on the ground, hair hiding most of his expression. "Who's Florrie's real father?"

I felt the blood rise to my face. "What?" I took a huge pull on the joint, followed by an enormous gulp of wine. Buying time, covering my confusion.

"Does she know it's not Alasdair?" Piers was looking at me now, properly, his features barely illuminated in the weak light that reached us via the kitchen. His eyes, huge, dark, lost in the shadow. Unreadable.

"That's two questions."

"Yeah."

What did he want? My heart was hammering in my throat, my skin reacting with goose pimples on my arms and legs. "What makes you think...?"

"Alys, I *know*. Ma and Alasdair have been trying for a baby since they got hitched. Six, maybe eight months ago they went for tests. Guess they both kinda thought it was her. I mean, she's what, forty-two?"

Oh God.

"Turns out he's got, now what was it? Oh yeah, low-motility sperm. Little bastards just don't wanna swim. And, you know what? The ones that *do* go round and round in circles. About as much chance of getting to an egg as I have of getting to the North Pole."

I only realised I was shivering when Piers draped his jacket around me.

"Shit. I didn't want to do this, Alys, believe me. I just thought you ought to be warned. I didn't do it to hurt you, or Florrie, or even Chrissake fucking *Alasdair*. I—Alys?"

"Flick," I said, distantly. The wine, the fragrant smoke, his eyes, they'd all reached me at last.

"Excuse me?"

"His name. Was Flick. Or, well, it wasn't, but I couldn't pronounce his real name. He was Polish. Flick was the nearest I could get."

"No shit." Piers took the joint off me. It was almost gone, but he sucked at it until the end glowed fierce in the darkness.

"I've never"—I drained my glass and shuddered as the bitterness cascaded down my throat—"*never* told anyone about this."

"You're drunk. And stoned. Maybe this isn't the time."

"Yes. Yes, I am. And I'm cold, I'm sad, I'm lonely, and my love-life has gone tits-up yet *again*, and I'm really tired and you're here. I can't think of any better time to tell someone."

Piers let out a breath. "Okay then. But look, you're fucking freezing. Give me a second." He vanished indoors again.

I waited, my heartbeat still filling my ears. What was I doing? This was *Piers*. But he was here and he listened and he was so *nice* and *pretty*, and bloody hell I was drunk. I could do with some peanuts. *I hope he's gone for some food.* Oh shit, fairly sure the garden wasn't meant to tilt that way.

"Come on."

"What? Where?" This time he'd got two bottles of wine.

"You'll see."

I clutched at the lapels of the jacket again, this time to hold it close around me as we set off down the garden. Piers loped through the long grass with me bobbling and weaving alongside.

"In here." Piers pulled a key from his pocket and unlocked the door to the summerhouse. "I think there should be—yeah, over here, there's some cushions." I sank down onto a pile of damp canvas and leaned back against the wall. Piers pressed a bottle into my hand and came to sit beside me. "I got crisps. Figured the munchies'd be striking about now. Guess I was right."

We sat and ate crisps for a while, listening to the sounds of the river and the very distant noises of the party, which occasionally crept closer in the form of vomiting in the shrubbery and what sounded like some vigorous copulation off to our left.

Piers eventually broke the crunch-filled silence. "I've been trying to say something to you since I found out. Didn't know how."

"That night in the wine bar? *This* was what you were trying to tell me? The family matter?" I started to drink wine out of the bottle; I was fairly certain that tomorrow wasn't going to be pretty. I failed to see how a killer hangover was going to make things any worse.

"Uh huh."

"I suspected. We tried for a baby when Florence was about three. Nothing happened and we both shrugged it off, decided that she was more than enough to be dealing with." I lapsed into silence for a bit, apart from the plopping sound my tongue made in the neck of the bottle as I prevented the wine from drowning me.

"You okay?" Piers asked eventually.

"I loved him," I said simply.

"Yeah, well I'm sure he loved you too. He often talks about—"

"Flick."

"Oh. Yeah. Okay."

"He was an art student. Lived in this incredible van on a patch of waste-ground outside the city. The coolest thing, all great slabs of artwork and chrome. I was only nineteen and he was the most beautiful man I'd ever seen."

"Did he know? About Florence?"

"I was young and stupid, thought he'd be *pleased*. There was an argument. Flick—he wasn't—he decided he wasn't dad material. And then I met Alasdair and he wanted to marry me, and he had a car and his dad's a laird and everything and…"

"He didn't know you were pregnant?"

"No," I said in a tiny voice. "I had to choose. Flick wanted me to get rid of it. Alasdair was absolutely ecstatic when I told him I was having a baby. He just assumed—"

"Oh shit. Alys. Jesus."

"Piers?"

"Hey." His arm came round me in the darkness and I was glad of his closeness. "I'm not judging you. I've not been there, so I don't know how it goes, but shit, yeah, I can imagine. Christ. No wonder you don't take money off him."

"I said that I didn't need his money, but Alasdair said that if Florrie needed anything or wanted anything she only had to ask, so she did. I couldn't stop her," I added sadly.

"So you live like you do, because…"

"Because that's what I deserve for what I did." I was slurring my speech quite badly now. "I used Alasdair because he was there. Because he said he loved me."

"And you didn't? Love him, I mean?"

"I was fond of him, yes. But. It was my fault. My fault he met your mother and left me. I couldn't—the marriage wasn't— it wasn't what he'd hoped for."

Piers's arm tightened around me. "Have you ever had it? That moment when you think, 'Yeah, I'd do anything for you. Die for you. Give you everything'? Ever had that, Ally?"

My head dropped briefly onto Piers's shoulder, my eyelids drooped. I could feel his heartbeat through the thin cotton of his shirt. Fast and deep. "No." The image of Leo swam into my head. "I want to."

Piers cleared his throat. "Florrie not being Alasdair's. I mean, I got there. I put things together. I'm clever, Alys, I'm sharp, but I'm not the only one. How long have you got before someone else does?"

"I don't know." I put the mouth of the bottle between my teeth, braced myself and poured. What was left in the bottle slid down my throat and I gulped at it, eagerly courting oblivion.

Chapter Twenty-One

I lay very, very still. With the return of consciousness came a montage sequence of events which I had to suppose represented the previous night—and then, nothing.

It was very quiet. This was bad. Meant I probably hadn't made it home last night.

Oh shit. I scrabbled about in my memory, trying to uncover some tiny glimpse into last night's events which would reveal just how deeply in the crap I currently was. Cautious fingers, still numbed with alcohol, let me know that I was wearing knickers and a T-shirt. My feet were bare and I had a bruised feeling at the top of my hip. Aha! I remembered that. I'd crashed into a table, Piers had given me some wine and I'd—

Oh God, please, no. The summerhouse. Dope, wine, Piers's arm around me. I'd told him about Florrie. About—*him.* Flick. The elven-faced, blond-haired artist who'd drawn me into his life and misled me, and ultimately who'd betrayed me in favour of his art.

Agonies flooded me, scrying and scribbling through my intestines like haruspices trying to divine the future. So now someone knew. Seventeen years of containment, of a memory dam which had resisted all other forces, gone in one night. Now, it wasn't so much a question of facing the music, more of facing a full symphonic orchestra with a nuclear string section.

I staggered out of bed, wincing as my feet touched the floor and my legs straightened. There was a cracking sound from my spine as I reached full height and dragged myself over to the small low window by judicious use of pieces of furniture. I had to lean quite heavily on the sill and close my eyes until the outside world stopped spinning, and I could get a proper look at it.

Oh *shit.* I mean, really, really *shitty* shit. With a big side order of *fuuuuuuuckkkk.*

The view wasn't familiar. Not exactly. But I did know where I was. Oh God, someone was going to *die* for this. It might be me.

"Oh, you're up and about. I brought you some orange juice. Reckoned it might be the best thing right now. Thirsty?"

"Piers, you absolute, total and complete *bastard.*" I spun away from the window, hissing like a boiling snake. "What the fuck possessed you to bring me *here?*"

Piers put down the pitcher and tray slowly and carefully, then, with great deliberation, began pouring a glass of juice. "What else could I do? You'd passed out, you were throwing up, like, every two minutes. I couldn't *leave* you. You might have choked."

"I don't remember." It was a half-lie. "I don't remember anything."

Piers drank the orange juice, looking at me over the glass. He had no *right* to look so bloody good. "Okay." He replaced the glass on the tray and sat down on the window ledge. "You were out of it, completely gone. I thought about getting you to hospital, but I figured you'd thrown up most of the alcohol anyway. I was going to take you to your place, but—" He looked down at his hands. "Don't forget, I was outta things too last night. Not thinking straight, know what I mean? And then." He looked at me and there was a whole book written in his eyes. "I didn't like to leave you," he repeated. "So I got a taxi, brought you back here. You'd stopped throwing up, but I couldn't be sure."

"This is your flat, yes? And you have been subtle about it? I mean, I'm not going to walk out through that door and find Alasdair and Tamar waiting to hear how I came to be brought home by her son, blind drunk and only half-dressed?"

"This is my place, yeah. Want to look round?"

I took a deep breath. "Piers, I'm only nominally sober, I'm still only half-dressed, and I feel like—you don't want to know. If I smile I'm convinced my face is going to fall off, put it that way."

"You look okay to me."

"I might *look* okay but I *feel* like a chemical toilet. Why didn't you book me into a hotel? And what about Grainger? I should have rung the vet!"

"The way you were last night? I had to pay the taxi driver double, he thought you were going to die on him. The only hotels that would have taken you were *not* places you'd want to be waking up in this morning. And, like I said, I didn't want to leave you. Don't worry about getting back home. I'll need to get to York, pick up my car. I'll drop you off on the way. Grainger will still be at the surgery whatever's happened."

There was a silence. I took the glass of juice he poured me, proper stuff, freshly squeezed. "Piers, what I said last night—"

"You said nothing last night. You want toast? I got a real class act, kick-ass toaster, does bagels too." He got up and headed out of the room, but I followed. This was too important to leave.

"No, I mean—"

He stopped, so suddenly that I collided with his back. "Alys. Listen up. You said *nothing* last night, right?" He turned around to face me, put his hands on my shoulders. "Nothing." His face bent towards me until I felt the soft drift of his hair on

151

my cheek, close enough to tell that his breath smelled of coffee. "It's okay." And he was gone, whirling away across bare-boarded floors to an island unit which stood in the middle of the best fitted kitchen I'd seen outside a *Homes and Gardens* magazine. "You should really be worrying about what you *did!* Jeez, you were crazy, woman. Thought you were going to jump in the river one time, up on the bridge dancing. What was it? *Rio,* something."

"Duran Duran? I was dancing to Duran Duran? On a bridge?" Trying to follow his mood, copy it, kid both him and me that I believed he'd really never mention last night again.

"Not just dancing. You were *singing* it! Fucking crazy. And that's when you threw your boots in the river too, case you were wondering. Can't dance in boots, apparently. You want eggs? No? And then you locked yourself in the john, did three lines of coke and insisted we went on to a club."

"I didn't!" This was truly horrific.

"Nah. Just kidding, you passed out. Had to carry you to the taxi." Piers juggled three eggs in the air, cracking each one against the side of a bowl as it came down. "Sure you don't want? I'm scrambling?"

"You're posing."

"Yeah." He struck a muscle-man attitude, then one-handed slooshed the eggs into a pan of foaming butter. "And I cook. Twenty-first-century man, right in front of your very eyes."

I shook my head and went and sat down in a cuboid chair until he'd finished. The smell of the eggs cooking made me nauseous, and the relentless resilience of youth made me feel crippled and weak.

I had to admit though that his flat was beautiful. Pale boarded floors from end to end, the kitchen with its lean-over worktop leading to the dining area, possibly the biggest TV I'd ever seen, and the clean-sheeted bedroom. I presumed there was also a bathroom to match. Anyone with a set-up like this was highly unlikely to be pissing in a bucket. I leaned my head back and closed my eyes. This much conspicuous consumerism in one place was narcotic and I must have drifted off again, because the next thing I knew was Piers gently shaking my shoulder.

"Alys. The taxi's here."

"Wha'? Oh. Need to get dressed." I shuffled into the bedroom and emerged wearing the pink skirt, but still in the T-shirt and with bare feet. I'd found the halterback top, but at some point during the night I'd obviously been sick on it. "I'll get the T back to you later."

"Keep it." Piers handed me a pair of flip-flop sandals. "Wear these for now. They'll stop you looking quite so—" He stopped and his cheeks flushed under his dark stubble.

"Quite so what?" He shook his head, but I insisted. "Quite so *what*, Piers?"

"Quite so slept over," he muttered.

"But I did sleep over, where's the problem?"

"I am so *not* going to spell it out for you, Alys. Let's go, taxi's waiting."

I frowned, and then his meaning rammed into my skull. "Oh!" and a second later, "Oh, God. You don't think anyone would think—would they?"

"My reputation's been shit for years, how's yours?" Piers flashed me a mischievous grin.

"Going downhill, I suspect," I said, as disapprovingly as I could.

"Yeah." Piers led the way to his front door. A short way farther down a gravelled drive lay the five-bedroomed, five-bathroomed home of Alasdair and Tamar. I felt a brief stab of pity for the two of them; this would have been the perfect setting for a clutch of kids. What the hell, they could always adopt. Tamar would no doubt insist on a matching pair of Romanian orphans and Piers would be kicked out to make way for a Norlands nanny.

"Darling." The voice cut the tranquillity I'd been feeling with the finesse of a chainsaw. "Did you want to come over for lunch?" Tamar's accent was still, after seven years in Yorkshire, entirely New England. I'd never put my finger on exactly how it was that she managed to make me feel superior and yet patronised all at once, but I suspected the accent played a large part.

"Uh, no thanks, Ma. Gotta get back into town." Under his breath he added, "Please go now." But instead Tamar advanced from around the side of the house until I couldn't help but come into view.

"Alys?" Tamar was clearly torn excruciatingly between the politeness she normally extended towards me whenever we met, and the thousand-and-one questions which had obviously sprung up, seeing me in the company of her son, wearing his T-shirt, a micro-mini skirt and suspect sandals. Particularly when she was as ever immaculate, with her feathery blonde hair, her oversized shirt emphasising her narrow shoulders and her sugar-pink pedal pushers with matching ballet pumps. She looked like Sunday Morning Barbie.

"Alys got mugged last night in York. She knew I was up in town at a party so she called me." Piers's eyes gleamed at me.

"And I didn't want to be alone, with Florrie away. I was a bit shaken to tell the truth so—"

"So I brought her back to mine for the night. We're off now to...er..."

"Report it to the police. I was too shaken last night, and they'll never catch him anyway. Them," I upgraded, knowing Tamar thought I was more butch than Russell Crowe simply on the evidence that I lived without a man and could wire a plug.

"Oh, Alys, that's terrible." Tamar looked me up and down. "They stole your clothes?"

"No, I—"

"Ma, we have to go, I don't want the car towed." Piers flung the taxi door open and waved me inside, rather wildly I thought.

"Sure. Okay. Have you heard from Florence lately, Alys?" Tamar continued, obviously trying to make conversation. You had to admire her really. After all, when it came to awkward social situations this must rank pretty highly.

"A couple of postcards, some rather brief phone calls. Have you?" I wanted the answer to be "no".

"Oh yeah. She sounds real happy, doesn't she? City life suits her."

The taxi started moving before I could reveal that Florrie had left herself limited time during her snatched phone calls in which to sound happy or otherwise, she mainly rang to shriek things like "I'm in the Tower of London!" Anyway, Tamar seemed to have satisfied herself that sufficient pleasantries had been exchanged. She was already heading back to her Aga-lined kitchen with resident cook. She probably had a little woman to do her sit-ups and pelvic-floor exercises too. I gave her a smile as we passed. She waved, but there was a thoughtful look in her eyes. Was it the sight of her son in my company or was she starting to make connections?

I was getting paranoid. I silently cursed Piers for telling me about Alasdair's fertility problems. But there was no reason for anyone to put things together. Alasdair's early influence on Florrie had made sure that she had a lot of his mannerisms, even his own parents had remarked on how like him she was. People seeing what they wanted to, I supposed.

"You okay?" Piers's voice shook me out of my delusions of discovery. "That was one wild party last night. Not surprised you're still hungover."

"I'm just tired."

"Yeah right. I know hungover when I see it." Piers smiled lazily and hauled his hair back off his face. "Can't take the pace."

He was trying to distract me, to stop me thinking about last night's revelations, to make everything all right again. A sudden wave of affection for him welled up inside me. "Know something, Piers? You are a very lovely guy."

The blush I'd seen earlier crept up his cheeks again. "Yeah, well." He cleared his throat and took a sudden interest in twisting his rings.

"I can't understand why you don't have a girlfriend. Surely they're queueing up for a gorgeous boy like you?"

He whipped around and faced me, the blush gone and his skin pale. "*Fuck*, Alys." Then he clenched his fists and breathed hard, obviously controlling himself. "I didn't say I didn't have a girlfriend, did I?"

"You told me that there was someone, but it was difficult. I assumed—I thought it was all over."

"It's not over." Piers was tensed up, I could see the muscles in his jaw locking his anger into place. "It's only just starting."

"Who is she?" There was the tiniest burn of envy in my chest. "Anyone I know?"

Piers turned away and looked out of the window. "Her name's Sarah. You wouldn't know her, she's at college in York."

"Oh." All the closeness and empathy we seemed to have been sharing was gone. It had drained away as soon as he'd mentioned her name. "Where's she from?"

"From? Manchester."

"Has your mother met her yet?" I couldn't stop myself. It was a curious feeling. Whilst I had never kidded myself to the extent of believing Piers found me attractive, or that I could see him as anything other than Florrie's stepbrother, some sub-atomic-level bit of me had been seduced by our intimacy. Hearing that all the time he'd been hugging me in a deserted summerhouse, he'd had this Sarah on the backburner made me feel profoundly guilty about opening up to him.

"I'm taking her down there Wednesday. Look, we're nearly at my car. I'll catch you. Sometime, yeah?" He pressed what looked like a lot of money into the cab driver's hand and leaped out of the door almost before we'd pulled to a stop. I frowned. Even with my well-known geographical dyslexia, I could tell that we were still a couple of miles from where Piers had parked last night. I must have upset him more than I'd realised. It had been a casual enquiry. Why had he suddenly got so touchy?

Chapter Twenty-Two

I remembered Grainger the second I opened the front door and went to call him, tell him I was home. I choked off halfway through his name. Somehow the flat felt wrong without his dear scowling tabby face frowning up at me from a cushion. I rang the vet, only to be told that Grainger was resting comfortably and doing as well as could be expected, which didn't help.

For a second I wished that Piers had come back with me to jolly me out of my despondency, but then I remembered his strange mood in the taxi and decided I'd rather be on my own. I'd had enough tantrums with Florrie. Anyway I really needed a shower.

The knock at the door made me jump, and the sight of Leo, carrying a bunch of red roses caused a near breakdown in all my faculties.

"Leo! You! It's—and all this way. Why are you—? And what about—?"

"Can I come in?" Leo looked me up and down.

I looked down too, at my unrestrained chest, the tiny skirt and the deeply unflattering sandals. "Err, I was about to do some decorating," I improvised. "Come through. How did you find me?"

"I have my methods." Leo smiled, and I was once again devastated by how good-looking he was. "These are for you. I came because I was worried."

"Worried?" Last night's memories had washed me clean of the painful conclusions I'd drawn after spending the night with him. A question of perspective and impact, I supposed.

"You left so quickly." Leo glanced around the hallway. "How's the clearing up going?" His eyes rested on the corner where the carpet was rolled away from the wall and several boxes of books and papers were stacked halfway to the ceiling.

I hustled him through to the living room, glad that, with the absence of Florence, it had stayed more-or-less tidy. "Err. Yes. I've got it under control."

We stood and looked at each other for a moment. Leo seemed obsessed with the position of his glasses. In my turn I fiddled with the roses he'd pressed into my arms, alternately sniffing them, and running my fingers over the baby-soft petals as we both thought of what to say next.

"I..."

"You seemed..."

We spoke simultaneously, him looking at the ceiling whilst I looked at the floor. The coincidence made our eyes meet, and we smiled properly at each other for the first time. "You first," I said.

"Alys." Leo pulled the roses from my embrace and dropped them on the table, stepping in to replace them. "I was worried. I thought it was me—something I'd done. You were—you *are*—the first woman I've cared about, the first woman I've slept with since Sabine. That night was amazing. Totally, totally unlike anything that's ever happened to me before. Then you got up and went away." He sounded so broken, so forlorn that I automatically closed my arms around him and he melted against me, seemingly with relief. "Oh, Alys," he spoke into my hair. "If you knew how I felt that morning."

I thought about it for a moment, but my own feelings of

inadequacy came pouring in. I stiffened and he pulled away from me.

"Is that it?" he asked quietly. The green of his eyes was deep. I found I couldn't break his stare, couldn't look away. "I'm not very experienced. There were only ever a few girls before Sabine. But I thought—you seemed to enjoy it."

"No. Oh, Leo, it's not you, it's me."

A rueful look dawned behind those beautiful eyes. "Ah. I see. Yes, well, er, in that case I—"

"No, it's not just a cliché, I really mean it. It *is* me." How did I explain it, the feeling that I was unworthy of love? "I've got issues," I finished, limply.

There was a moment's silence so deep that I could hear the rumble of lorries passing along the inner ring road. Leo spoke, hesitantly, as though he was afraid his words might panic me. "Look, Alys. Neither of us is a teenager. We've both had—relationships that have gone wrong. But I'm sure, if we take things slowly. I mean, we like each other, don't we?" His lips were close to my ear, when I turned my head our noses collided but then our mouths met and we indulged in a slow kiss. I tried not to think about how I must taste.

"I've done nothing but think about you since you left," Leo whispered, breaking contact. "I wrote sheaves of poetry last night, didn't know what else to do. Couldn't concentrate, wanted to get my thoughts down, get my head around what was happening."

"Poetry? About me?"

"Of course, you." Leo caressed my cheek. His eyes were raking my face more thoroughly than if it had been a Zen garden. "Some of it came out the best I've ever written, and I'm sure that's because of the way I feel about you."

"Can I read it?" No one had ever written anything about me before, if you don't count that time at school. And that was only in the boys' toilets. *And* a complete lie.

"Ummmm. Don't be offended, Alys, but I don't let anybody read my poetry. It's not written to be read, if that doesn't sound too mad."

I looked down at our hands, fingers entwined, liking the way his tanned, capable hand made mine look ethereally pale and my fingers long and elegant. "So, why do you write it?"

Leo gave a sigh. "It's my form of expression. I use poetry to kind of capture emotions, moments. Do you see?"

"But not for anyone else's consumption?" Right at that second I would have *killed* for him to put into words one tenth of the emotion I'd read he was capable of. Just so that I could know how it felt.

"They wouldn't mean anything to anyone else." He smiled at me, his face relaxed now. "I like your flat. It's very colourful. Very exciting." His gaze flickered over my rescued-from-a-skip sofa with its homemade cushions and the boot-sale rug. I hastily stood over the most conspicuous of the stains, which made me look like I was playing an advanced game of Twister.

"Are you hungry? I could cook."

"Oh. Umm." To my horror Leo looked at his watch. "Sorry, Alys, but I really have to go."

"Oh." I heard myself sound disappointed. "That's a quick turnaround."

"I know. But I came on the spur of the moment—had to deliver the two youngsters to Builth Wells, and when I'd driven that far I thought, well, it was only another few hours to get here. But I have to pick the trailer up on the way back. I'd better get going so I'm there before nine. It's hell coupling-up in a yard in the back of Welsh beyond, in the dark."

I gave a rather tight smile. He was just so bloody *practical*. But, like he'd said, neither of us were teenagers any more. There was a large matter of Life to be getting on with. And he

161

had brought me roses. Thinking of him sitting, writing, pouring it all out in poetry gave me a little frisson, a sexy kick.

A couple more entwined kisses and he was gone, leaving the flat feeling twice as empty but smelling twice as fragrant. I was putting the roses in the sink with some water, when the phone rang.

"Alys?"

Good Lord. Alasdair. This must be the first time he'd rung me directly since Florence became old enough to arrange her own visits. I was still wrestling with my guilt-hangover and therefore trepidatious about what he might have to say. "Hello, yes."

"Tamar said she'd seen you this morning. Said you'd been mugged?"

I hoped this wasn't going to be one of those spontaneous little lies which come back to bite you on the bum. "Well, sort of, but it was nothing really."

"And you'd rung Piers? Spent the night in his flat?"

I was instantly defensive. In my mind's eye I could see Alasdair now, probably sitting in his study. He'd be wearing loose jeans and an M&S jumper. His greying auburn hair would be tidily trimmed. He would be, as ever, looking like Tamar's ideal partner—Upper Class Ken. And now, in his usual persona as the only person with any sense around here, he was going to give me some good old Scottish Methodist moralisation.

"So? I can see who I want to, you know, not that I am. Seeing Piers that is. He happens to be—look, why am I justifying myself to you? He's an adult, I'm an adult, if we wanted to—which we don't, obviously, but if we did, then it wouldn't be anyone's business but ours."

"I have no idea what you're babbling on about." Alasdair's calm, measured tones seemed designed specifically to enrage me. "I was only ringing up to make sure that you hadn't been burgled."

"Burgled?" I'd been so full of ethical righteousness that this sudden change of direction left me morally winded. "Why on earth should I have been *burgled*?"

"I know what you're like for leaving keys and things in your bag. I was concerned that, if you spent the night at Piers's, anyone could have got into your flat."

As usual, whenever I talked to Alasdair I started off feeling that I held the moral high ground, and by the end of our conversation, I was left with the sensation I was wallowing around several fathoms under moral sea level. In some ways it would have been better to admit I'd been totalled rather than pretend to have been mugged.

"Well, I haven't."

"Are you *sure*? You can be a bit woolly minded sometimes, Alys. You might just not have noticed."

"Not have *noticed*? What, that someone had broken in and stolen things? Now, let me see. Oh yes, the Van Gogh is still here, and the Ming. No, I'm pretty sure I've not been burgled, Alasdair."

"There's no need for sarcasm, you know. I was ringing up to say that if you *had* been robbed, my insurance might cover some of Florence's things. That was all. I might have known you'd take it the wrong way. Do you always have to be so *spiky* these days?"

"Sorry." I had my fingers crossed when I said it though.

There was a short pause. I wondered if Alasdair was trying to get round to saying something about Florence. Something dating back seventeen years. So I leaped into the silence. "Piers was telling me that he's bringing his girlfriend home on Wednesday to meet you both."

"Girlfriend? What, Dominique? I thought he'd stopped seeing her."

163

"Girl called Sarah." I took positive pleasure in knowing something Alasdair didn't. "From Manchester, apparently. Very pretty girl." This was pure assumption, but it was a fair bet.

"Oh. Tamar hasn't mentioned—neither has he, come to that. Well, I'll look forward to meeting her then. Now, if there's nothing else?"

How come he made me feel as though *I'd* been the one making the call? I hung up, mildly pleased that I'd managed to score back a few I-know-something-you-don't-know points in the Divorced Parents' Sunday League tables.

Chapter Twenty-Three

When I met Florrie from the London train she seemed to have grown a couple of inches and she smelled different. Exotic. My familiar-as-my-own-face daughter was suddenly angular and foreign. "Good trip?" I eyed her outfit, not one item of which I'd ever seen before.

"Pretty good, yeah." This was new too, the cool offhandedness. "London is a wild place, there's so much to do. So, what did I miss? Piers got a new flat yet?"

"No, but he's got a new girlfriend, apparently."

Florence stopped walking. I thought for a moment she'd snapped the heel off her Red or Dead sandals. "*Piers?*" She couldn't have sounded more surprised if I'd said the Pope. "He told *me* he was sick to death of those brain-dead bimbos always hanging round him, he was giving himself six months celibacy to decide what he wanted. She must be really something?"

I didn't know Florence knew words like celibacy. London must have done her vocabulary good, if nothing else. "I don't know. No one's met her yet."

Florence wheeled on her spike heel, her gypsy dress flowing against her minimal curves with maximum effect. A platform sweeper nearly drove his cart into the newspaper stand. "Then I guess *I'll* have to find out all about it, won't I? Are we taxiing home, only I'm really shattered and these shoes are bloody killing me."

Given their pointed toes, pointed heels and very little superstructure in between, I wasn't at all surprised but refrained manfully from pointing this out. They certainly looked spectacular with the frilled layers of her dress which made her waist impossibly tiny and her B-cup bosom incredibly bountiful. The taxi drivers were falling over themselves to take us home. Luckily Florence didn't ask what I'd been up to whilst she'd been away, but began a commentary about how much better life was in London compared to York. How much there was to do, how fantastic the shops were. It even appeared that she'd visited a museum or two.

Back at the flat, Florrie reverted to her normal at-home persona, grabbing the phone and talking to her entire collection of friends. I slumped down on the sofa. Although I'd missed her, the flat seemed to shrink as soon as she came in, the sound of another voice in another room pulling the walls and ceiling towards me until the place became uncomfortably oppressive.

I cupped my hands over my eyes and pressed, trying to relieve the tiredness. My eyes felt like a couple of ripe boils wrapped in sandpaper. Jace hadn't been in the shop so I'd suffered a day of Simon's vigorous attention to detail without the usual relief of being able to snigger about him behind his back. Oddly though, when I'd asked Simon if I should phone Jace to find out how she was and whether she'd be in tomorrow, he'd come over all awkward.

"I should leave her for today," he'd said, eventually. "She'll be in tomorrow, I'm sure." Which made me wonder. Did he know what was up with Jace? Or did he not know, but care even less, in which case, was her job safe? She'd certainly been taking quite a lot of time off lately, usually with some fairly feeble excuses. If she wasn't in tomorrow, I was ringing her for sure and warning her.

A high-pitched shriek from Florrie made me jerk to my feet and hurtle through her door. "What is it?"

She'd seen the letter from the vet, stuck to the side of the fridge. It detailed treatment so far, and the cost. I was keeping it so I could track how much I owed Piers. All the sophisticated trappings of Florrie's London fortnight fell away, and she was just a scared child crying in my arms, as I explained my predicament over the world's scabbiest cat. "Don't have Grainger put to sleep, Mum. Don't."

"We can't let him suffer, Florrie." I stroked her back. Under the filmy dress I could feel the bones of her spine, vulnerable. My daughter fragile for all her worldliness. She looked up at me, her highlighted hair stuck to her cheeks, her eyes washed free of the make-up and cosmopolitanism. She was seven years old again, wanting me to make everything all right.

"But he's always been a healthy cat, he can get over it. The vet must think there's a chance or they'd have put him to sleep. Straight off, no messing."

I didn't tell her that this had been the vet's first suggestion. "I'll ring the vet's tomorrow, early. See when they'll let us bring him home." I thought this was unlikely to be any time soon, but my need to appear confident and in charge stopped me from breaking down alongside her. It's lesson one in the Mother's Handbook. Never let them see how panicked you really are.

Florence sat up and wiped her eyes with her hand. "I couldn't imagine life without Grainger, could you? Remember that time he brought that rabbit in alive and left it in the living room, and you had to catch it under the rubbish bin?"

I smiled back at her, but the thought of a catless house made me remember the tabby body curled in Piers's arms, which had triggered the guilt again. Now, with Florrie here, that house in York seemed an interplanetary distance away. That night in the summerhouse with Piers. A space seen through alcohol, filtered through a dream.

We sat companionably for a while longer, chatting about nothing very much. It was wonderful, amazing, my daughter

167

seemed to have matured into the kind of person I'd actually *want* to spend time with. I was congratulating myself on the terrific job of motherhood which I'd clearly done, when her mobile rang, and she turned instantly back into the sulky child she'd been before.

"Yeah?" she demanded, snatching up the handset. "What?" I rolled my eyes and got off the bed. "Yeah." Florence looked at me over the phone, her tone a little softer now. "It was great. Hey, what's this new girlfriend like? Mum told me you'd—"

There was a moment's pause, and Florrie lifted the phone away from her ear, stared at it, then pressed a button.

"What happened?" I asked.

"Dunno. Bad signal maybe?"

"Piers?"

"Yeah. I'll call him later." She shook her head briefly. "Now, Mother dear." I paused in my attempts to leave the room. "What about this *man* you've been hinting about the last couple of weeks?"

"Man?"

"Tell you what, I'll make us some tea and you can tell me *all* about him." That was it. Proof positive that my real daughter had been stolen away by the pixies and replaced by a Stepford teenager. She went out of the bedroom, but popped her head back around the door a second later. "Only not the sex stuff. Cos that would just be *gross.*"

Probably still the real Florence then.

I updated her on the Leo situation as best I could over tea. I wanted to give her as true a picture of the man as possible whilst all the time aware this could be a person she might be forced into proximity with in the near future. Didn't mention the poetry. I had the feeling that it would make him sound too nerdy. I needn't really have worried. As soon as I mentioned the ponies, she was all for moving down to Devon on the next train south.

"Look, Florrie, Leo and I haven't even *discussed* moving in. I think he likes his own space. After all, we hardly know each other yet."

"But you would if he asked you, wouldn't you?"

"I don't know. I don't even really know how I feel about him. He's a bit shy. Quiet."

"Yeah, but, Mum, you have to realise, your chances are going to get less as you get older. I mean, you've still mostly got your looks, and your body's *okay*, I guess. Maybe you should go for it while you still can."

A little blunter than I'd been with myself, but echoing quite a lot of my own feelings.

"And if he's got cash, you can always have plastic surgery," Florence continued, practical to the end. "Right. I'm going to call Piers," and she skipped off, leaving me with the washing up and no doubt that this was *definitely* my real daughter back.

I was settling down on the sofa with Iain Banks and half a bar of fruit-and-nut, when Florence came wandering back through, phone pressed tight against her ear. She began to make herself a sandwich. "Yeah, I guess," she was saying, "but he was so cool I couldn't turn him down."

I tried really hard not to listen and she was clearly trying to change the subject.

"Why won't you tell me about *her*? What've you got to hide? She's not a big ug, is she?"

My head whipped round. "You're not still talking to Piers, are you?"

Florence flicked a dismissive finger at me and carried on buttering bread. "Yeah, just the Old One giving me grief, you know how they get. Look, you want to come over? You can bring whatever-her-name-is if you like, we can go get pizza..."

"Florrie! It'll be costing a fortune."

Wearily Florence lowered the phone from her ear. "That's why I asked him over," she said, as though I was an idiot child, then back into the phone, "Yeah, I'm going over to Dad's tomorrow, probably see you then. Okay. Cheers."

"He didn't want to come?" I felt a bit downcast about that. I'd been wanting to apologise to Piers for our falling out.

"Nah." Florence looked slightly puzzled. "Dunno why. He got a bit weird when I asked him—you haven't said something to him, have you?"

"Like what?" My eyes wouldn't focus. Oh God, was Piers avoiding me? Was it something to do with Sunday night? No, surely I'd offended him in the taxi, that was all. But what if it *wasn't* all? What if he'd let something slip, and now he couldn't face me because he knew—shit. Paranoia.

"It's just that usually he's dead keen to come over here, always on about how cool you are, how much he likes hanging out with us."

"Maybe he's out with his new girlfriend and they want to be—you know. Alone together."

"Well she'll be pretty pissed already. He's spent three-quarters of an hour talking to me."

I felt itchy, edgy. *Was* Piers avoiding me? Seemed a rather extreme reaction, considering. I had to know. "Have you finished with the phone, Florrie? I've got a couple of calls to make."

"I wanted to phone Jude."

"Use your mobile." Behind the safety of my bedroom door, I flopped onto the bed and dialled Piers's mobile.

"Hey, Flo." Piers sounded bright, not conscience-stricken at all. Neither did he seem reluctant to talk, or as though he'd been dragged from the arms of his beloved to answer. "What's up?"

"It's me," I said, in low tones. "Alys."

"Hey, Alys, then." A little of the brightness died, a guarded edge creeping in. "Did you want something?"

"Just wondered why you didn't want to come over tonight." I tried to keep the worry out of my voice, but even I could tell there was a tremble in it. "You can bring Sarah. Obviously we quite understand if you'd rather have a quiet night with her, but Florrie would *so* like to see you—"

"I'll see her tomorrow at Ma's."

"Is everything all right?" A telling pause. "Piers? Have I done something to—"

"No." I heard him sigh. "Look, it's okay. I'm not going to say anything to anyone about the other night, you can trust me on that one."

"Then?"

He sighed again. "I just thought—a bit of space, you know? I mean, I've got things. You know, like, *things.*"

"Yes. Yes, you're right, of course." I listened to the background at his end for a moment. It was almost silent, no sounds of anyone drinking or talking. If he was with Sarah, she must have no bodily functions at all. "So, you'll see her tomorrow."

"Yeah. Guess so."

"All right. Well, thanks, Piers."

A bit more of a pause. "You take care of yourself, okay?"

I smiled down the phone. "Yes. I will. See you soon, Piers."

"Sure." He hung up. I still wasn't certain whether he'd been with anyone or not.

The next morning Florence repacked most of her London clothes and set off to visit her father. We said our goodbyes at the bus stop, then she headed west, making me promise to update her on the Grainger situation, as soon as I got in touch with the vet. I journeyed into town, arriving at Webbe's exactly the same time as Jacinta. This morning she was dressed like a wallpaper sample book, in huge clashing floral patterns. She was touchingly pleased to see me.

"Alys! You are being here! This is most early time for you. Have you come from more partying with Piers? I am telling you, Alys, Piers is *big* hot. Verrrry sexy boy."

"Yes, you *do* keep telling me that, don't you? But I notice you turned down the party invite. You should have come, Jace. All those very young men—it was a bit like a sixth-form nightclub. Anyway, Piers and I had a bit of a disagreement so I think we might not be seeing so much of him for a bit."

Jace just snorted and hustled off behind the curtain to put the kettle on.

"Good morning, Alys. Is Jacinta here yet?" Somehow Simon had managed to get into the shop unheard by either Jace or me. Presumably he'd come in the back way whilst we'd been talking on the step. Either that or he had his spartan bedroll laid out in Biography and never actually went home.

"She's making tea." I followed Simon as he went round, which meant both of us caught Jace in the guilty act of shoving a chocolate HobNob between her deep red lips.

"Simon," she mumbled around the crumbs. "You are early also."

"So I am," he said dryly. "Look, Jacinta, I need to have a word with you." He turned to me, standing in the doorway. "In private, Alys, if you don't mind."

I felt myself blush as though I'd already been eavesdropping. "Oh. Right." I began to shuffle my way over to the counter as slowly as was compatible with retreating behaviour. I fired up the till and wondered was Simon really going to sack Jace?

A customer came in, and I stopped pacing back and forth beyond the curtain, trying to overhear. There hadn't been any tears so far, nor shouting, and they'd been in there nearly fifteen minutes. How long does it take to sack someone anyway? A couple of minutes should do it, surely? I sold a book absent-mindedly, still straining my ears for the sound of sobbing. On either part since, if riled, Jace could have done Simon some serious damage.

Then the telephone rang and took my mind off things. I hoped it wasn't for Simon, since I didn't fancy putting my head round the curtain after the no-nonsense way he'd already told me to butt out, but it wasn't. It was Leo, for me.

"Good morning, Alys." He sounded bright and breezy. "How are you today?"

"I'm fine, I think. How about you?" I was still uncertain about the whole me-and-him thing, but I was having little waves of good feeling towards him, and that was a start.

"Yes, I'm fine too. Look, I'm ringing"—he dropped his voice and I wondered who was listening—"to ask if it would be possible for me to come and see you tomorrow. At your flat? I can be there by, oh, sevenish, I should think. Would that be all right?"

Oh God, was he going to give me the final talk? "I'm sorry but this just isn't working." Followed by an excuse picked from the Man's Get-Out Clause list? Just as I was beginning to get my head around the idea of a relationship? My heart pounded as I switched from being offhand to concerned. "I think that would be very nice," I said inadequately. "Will Jay not mind being left in charge?"

There was a short pause and I hoped he wasn't going to ask if he could bring her too. "Jay—" He broke off and restarted. "Jay is having a few days off. She's considering taking up another position."

It might not be the Dear Alys talk after all. Leo sounded too happy. Unless he considered he'd be well rid of me and couldn't wait to move on to someone who knew a fetlock from a crupper.

Leo was hesitant again and my heart took a dive. "I've written a poem I think I'd like you to read."

Behind the curtain to my left there was a sudden movement. Something poked the fabric until it bulged, then swiftly subsided like a cheap erection. Half my mind was on this, while the rest crept around the implications of what Leo had said. "You want me to *read* something you've written?" I sidled around trying to catch a glimpse of what was going on, but the curtain was tightly pulled across the cubby hole. Not so much as a sock was visible.

"Er, yes. I think so. Well, don't be disappointed if I change my mind, will you? I mean, I'll still come to see you, the poem isn't—I mean—it's not just—" Mr. Diffident had clearly taken control of Leo's body again. "About sevenish," and he was gone, leaving the phone to feel the heat of his embarrassment.

"Gosh." I stared down at the replaced handset, my mind ringing like a bell.

"You are looking serious." Jace popped up at my elbow like an economy-sized Jack-in-the-Box. "Is it that you are having some news?"

I stared at her. She was smiling, her mascara was unimpeachable, her lipstick unsmudged, evidently neither sacked nor rogered. "Leo's coming visiting tomorrow night." I followed this bald statement with a quick update on the events of his previous visit.

"Ah." Jace sat on the stool next to me. "So."

"So? What did Simon want with you?"

"It is nothing. Just wishing to talk about my privates, you understand? Personal."

I felt momentarily hurt that Jace expected me to give her

the down-and-dirty on my life while she kept her own locked away, but then I thought of all the things about me which I'd never told her, and forgave her. "Leo's such a nice guy, Jace."

"And you are not knowing what to do with nice, are you, Alys? The men you are having, you are always choosing because they are not wishing to have relationships with you. They are wishing only for quick sexing."

"No," I said indignantly. "It's just that that's how it's always turned out."

Jace looked at me sternly. "Alys. I am seeing for myself. You are not wanting men to be close to you, so you are picking men who are not wanting to be close with anybody. Then you are saying 'Boo hoo, he is not staying with me.'"

"I couldn't really have any kind of full-time relationship though, Jace. It wouldn't be fair on Florrie."

"But, Alys, this is always being your excuse. You are not seeing properly. Florence, she is a woman now, soon she will be going away into this big world and you are needing someone to show you that you can be a sexy woman again. Is like you are *afraid* to be loving a man."

I sighed. "But is Leo that man? Is he the big *IT*?"

Jace inclined her head towards me. "Only you can know these things. I hope that you will let me be meeting with him tomorrow."

"Oh yes. Look, come over about eight. I'll get Florrie to come over too. Maybe Mrs. Treadgold would like to pop in as well. It might be time to break it to the group that I'm not really dating Piers. I've got a book to drop off for her. I'll ask her while I'm there."

"Hmm. I will come." Jace stood up and the heels of her shoes squeaked as they took the strain. "You are needing my vision of this man." She sauntered off into Science Fiction with Neil Gaiman under one arm, leaving me to wonder what she

175

was going to make of Leo and what he would think of her.

Chapter Twenty-Four

Mrs. Treadgold had been baking and her wig was coated in flour. It made her look a little like a Christmas-tree ornament. "Hello, dear. Would you like some cake?"

"No thanks. I've just dropped by to let you have the new Mills and Boon book you were wanting. Oh, and to ask if you'd like to come over to my flat tomorrow night."

Mrs. T shuffled backwards over her doorstep to allow me into her tiny house. It always reminded me of an illustration in a children's book, a four-square building with a wiggly path up to the front door. "Is it a special occasion, dear? Or just a get-together?"

"I'm having a visitor." I eased my way along the narrow hall into the brightly lit kitchen. "I'd like everyone to meet him. Oh." Under the fluorescent tube which illuminated her surprisingly modern kitchen, Mrs. Treadgold looked pale. Even her bright blue eyes had a faded look to them. "Are you all right?"

She turned to the scrubbed table in the middle of the kitchen and began parcelling up slices of cake into greaseproof packets. "Old age, my dear. Comes to us all. Is this visitor something to do with your young man?"

"I—" I sat down on one of the pine chairs. "I think I really want some advice."

A cup of tea materialised, poured from the stoneware pot

which hid under the cat-shaped tea cosy. A slice of cake joined it.

"What sort of advice?" Mrs. Treadgold sat next to me, on the chair with the embroidered cushion. That had cats on too. She was a woman in the grip of a serious feline obsession. "And is it advice you really want, my dear, or someone to agree with something you've already decided? I mean, I can give you all the advice in the world, but if you don't want to do something, you're not going to, are you?"

I slumped even deeper into the chair and thought of Jacinta's opinion. That I was too afraid to take a chance and deliberately chose men who just weren't that into me to prevent myself from ever having to work at a relationship.

"If you fall in love with someone," I said slowly, "do you think it happens all at once? Or can you, for example, quite like someone for a long time, then find that it's turned into something else? Or do you just look at someone for the first time and go—yep, he's the one?"

"Eat your cake, dear. Philosophy always goes down better with a cup of PG Tips and a slice of banana loaf."

Obediently I ate. "So I suppose what I'm really asking is, do you believe in love at first sight?"

Mrs. Treadgold sighed. "When I met Mr. Treadgold, I didn't fall in love with him. Not at first. He was wearing a slaughterman's apron and the most ridiculous hat I ever saw. But. The first time I looked into his eyes, I knew."

"Knew? What, that you were in love?"

The teapot clanged against the side of her cup, as though her hands were shaking. "I can't say that it was love, not exactly. But it was something. I just felt—different. As though he knew me from the inside out. Oh, I can't explain, not really, but to answer your question, no. I don't believe in love at first sight. And anyone who does, in my opinion, is getting love and lust mixed up. I believe that when you're with your true love, you don't feel you have to hide any more. Does that make sense?"

"Yes." It was true. I didn't have to hide with Leo. He let me be who I was, without question. My heart gave a little skip. We *could* make it work, Leo and I. Maybe this confusion I felt about him was the first part of falling in love? Perhaps I should stop worrying and just go for it, let myself fall.

At precisely seven the next evening, I was showered, dressed in a form-fitting sweater and embroidered trousers. The flat was tidy and had been hoovered so thoroughly that most of the remaining thread had left the carpet. I'd put the roses in vases, borrowed from Mr. Roberts-next-door, around the living room. With the few tea-light candles I possessed lit under tinted glass shades, the place looked inviting and slightly romantic.

At seven thirty-seven, there was a knock. I left a long enough pause to indicate I wasn't standing right inside the doorway, but was instead pursuing any one of my varied, fascinating hobbies, then hurried to answer the door. Leo stood on the step wearing a sexy grey top and faded denim jeans, and with his hair rumpled attractively as though he'd just got out of bed. My heart did a little double-thump at the sight of him and I smiled into his green eyes. This was it. Did I feel different? I felt—yes, something. Was this love? It was warm and enveloping, and sent a little row of tingles down my spine, a burning press through my body. I knew I wanted him.

"I'm so glad to see you," I said.

"Oh, Alys." Leo stepped forward, and for a moment I thought he was going to hug me. I moved towards him, anticipating the hug, but his arms didn't move from his sides and I ended up standing almost under his chin. "It—you—I'm glad to see you."

I led him in to the living room as he chatted slightly shakily about how badly the journey had gone, then rolled his eyes like

179

a nervous pony at the table of food I'd set out.

"Florrie's coming over from her Dad's later," I explained. "I thought this would be a good chance for you to meet her."

"I'd love to meet your daughter."

"Oh, and my best friend, Jace, might drop by."

"That's nice," he said hesitantly.

"And Mrs. Treadgold from my book group. She might pop in too."

"Um. There's not anyone *else*, is there?"

"Anyone else?" Immediately I thought that he was calling my fidelity into question. Why did that image of Piers in the summerhouse keep floating through my head?

"Coming over. Tonight." Leo shifted from foot to foot. "I mean, you're not having a party or anything? I know it was short notice and everything, so I wouldn't expect you to cancel your arrangements but—"

"Oh! Oh no, they're coming over to meet you."

"That's nice," Leo repeated. "Look, Alys. I wanted to—"

He was interrupted by the sound of a key in the lock and Florrie calling, "Mum!"

"In here," I called back. Florence's head appeared cautiously around the door.

"Are you...oh good, you're not," she said ambiguously. "Hello. You're Leo. I'm Florence." More of her arrived in the room, and there was quite a lot of her on display in a little cropped top and low-waisted Capri pants. I wondered quickly whether she'd dressed like that deliberately to flirt with my boyfriend, then dismissed that as overly paranoid. Florence thought everyone over thirty was completely past sex and was staggering rapidly towards the grave.

"And I'm Piers." Piers walked in behind her and stood with one arm draped across her nearly bare shoulders. "Sorry to invite myself over, Alys, but Flo wanted to cadge a lift back later. Alasdair's taking her and Ma to Harrogate tomorrow."

I waved an airy doesn't-matter hand whilst staring at him. His Sarah must have had a word with him about his terrible taste in clothes because today he looked all-out gorgeous.

"I got your text, Mum. About Grainger." Florence shrugged herself away from Piers. "Are they sure he's okay?"

"Doing as well as can be expected. They haven't said when we can fetch him home. And they've said not to visit in case he gets upset. Or, more upset than he already is. Apparently he tried to eat someone yesterday."

"That means he's getting better. Doesn't it?"

I fixed a reassuring smile. "Yes." I couldn't look at Piers. He had, according to the vet, already paid two hundred pounds for the consultation, drugs and accommodation fees. I squirmed at the thought of how much overtime I was going to have to work for Simon to pay it back. I'd probably be shelving until I was seventy.

"And are you Florence's boyfriend?" Leo shook Piers's extended hand, clearly baffled by this unexpected person.

"I'm her stepbrother," Piers said rather unhelpfully.

"My ex's wife's son," I filled in quickly as Leo glanced at me. "He's driven Florrie over from Thirsk for the evening." I allowed my gaze to meet Piers's and was disconcerted when he gave me a tiny wink. "I, er, I—look, everyone grab something to eat and ummm...mingle."

The three of them, bless them, did their best to mingle while I went into the kitchen and took some deep breaths. When I came out armed with two bottles of wine, Florence was talking to Leo about ponies. Piers had vanished.

"You didn't tell me Leo owned the Charlton Stud." Florrie turned accusing eyes on me. "Dylan was by Charlton Thistle. His mother was a thoroughbred mare." She lapsed back into

181

horse talk, Leo hanging on her every word, interjecting now and again with even more jargon about straight pasterns and cow hocks. I was glad they were hitting it off so well and ate a sandwich to celebrate.

"The door is open." Jacinta sashayed her way into the living room. "I am hoping you have food, Alys, I am most hungry." Her eyes fell on Leo. "You must be man."

I introduced Jacinta to Leo, who shook her hand and winced. Jace had obviously given him her no-nonsense handshake, which could have brought tears to a docker. She fixed him with eyes carrying enough makeup to have rendered a corpse presentable in society.

"You are able to be leaving your tiny horses tonight?" she asked, as though she suspected he might have one or two tucked into pockets or shoved under the sofa.

"Er. Yes."

Florrie and Jacinta began a discussion about their relative outfits and the purchasing thereof. Florrie's entire outfit would have just about made a nice belt for Jace, and the latter was wearing a purple silk number which made a noise like a cellophane-rolling plant whenever she moved. Leo carefully removed himself and came to stand beside me at the food table.

"Your daughter seems like a nice girl."

"She is. Mostly. And Jace is all right, once you get the hang of her." We looked at the pair of them chatting and comparing labels, Florrie so slim, Jace so large and sturdy, they looked like punctuation on legs. "I'm glad you're here, Leo."

I reached out and squeezed his hand. "So am I, Alys," he whispered back. "But they are, you know, going to go away, aren't they? So that we can talk?"

"Oh, yes. Wait until the food's gone and you won't see them for dust." I ate another eclair to help things along. "What prompted this visit anyway?"

"Do I need prompting?" Leo picked at some nuts, watching Florrie and Jace still chatting. "I found that I could get away for a couple of days and—well—I felt that we had some talking to do. Things to discuss. About us." He looked around. "Where's the young chap gone?"

"I don't know. I ought to find him. Knowing Piers he's probably holed up in Florrie's room smoking spliffs." It was meant to be a joke, but from the way Leo rolled his eyes at me he'd clearly already marked Piers down as a crack dealer. I left him in charge of the nuts and went in search.

"What are you doing in here?" I found Piers in Florrie's bedroom, stretched out at full length on the bed with his mobile pressed to his ear.

"Sssssssshh." Piers waved a finger at me. "No, not you. Carry on," he said into the phone.

"Oh, right. Just checking where you'd got to." I pulled back and went to close the door, but he jumped up, waving an impatient hand at me to stay. Beckoned me over.

"Could you just say that again, please?" He gathered me up against him with the arm not supporting the phone, holding the tiny clamshell between us so that I could hear. "Just that last bit."

The tinny voice at the other end of the mobile gave a sigh. "Your cat. Making a remarkable recovery. Quite astonishing."

I gave a little squeak and Piers squeezed me closer, grinning. "Yeah, well thanks for letting us know. I'll be in touch later about when we can fetch him home, yeah?" He flipped the phone shut with a casual twist of his wrist and slid it back into one of the almost invisible pockets in his suit. "Good news, eh, Alys? The vet had my card, so they called me. Hope you don't mind, Grainger being your cat and all. Apparently, after you phoned this morning, he tried to dig his way out of a solid metal cage. Now they reckon he's really on the mend."

"That's brilliant." I tried not to think about the bill again. "It's just so good. I mean, seeing him like he was, I didn't think he'd..." An alternative future rose up and I blinked back tears. "It's so good," I whispered through the thickening in my throat.

"Yeah. Tomorrow we could go see him if you want." Piers swivelled around so that he was facing me, still with an arm holding me in a half embrace. "I know they told you no visitors, but, hey, I'll use my charm. Maybe we could make an evening of it, yeah? Catch a movie, grab a meal—"

"I don't know. There's—well, Leo's here and..."

Piers let the arm fall. "Oh yeah. I forgot. This guy who's really into horses. You and he—is it, you know? Kinda serious?"

"I don't know *what* it is. But we get on, we've got a lot in common. Well, it's not like I'm beating them off with a stick, is it? Talking of which—" I took a tiny step back. "I'm sorry I upset you. In the taxi."

"Don't worry about it." Piers had an expression on his face that I couldn't read. "I shoulda been flattered, I guess."

"I didn't know about Sarah. I'd assumed, which was stupid. Just because I don't see you with a woman on your arm every five minutes, doesn't mean you don't have—girlfriends."

"Oh, yeah, Sarah." There was a deadness in his voice. "Well. You weren't to know."

"I told Alasdair that you were taking her down tomorrow. They're looking forward to meeting her. She must be quite some woman if she's managed to get you into something as stylish as that suit." I looked him up and down again. "You look fantastic."

"Fantastic, huh?" Piers sounded smugly pleased, then... "You told Alasdair *what*?"

"It's only what you said. Only passing on what you told me."

"Jeez, Alys. Sometimes you're *so* fucking..."

"Alys? Is that you?" Leo's voice made me jump. I pulled away from Piers and took another step back, so that I couldn't feel him against me any more. "What are you doing in here?"

"Long story." I was rubbing at my arms, as though my skin was chilly. "Let's go find some more wine." As I left the bedroom, Piers was standing in the middle of the floor twisting the rings on one hand. Staring down at the carpet with his features set, as though he was thinking hard and fast. Leo looked over his shoulder at him, and I noticed his expression change. "Is something wrong?"

Leo took my arm and guided me through into the kitchen, shutting the door behind us very quietly. "That man." His face had slumped down into lines of weary seriousness, and he took his glasses off to rub at his eyes. "You and he—"

"The vet had phoned him about my cat. He's at the vet's— that's the cat, not Piers, obviously. I thought he was going to die. But he's not. That's still the cat, you knew that, didn't you? He's up and about apparently." I wondered even as I said it why I felt that I had to justify what I'd been doing.

"Never been very fond of cats." Leo stared over my shoulder and then met my eyes. "Bit allergic. And there's something about the way they jump at you. I knew there was nothing to worry about, but I can't help myself, Alys. I'm sorry."

"What were you worried about?"

"You and that man. You looked— Oh, it's me, wrong end of the stick, misunderstandings, all that."

"For goodness sake, Leo. He—there's absolutely nothing going on between me and Piers! I've known him since he was seventeen," I added, as though this made a difference, impatience boiling from every pore that Leo could even *think*, even remotely *suspect* that I would do anything behind his back. And with *Piers*?

"Yes." Leo was still rubbing his eyes and now he'd extended the motion to take in his cheeks. I watched his whole face rising and falling like Eeyore on happy pills. "Baggage, Alys."

"Baggage? I don't understand."

"From Sabine. I lost count of the number of times I watched her flirting with other men, whether it was to get their attention or to make me jealous, I never knew. It was almost as though she couldn't stop herself. Like an addiction, a drug, do you know what I mean?"

"Oh, Leo." I looked him square in the face. "Honest, cross my heart and hope to die, I was *not* flirting with Piers." Looking into Leo's beautiful green eyes as deeply as I could, I whispered, "I wouldn't do that."

Unfortunately, coming to sabotage my openness was the memory of Piers's arm circling my waist. The feel of his body tight against me. My awareness of him so close. But surely that wasn't flirting, was it? My eyes must have clouded, because Leo frowned. "What? What is it?"

"Nothing. Really, Leo, nothing." Thankfully, I heard the telephone ring in the living room. "Perhaps we'd better go through. They'll be wondering what we're doing in here. And it might be a call for me."

"One minute, please." Leo started scrabbling about in the pockets of his jeans. "I wanted to give you..." he withdrew a piece of paper, folded so many times it formed a small square, about the size of a matchbox, "...this to read. But, can I just ask. Will you let me leave the room before you open it? I'm a bit shy, I suppose, about these things."

He took my hand, opened my palm and dropped the paper into it, then went out of the kitchen, leaving me listening to the sounds of my own party going on. Was this the poem? The paper had been so tightly folded that it seemed to weigh heavily against my hand. It felt cold.

On the other side of the wall, the whole decibel content seemed to drop. Was I being oversensitive or were they all listening to me? Was Leo in there with them? I began to unfold the paper between my fingers. As I did so, something heavy dropped away from between the creases, making me jump. Was it a beetle? I didn't see it land, my attention was distracted by hearing Florrie, distinct through the wall and the silence on the other side of it, say, "I'll tell her, yes." I stroked the now-open sheet of paper smooth on the work surface and put myself into poetry-reading mode, letting my eyes run over the words arranged in sentence-like structures on the page.

Dear Alys

I know that we haven't known each other very long, and opportunities to be together have been few. However, I am totally and completely certain of my feelings in a way I never have been before, and since we share a depth of communication and understanding, I truly believe that we also share these feelings.

Since we last met I have thought long and hard over the best way to resolve our situation and find it impossible—I just want to be with you.

Please, darling Alys, would you marry me?

Love Leo

I stood totally still, as though I'd been shot and had yet to fall. I read the words over again, moving my lips as I searched for a rhyme scheme or structure. What—?

He'd *proposed?*

But...

But what? He's attractive, sensitive, gentle. You reckon you don't deserve this by now, Alys?

It's so sudden. *No, not sudden. More than that,* abrupt. *I*

187

hardly know him! We've spent only a handful of days together.

So? You'd barely known Alasdair's name when you decided you were going to marry him, had you? Stability, Alys. Stability for you, and *Florrie, and she seems to like him too. And remember the poetry...*

But I hate horses.

Look, love. You're thirty-six and, as Florrie so generously said, things won't stay pointing upwards forever. Maybe you should stop agonising and go for it. After all, at your age you shouldn't look gift horses in the mouth. Ha ha.

I shifted my weight and stood on something prickly. Without thinking I looked down and moved my foot to reveal a square cut sapphire, surrounded by tiny diamond chips set into a gold ring. Shit. Well, no way now I could assume it was a particularly unusual free-form poem. What should I *do*?

Half of me wanted to leap up and shout *yes!* But was that because it was *Leo* proposing, or because I'd actually got a proposal, and from a man who didn't think football was better than sex because it lasted ninety times as long? The other half of me—the tiny, slippery half—was floundering. Why? Why me? What had I done to make him want me? *What happened when he stopped?*

Without knowing what else to do, I walked back into the living room at the same time as Leo came in from the bathroom. We tried not to meet each other's eye. He looked poised, although whether it was for triumph or disappointment I couldn't tell. Jace, Florrie and Piers were just standing. Did they know? Had he told them? Were they also waiting for me to say something?

"I..." I began, but Florence interrupted.

"Mum." She sounded strained. "That was the hospital. It's Mrs. Treadgold."

"What's happened?" And then I had a clear vision of Mrs.

Treadgold's faded blue eyes in that china-pale skin. *She was ill. And I'd hardly noticed.* "Shouldn't they be calling her family? Oh God."

Mrs. Treadgold had a son and a daughter, I knew that. And quite a lot else besides, Mrs. Treadgold being something of a chatterer where her family were concerned. Thomas was a veterinary assistant in Abergavenny, had a very nice partner called Dave but that was all right as long as he was good to Tom. Vivienne was a flight attendant currently on long hauls to Dubai, no plans to marry but happily seeing a pilot who was suspected of being married himself but no proof yet. And Mrs. Treadgold didn't like what she'd done with her hair.

"Apparently she's asking for you."

"I'll go now." I felt a sudden pang of guilt, quickly stifled. I'd taken her advice, hadn't I? Leo loved me as I was, I felt different when I was with him. I felt *myself.* "I'd better ring the hospital. Make sure I'm allowed." I sat down and picked up the phone.

"Of course this is so." Jace began bustling around. "I will be going to my home. Piers, you is to be taking Florence away, and you." She flicked fingers at Leo. "Are you staying?"

"I don't know." Leo looked uncomfortable. "It's up to Alys really." I saw him glance down at my hands and wondered what he was doing, before it dawned on me that he was trying to see whether I'd put the ring on.

"Jace, don't go. I need to talk to you."

"You need to be doing other talking more."

"I'm not going until I know what's happening." Florence sat herself down firmly next to me on the sofa. "Mrs. Treadgold is a nice old thing. I hope she's not *too* poorly. She knitted me a rabbit once."

"Then it looks like you're stuck with me too." Piers sat in the armchair opposite, looking like James Bond's younger, more disreputable brother. I wondered idly why he'd worn that sexy suit and bow tie.

"Do you want me to stay, Alys?" Leo was hovering, having opened the front door for Jace. "I mean, I can go, if it makes things easier for you. I could phone you." He left the words *for your answer* unsaid, but I could feel the pressure building already.

"Yes, you might as well stay too." As I said it I realised that I'd been ungracious and tried healing my words with a smile in Leo's direction, but he'd already adopted a slightly wounded expression. "I'll call the hospital and take things from there."

The hospital refused to tell me anything since I wasn't a relative, only that Mrs. Treadgold had indeed been asking for me, but was now sedated and couldn't see anyone until tomorrow.

"You want me to drive you?" Piers asked after I put the phone down. I turned. There was something in his eyes which rolled my heart over. Maybe we looked at each other for too long because the next thing I knew Leo was inserting himself between us.

"*I* could take you." Leo rested an arm around my shoulders. He couldn't have spelled out *she's mine* more clearly if he'd taken out a full-page ad.

"Yeah, but we were going out anyway. To visit the cat and, like, maybe do stuff."

"I'll get myself to the hospital, thank you both." I stepped away from Leo, away from Piers. "It's hardly a cross-continental epic journey. Now, Piers, Florrie, you go."

Muttering about being left out, Florence picked up her trendy shoulder bag and shuffled to the front door, Piers trailing behind. At the door he flicked his eyes to Leo, who had his back to us, piling plates from the table on top of one another, and mouthed "I'll call".

I shook my head but he flashed me a smile, tossed, "Nice to

have met you!" into the flat over his shoulder and shepherded his stepsister, trailing shoelaces, down the stairs.

Energy fell out of me through the soles of my feet.

"I'm sorry, Leo. I don't think I'm going to be any kind of company tonight." I slumped against the wall. "I feel completely exhausted."

"I'm not surprised." He came and stood in front of me, taking both my hands. "Do you want to talk?" He turned my hands over and examined them closely. I think it was an excuse to avoid my eyes. "It wasn't a great way to spring a proposal on you, was it?"

Carefully, so as not to cause offence, I slid one of my hands from his grasp and used it to push my hair out of my eyes. "I am going to need time, Leo. I mean, I'm assuming that you'd want me to move down to Devon, that you weren't thinking of selling the stud and moving up here?" His horrified expression told me that this hadn't even crossed his mind. "So I'd have to leave my job. And Florrie, her father lives here. She'd not see nearly as much of him if we moved south."

Leo came towards me with new eagerness. "Yes, yes, I've thought about all these things. You could get a part-time job in the bookshop in Charlton. Isabelle knows the owners. I'm sure she'd put a word in for you. It'd give you plenty of time to learn all you need about the stud business. Florence could have her own flat in the house, a job down on the yard. And there are trains, Alys, if she wants to go and see her father or"—Leo seemed to swallow the words but they crept out anyway—"her stepbrother."

The walls inched towards me. He'd thought it all out. From where I'd work, to where Florence would sleep. I looked up at him, into his face. There was no guile there, just a keen and loving enthusiasm.

"I love you, Alys." Leo let go of my hands and turned away,

talking to the opposite edge of the carpet. "I love you and I would like us to be together."

"And I..." I *wanted* to say it, wanted to throw him the crumb of comfort he deserved but in the end what came out was, "...and I need time to think about things. Forgive me, Leo, if I seem to be messing you around but I really, *really* want to think carefully about this."

"But you're not saying no, are you?"

Say no? To a sexy man in possession of all his faculties, own teeth and hair, and a sizeable slice of Devonshire real estate? Who professed to love me, wrote heart-stoppingly beautiful poetry (although admittedly not to me) and who drove a car with a current tax disc? I'd have to be insane. "I'm thinking, all right?" I smiled. "A girl's allowed thinking time. It's traditional."

Leo returned the smile. It softened the contours of his whole face, and I realised how stressed he'd been. "Maybe I'd better go. You'll think clearer if I'm not here, and you've got enough to worry about, with your friend being ill and everything." A momentary pause. "You're not going to go out with—what's his name, Peter?—are you?"

"Piers. No! He's—Piers is a friend, that's all. He's been very good." Another tiny shiver at the memory of Piers standing so close. God, I needed to get a grip. "To Florence," I finished.

Chapter Twenty-Five

I lay in the darkness trying to sleep. It wasn't quite the romantic postproposal night of passion I had envisaged, but that hadn't been Leo's fault. He'd sweetly and uncomplainingly gone back to Devon, leaving me with my worries and uncertainties and a sapphire the size of a small dog.

In the living room, the telephone rang. Who'd ring at four a.m.? Maybe the hospital? Or—no, he wouldn't, would he?

"Hey, Alys."

"Why don't you just fuck *off?*"

A sharp intake of breath. "Oooh. Hissy fit!" But Piers sounded as though he was laughing. "So, when shall I pick you up?"

"Look, I told you, I'm going to the hospital on my own. On the bus. No picking up. No lifts."

"So, I'll come by about nine, then?"

"Read my lips. *No.*" There was a pause. "Piers?"

"Yeah?"

"I'm sorry. But everything's got very complicated. Leo thought you and I—and so he's a bit sensitive about me talking to you. Do you see?"

"How complicated?"

"He thought we were—oh it's stupid. I'm not even going to

bother to explain. Look, thanks for offering and everything, but I'm fine."

"Okay. If you say so."

My breath caught and a tiny soblike gasp escaped. "Yes. Yes, I'm fine."

"*Ally.*" The sympathy in Piers's voice was almost touchable. The receiver was suddenly slippery between my fingers.

"I'll—I can't do this right now. I'll talk to you later." I hung up very carefully and wiped my eyes and nose on my dressing gown. What the hell was *wrong* with me? Losing it over the phone to Piers? I mean—*Piers*—what the hell was I thinking? Was I thinking *at all?*

Next morning I set out for the hospital bright and early with my ring stuffed in a pocket. It looked too valuable to be left kicking around an empty flat, and I couldn't bring myself to put it on, so I'd wrapped it in my handkerchief and shoved it in the recesses of my jeans. Diamonds and sapphires. Leo thought I was *worth* diamonds and sapphires.

I walked down Monkbar and turned up Gillygate, against the flow of tourists. It was another bright morning, and despite my errand, I felt my heart rise. I *was* worth diamonds and sapphires. I nearly stopped to put the ring on, wanting everyone to see. Hey, everyone. Diamonds! Sapphires!

The throaty roar of a restrained sports engine began trickling along beside me. At a break in the queue, the car speeded up, then bumped up onto the pavement at an angle which blocked my path.

I recognised the car after a second of panic. Particularly when the driver sprang the passenger door open. "C'mon. I'll get a fucking ticket."

It was the inevitability which did for me. I *should* have kept walking, of course I should. Ignored him and marched off, leaving the Porsche skewed across the pavement, impotently kerb crawling. But somehow the fact that he'd second-guessed me was some kind of admission. I slid into the seat and closed the door, sitting bolt upright and not looking at him. "I'm doing this *under protest*. I thought I made it clear," I said between clenched teeth, "I was going *on my own*."

Piers was wearing glasses tinted so dark I hadn't a hope of reading his true expression. "This morning, on the phone. I *heard* you crying, Alys. You need someone to talk to."

"Where the *hell* do you get off, using these bully-boy tactics on me? You just can't—" To my shame my voice cracked. I was tired and my nerves were stretched so tight that you could have played the opening bars of "Layla" on them. I squeezed my eyes shut to prevent the betrayal of tears.

"Actually, I kinda think I *can*."

I squinted out between my eyelashes. Piers was staring out of his window, tapping his rings against the wheel, his hair scragged back from his unshaven face. It was like being abducted by a hitman from Models 1.

"At least you're not wearing any of your truly scary wardrobe," I muttered. "That would be too much to cope with."

"Be glad that you can't see my underwear."

"Oh, I am, Piers. Trust me, I am."

He smiled. I felt my heart give a catch in my chest and bit the inside of my cheek to stop it. Shit. I must be feeling more vulnerable than I thought, to start getting all knee-trembly over Piers. Although it had to be admitted that he did look alarmingly sexy. Oh God, please, make me stop this, now. It's *Piers*. He can't *help* being eye-poppingly gorgeous, can he? I'm just having an attack of unhealthy lust, that's all. But—Jesus Christ—

"So, Ally. Anything you want to tell me?"

"I think I've told you quite enough already."

"Yeah, and have I used it against you? Have I repeated even so much as *one fucking word* to anyone else? What is it going to take to make you trust me, Alys?"

I opened my mouth to ask him why it was so important that I trust him, but what actually came out was "Do you think I've wasted my life, Piers?"

"What brought that on? Did that...did Leo say something?" He powered down the Porsche, pulled it to a standstill at the side of the road. A couple of passing cars tooted but he flicked a finger at them without even looking. "Ally?"

I wiped my eyes with the back of my hand. "Sorry, Piers. Sorry. I didn't mean to. You wouldn't understand."

"Why? Cos I'm young? Maybe, but maybe things are clearer to me, not cluttered up with all that life crap. Maybe I see what's really *there* cos I'm not looking through some cloud of duty." He whipped the trendily dark glasses away from his face and glanced at me, sharp brown eyes seeming to steal some of my doubt. "Don't be scared."

I took a deep breath. Ready to be reasonable, to ask him to leave my private affairs to me.

"Look." But it was no good. It was as though the magnetism which undoubtedly surrounded Piers was pulling everything to the surface. "Leo's asked me to marry him. But he seems to think that I'm going to be this little woman, working a few hours a week in a bookshop and looking after the house and him and—"

"Holy fucking *shit*." Piers wrapped his long fingers around my hands clenched in my lap. His hands were trembling. "Tell me."

"I searched Alasdair out." My voice shook. "I knew he fancied me. I'd seen him watching. When Flick said he wanted nothing to do with me and the baby I—oh, I made it look like an accident, but I already knew who Alasdair was, his family, everything. I knew he'd be able to support us. The baby and me. I wasn't going to be able to finish my degree and my parents were dead and his father owns an island, you know that?" I sniffed. "Not a very nice one, admittedly. It's full of midgies and people shooting deer and stuff."

Piers moved one hand to my shoulder blades and rubbed my back gently. He smelled of coffee, of something lemony and rich, like scents in the night air. "Hey, Ally. It's okay." His voice sounded a bit shaky too. "You didn't go looking for Leo though, did you? Or did you?"

"No, but I knew who he was and pretended I didn't. It's all repeating itself."

"And he's asked you to marry him." Piers's voice dropped. "Are you going to?"

I gave a cracked laugh. "I have absolutely no idea. And how stupid is *that*? He's got everything I ever thought I wanted. All these years of struggling and not enough money and second-hand clothes and stuff and—*I don't know.*"

"Oh, Ally. You're so fucked up about this, aren't you?"

"Look, I'd better get to the hospital." I opened the car door. "Thanks for the lift and everything, but I—"

"Uh-uh, you're not running out on me now." Piers leaped out of the driver's seat and grabbed me as I tried to head off up the pavement. "You need someone. I'm here. Talk to me, Alys, for Chrissake."

"There's nothing more to say. I'm going to see Mrs. Treadgold now. You'd better move the car, you'll get a ticket."

"Fuck *that*. I'm coming with."

He swore a trail of Spanish as we entered the hospital along a corridor where the smell of bandages and the ghosts of long-dead cabbages filtered into my lungs. The buckles on the boots he wore jingled and the hems of his overlong combats trailed on the floor. He was still all legs and hair, but at least that weird

197

longing feeling had gone, and I could look at him properly again.

I found Mrs. Treadgold propped on pillows in the geriatric ward. She looked pale and old and pleased to see me. "Alys. You came! And brought your young man." She lowered her voice. "You saucepot."

I decided not even to attempt to explain. "They said you were asking for me?"

"Yes. Tom and Vivienne will be on their way. They've been expecting this for a while. I'm ill, Alys, I expect you knew that?" I gave a kind of half-nod. "And I've come to think of you as a surrogate daughter, I suppose."

A sudden outburst of coughing doubled her forward across the blankets and I looked on helplessly, ineffectually patting her blue-veined hands. Piers piled pillows behind the old woman's head and winked at her when she finally got her breath back. To my slightly appalled surprise, she winked back at him.

"I'll go get you a drink of water." He loped off with her empty drinking jug. No doubt he'd spotted a good-looking young nurse somewhere and wanted an excuse to chat.

"An American," Mrs. Treadgold croaked at last. "Ah—I had an American sweetheart after the war. He was a good-looking boy too. Had an enormous willy, as I recall."

"Mrs. Treadgold!"

"Not much point in being coy when you're dying, is there? It's all right. I've come to terms with the whole thing. Arrangements have been made and suchlike. Which brings me to why I asked for you." Mrs. Treadgold scrabbled about in the confines of the bed. "Before Vivienne gets here. I've got a present for you." A cold, bony hand pushed something into my palm. "It was mine from before Mr. Treadgold. Vivienne and Tom don't know about it, but I'd like you to have it. To remember me by. You and your young man. Please wear it when you agree to marry him. For me."

I opened my mouth to prevaricate. This had all gone far enough. I really couldn't accept something like this under false pretences, but Mrs. T went on. "That little chat we had the other day? Don't worry, Alys, it's obvious that you're in love."

The coughing came again. Harder and harder she choked until a couple of nurses came over and elbowed me aside, pushing the bed to who knew where, the fragile hand being snatched from mine.

I collapsed into a chair. Piers had returned, thrust his hands into his pockets and was staring at the floor, occasionally shaking his head, muttering to himself under his breath. Finally he looked up. "Mortality. What a *fuck*."

I opened my hand a crack, looked at the object Mrs. Treadgold had been so desperate for me to have and had to bite my lip to prevent a hysterical giggle escaping. She'd given me an engagement ring. Oh, not diamonds and sapphires. A much more understated little item in white gold with a ruby cut into a heart shape set in the centre. A giggle escaped over my tongue clamped between my teeth. The ring was beautiful.

"Let's get outta here."

I was hardly aware of the tears rolling down my chin until we got outside. The ring was clenched so tightly in my fist that the ruby was making little heart shapes on my palm, but I didn't kid myself it was just for Mrs. Treadgold that I was crying.

Piers didn't ask. Instead he stood, back braced against the Porsche, smoking what I hoped was an ordinary cigarette. Then he looked at me, said, "Oh, *Ally*," in a heartfelt way, and closed his arms around me.

I could really do with more friends like him.

Chapter Twenty-Six

Jace took another Jaffa cake. "So, you are telling me that you are having Mr. Small Horses Man asking you to be marrying with him?" She looked at me over the top of the spongy morsel which she ate in her usual fashion, by folding it in half and popping it into her mouth in one go. Her expression was absolutely deadpan. I couldn't get any kind of impression as to what she thought about this, other than that the emotion it generated was making her get through confectionary products as if there was about to be a prohibition order on Kit Kats. "You must be very exciting."

"Exc*ited*. Yes, I suppose I am. It's a lovely ring, you've got to admit. Leo's got taste." We looked at it jointly for a few moments and if the weight of our gazes had been physical, the ring would have been atomised in milliseconds.

"Forgive me, Alys." Jace grabbed me by the wrists suddenly and pulled me towards her until my face nearly rested on the shelf of her bosom. "But as your friend I must be speaking. This man is not the man for you, I am thinking."

I disengaged myself gently from her grasp. "What on earth makes you say that? He's good looking, he's got money, he's very *nice*." And Mrs. Treadgold had spotted that I was in love. Even if I didn't know it myself.

"Well, I would not be asking you to marry me in a letter." She sounded contemptuous. I hadn't known Jace was quite so opposed to Leo, but now she seemed quite vituperative. It was strange how this attitude of hers made me even more determined to see his side of things.

"Florrie likes him."

"Florence is liking Eminem. You are not wanting to be marrying *him*, are you?"

I reached for a biscuit and lackadaisically bit the chocolate off around the sides. "Oh, Jace. Why does it have to be like *this*? It should be all lovely and happy. We should be drinking champagne with you telling me how lucky I am to have a man who loves me and wants to give me a better life. Instead, here we are, ingesting a lifetime's worth of calories in one sitting. He's hardly going to want to marry me if I turn up with a bottom the size of a principality, is he?"

Jace snorted like a bullock and declaimed in Spanish, but when I asked for a translation, she just shook her head. "So, what else is news? I was hoping you would be coming to the shop yesterday, after you are visiting your sick person."

"I was feeling a bit shaken up."

After the hospital Piers had taken me to some bar he knew and bought me sneaky, vicious little cocktails all day and well into the night, which tasted like a potent treacle and weedkiller mix with umbrellas in. They all had improbable names like *Scrubbing the Puke off the Carpet on Sunday Morning*. I'd become incoherently drunk and probably cried a good deal too, but my memory of that was hazy. Piers had taken me to visit Grainger, I remembered that. I had the teeth marks to prove it. And Piers's arm around me reassuring me that I needn't feel guilty, that Grainger was fine where he was for another day or so.

Then he'd listened to my list of things I *did* need to feel guilty about, held my head while I was sick in the toilet and given me a huge hug when I tried to apologise. This morning I'd had an economy-pack headache and a horrible itchy feeling in the back of my mind when I tried to remember getting home.

"You were gone on a day with Piers, and you are having nothing new to be saying? I am finding myself hard to believe." Jace waggled a finger at me. "And Piers is lovely, lovely young man, veerrrry pretty. I am not blaming you if you are sweeping him backwards."

I loved Jace dearly, she was my best friend and everything, but sometimes she just plain got on my nerves. "No. No sweeping backwards." Our eyes swivelled back to the ring. I ate another biscuit and was sure I felt my hips expand. At this rate they were going to need planning permission.

"So. You are going to be saying yes to the man who is always being with his horses."

"Florence was mad keen. She'll love it in Devon. Horses on tap."

"But you will not be marrying to please Florence, will you? Is this what *you* want?"

I made some noncommittal remark and we left the subject, but that night I woke in a feverish sweat.

"Charlton Hawsell Stud, Leo Forrester speaking."

It was three a.m. and Leo was answering the phone like it was midday. "It's me."

"Alys? Good Lord." Then his voice softened. "Can't you sleep?"

"No. Sounds like you can't either." I tried to think how to say what I needed to say. *Before we get married there are things I need to tell you, things you should know about me.* "Leo, I need to talk to you."

"Yes, and I'd love to talk to you too, but, actually I've got a mare foaling."

"Not that kind of talking."

A sudden silence. "Ah. I see. You mean serious stuff." Another quiet space. "Well, look. We can't really do this now, can we? Is there any chance you could come down here? We could have some proper time together, get some proper talking done—how does that sound?"

There was a silence across which metaphorical tumbleweeds blew and timber wolves called. "Yes. I'd like to do that. I'll talk to Simon, see if I can get some time off."

There was a huge relief in his voice. "So, this isn't the Final Speech you want to give me? You haven't. Decided. Yet, that is."

"No. I was just ringing. Oh, I don't know why." The howling empty sound of the phone line was doing nothing to bridge the miles. "To say that I wanted to talk."

There was a sudden shuffling sound, an echoing voice said, "Oh, she's down," and a straining, groaning noise like a hot-water system in distress. "Things are getting moving here, I'd better go." Leo was already distant. "Let me know when you can come. Sleep well." The phone clicked off to a hum in my ear.

While I was waiting for the kettle to boil, I flopped onto a stool and considered Leo's ring. Slid it onto my left hand, third finger, held out my hand at arms length and twisted it around. Made tea with the unfamiliar weight on my finger, clinking the gold band against the side of the cup for the sheer novelty of it.

I went to pull the ring off, but although the fit was perfect and it had gone on without any kind of a hitch, suddenly the metal seemed to have shrunk. I pulled and twisted, twisted and pulled, poured washing-up liquid over my finger to such an extent that I worried my hand would froth in the rain, but it remained immovable. What had begun as a charming conceit was now beginning to look actively malign.

Jace's eyes widened the following morning as I followed her into the shop. "Alys, you have said yes!"

I put my hands behind my back. "No, I haven't. I was just

trying it on and look." I gave a couple of exploratory tugs to reveal the problem.

"We must remove it." There was a determined expression in her eye which I didn't like the look of. "Have you tried washing liquids?"

"And soap. And butter, lard, motor oil, beef dripping, Vaseline and I even rubbed half a banana on it. I smell like the strangest restaurant in the world and dogs are finding me incredibly attractive."

Half an hour of protracted tugging later, even Jace had to admit defeat. She'd gone off in search of a final remedy, and would probably come back with a meat cleaver and two packs of Elastoplast. I began sorting shelves. There had apparently been a small party of schoolchildren in yesterday like a marauding band of antilibrarians.

"Hey. How's it going?"

I snapped around so quickly that my spine made little protesting crackly sounds. "Piers! Hello—oh."

Piers stood at the entrance to Fantasy wearing black velvet jeans, a pure white collarless shirt and red cowboy boots. His hair hung loose, he sported enough stubble to highlight his cheekbones and he'd put a couple of studs in each ear. Not that I noticed, you understand. No, my eyes were too busy staring at the girl he was wearing down one side of his body, standing so close they appeared to be occupying the same shoes. "Alys, this is Sarah. Sarah, Alys."

The girl and I eyed one another for a moment, then she clearly wrote me off as any kind of potential rival.

"Hi, Alys." She even had a sultry, attractive voice, the kind that growls its vowels.

"Thought—well, coming past, just kinda—you know." Piers stepped slightly away from Sarah. I could almost see daylight between their bodies. "See, y'know, like, how things are."

"Almost a complete sentence there, well done," I said, slightly tartly. "I'm okay, Piers, thanks. Keeping busy. Is Florrie coming back tonight, do you know?"

Sarah snuggled against him and I watched his arm curl around her bare midriff with a crystalline feeling somewhere in my stomach. This must be how it feels to have gallstones, I thought distantly, if gallstones were hard and green and comprised mostly of jealousy that I would never again be that slim or have that flat a stomach.

"Er, sorry Alys, I dunno. I guess I'll not be over at the house tonight, we're"—he threw a glance at Sarah, who tossed her predictable blonde hair and giggled—"we're going to a movie."

There was a crushing, squeezing sensation in the region of my heart and I felt slightly breathless. "That's nice," I said, with an effort. "Enjoy." But she was so *thin,* it would be like having sex with a pipe cleaner.

"Uh, yeah."

Why weren't they *going?* I pointedly turned back to my books but had to face them once again when I moved a Frank Herbert from one side to another.

"So. You're from Manchester?" I said to Sarah, who was still leaning against Piers whilst he leafed through a Neil Gaiman. His head flicked up.

"No, I'm from Durham. I'm in York on a placement, got another six weeks to go."

I looked at Piers who shrugged.

"Are you going to buy it or read it here?" I indicated the book. "Only, it's quite a long story and I notice you didn't bring sandwiches."

Piers was focussed on my hand. "You—you've said *yes?*"

"Um." I snatched my arm back and folded it behind me.

"Oh, Jesus, no. God, Alys, tell me you're kidding. I mean—"

He seemed to grasp around for something to say. "What about—Grainger? Yeah, how's he gonna feel if you go shooting off to Devon? Poor guy, he'll be—yeah, he'll be *wrecked*."

I opened my mouth but no explanations came out and a sense of annoyance crept in. Here he was, flaunting this *stick*, who had less boobs than your average *bloke*, and he was getting uptight with *me* about *my* choices? "Look, if it's any of your business I'm still thinking about it."

Jacinta chose that moment to come bowling through the door clutching a Brown's bag. "Alys. I am saluting you!"

"What?"

"I have the salution to the problem with your finger." She noticed Piers and smiled. "Hello, lovely person."

Piers didn't introduce Sarah, I noticed, but said something I didn't catch. Jace moved smoothly into her native tongue and the two of them undertoned Spanish at each other for a few moments, Piers getting louder and quite emphatic. Finally, Jace muttered something which sounded like *que puedo hacer*, shrugged, causing this morning's blouse of ruffles and flounces to cascade across her frontispiece like tidal waves. Piers turned to go.

"Catch ya later." He headed for the door with Sarah stapled to his side trying to match his stride. He didn't turn back and pulled the door closed behind him so firmly that the bell fell off its hook.

Jace stared after him with a faint frown furrowing her smooth skin. "This is being most strange."

"Oh, that was Sarah. Which is odd, because he distinctly told me she was from Manchester, and *she* told me she's from Durham."

"This is not what I mean. Piers is telling me he is not seeing womans at the moment. He has big thinking to do."

"Apparently it's taken them a while to get it together,

maybe that's why." I had rarely seen a woman look so *much* like a girlfriend. Well, less a girlfriend, more a skin graft that talks.

"Perhaps. Now, do you wish to know how we are saluting your problem?" Without waiting for my answer, Jace wielded the Brown's bag with a flourish. "Is in here. Look."

"Jace, it's a pair of gardening gloves."

"I know." Jace pushed the gloves under my nose and wobbled in a manner which indicated that if I turned them down she might cry. "You can be using them for concealing your ring."

I put the gloves on. They had clearly been designed to prevent the Incredible Hulk from snagging his fingernails. "They're a bit big."

"Then we must remove the bits of fingers." Jace popped behind the curtain and emerged brandishing Simon's best scissors. I stood like a rock while Jace snipped the tips off the gardening glove fingers with some effort until I was left wearing something like Alan Titchmarsh's mittens. "There. Now no one is able to see that you are making a big mistake."

God, if I ever *did* marry Leo, Jace would probably insist on my wearing a full bodysuit. "Er, thank you, Jace."

With little clucks of pleasure and self-satisfaction, Jace went back about her work. I tried to carry on sorting out the shelves but it was like having flippers.

My daughter sprang through the doorway wearing a pink vinyl miniskirt, boots and a top which looked as though it had started life as a feed sack. "Hiya, Mum. Hey, Jace."

Jacinta gazed in admiration at Florrie's outfit. "Florence, where are you buying such amazing skirts? I must be finding some for myself."

I widened my eyes in pleading at Florrie. Jace in pink vinyl was best kept purely a vision. "What brings you in here?"

"Oh, Dad ran me over. Hey, Mum, I got my results."

"God yes, it's GCSE day, isn't it?" Then, suspiciously, "You said you didn't want me to come over to the school with you. You said I'd show you up in front of your friends."

"Well, duh. I made Dad stay in the car. But, guess what, I got four A's and three B's! Isn't that amazing?"

"Bloody hell." I sagged at the knees and had to lean against the counter. "You must have done loads of revision—I never saw you."

Florence looked at me pityingly. "Mum, *no one* does revision."

I instantly felt like the worst mother in the world again for having forgotten that today was the day the GCSE results came out. "That is absolutely fantastic, Florrie."

The three of us linked arms and did a little celebratory dance around the shop, kicking our legs in the air. "So now you can do any A levels you want," I panted eventually, collapsing out of the dance routine and onto the stool at the desk.

Florence looked down and flicked her hair over her face. "I dunno. Need to think about—ohmigod. *Muuuuuum!*"

During the frenzied prancing, my huge gloves had somehow become detached and Leo's ring was shining as though someone had poured glycerine over it.

"Ah," I said. "Now. There's a funny story."

But Florrie wasn't listening. She'd grabbed my hand and was turning it this way and that. "Wow. That is so cooooool. When did he ask you? How did he do it, go down on one knee kind of? Oh shit, wow, this is...wheeeeeww, what a day! So you going down to live on the farm?"

"I thought that was what you wanted to do."

"Me?" Florence looked astounded. "Me? But I—well, look, I mean..."

"All that talk about having a horse and going to work in the stud?"

A slightly sly look crept over her face. "But what about my A levels?"

"They have schools in Devon you know. Apparently it's not all mud huts and tribesmen."

"Or I could stay here. Move in with Piers."

"Piers was in here with a girlfriend." Jacinta was still admiring Florrie's costume from all angles. "Woman who is *saying* she is his girlfriend."

"Oh, come on, Jace. It was like the Siamese-twin show!" I got up and fiddled with papers. "But I don't think he'll be overjoyed if you announce you're intending to move in with him just as he's got himself nicely settled. Don't you want to come to Devon with me?"

Florrie raked her hair back with her immaculately pink painted fingernails. "Mum, Devon is *dead*. I mean, no dissing Leo or anything but...what would I do in *Devon*? All my friends are here, Dad is here, Piers, and I want to live my own life. Go out with my mates, chill, go clubbing, you know. I'm not your little kid any more." I must have recoiled because her voice softened. "I mean, yeah, it sounds really lovely, but I grew out of ponies a while back."

"But you and Leo talked about nothing else," I said indignantly.

"I was being *nice* to him." Florrie was equally indignant. "And besides, Mum." She lowered her voice. "I'm not sure he *does* talk about anything else."

"This I have also said." Now Jace had to put her two pennyworth in. "Your mother knows nothings of the tiny horses."

"*I* think he's lovely. Go for it, Mum."

Into this three-way Mexican frown-off walked Simon. "Hello!" he called innocently and was instantly caught in the crossfire of outrage.

"...not what it looks like..."

"...be telling her, Simon."

"...great idea. I think..."

"...is not seeing real Alys..."

"...stupid accident and I haven't..."

"Now, girls." Simon held up a hand. "*I* think"—we all held our breath, as though waiting for the judgement of Solomon—"that I'm *trying* to run a bookshop here, so can all this domestic disputation just wait awhile, hmm?"

Florence sighed hugely. "Well, all *right*," she breathed. "I'm going to see if I can find Piers. We'll talk about this later, Mum."

"Don't get portentous with me, young lady."

"Honestly. Can't you make up your mind and go move to Devon?"

"It's not as simple as..."

Once again Simon held up his hand. "In deference to the situation and the fact that I'm paying you *hourly*, Alys, save it for later."

Florence gave another exaggerated sigh and, with a totally redundant tug at the hem of her skirt, flounced out of the shop. We watched her go, the three of us grouped behind the desk slightly forlornly, like the Teletubbies watching Dipsy emigrate.

"Is still lovely skirting." Jace looked rueful.

"You should buy one. It'd have great pulling potential."

Now it was Simon's turn to sigh dramatically. "Don't you two ever think about anything else?"

I looked at Jace who made a little rueful face at me, all downturned mouth and partly raised eyebrows.

"Really, you should." I ignored Simon. "There's apparently this great new speed-dating club opened up in the city."

Jacinta rolled her eyes at me and wandered off, a box of books under each arm, towards the back room. I'd miss her. If I moved to Devon, that is. Who the hell would I get to be my best friend? Jay? Isabelle?

"Um. Alys." Simon was at my elbow, all hushed voice and bone structure. "What exactly *is* a speed-dating club?"

Chapter Twenty-Seven

At the book group that evening, we were all very subdued. Even Mr. Mansell restrained himself from his normal lecherous pursuit of my bottom and merely patted my hand in a distracted way when I sat next to him. Mrs. James reported that she'd rung the hospital to be told that Mrs. Treadgold was in a coma, and her son and daughter were with her. I didn't mention my visit, just sat sympathetically while the remaining four shored up Death's Maginot Line between them with jocular comments and heavy lightheartedness. Mrs. Munroe had baked tonight, but her lemon sponge had become infused with imminent death and refused to rise. So we ate flat citrussy cake without comment and discussed the Booker shortlist without enthusiasm.

I got home before Florence and began washing up with extreme prejudice. As I scrubbed I wondered about Grainger. Piers had a point. If—*when* I married Leo, where would he live? Devon was largely ruled out by virtue of the state of Grainger's unreliable bowels, Leo's dislike of cats and Leo's dogs. Would Florrie look after him? Alasdair wouldn't let him in his house either, pleading Tamar's allergies. It seemed Tamar was allergic to anything with a value in single figures. Piers? Maybe it would be kinder to... No. I'd let him see through his recent indisposition rather than face putting him to sleep. I certainly couldn't justify it simply to save myself the difficulties of rehoming or moving him.

The front door banged open and shut. I hastily pushed the as-yet-unwashed dishes into the sink and wiped my eyes on the back of my hand. "Hi, Florrie, I'm in here."

"Hi Mum!" Florrie's voice sailed through, followed by:

"Hey, Alys."

"Piers!" I quickly checked my appearance in the reflection off the kettle. If the wraithlike Sarah was with them, I didn't want to look like the dandelion in the flowerbed. "What brings you here?"

"Met up in town." Piers came wandering through to the kitchen and took a biscuit from the jar on the side.

"Sarah not with you? Thought you were going to the pictures?"

"We were. But, hey, y'know, shit happens." Piers went back out into the hallway. "I brought you something."

"You did what?"

Florrie came bowling through in his place. "Oh Mum, it's so *cute*. Oh you wait, you're going to love this."

You think? I thought, my heart zigzagging through my chest at the thought of Piers bringing me anything which might be called cute. Especially when Florence's idea of cute encompassed teddies in sweaters bearing slogans, brushed angora dresses and Jake Gyllenhaal.

Piers appeared in the doorway, framed artfully by the domestic chaos. In one hand he held a plastic basket which barely contained a furious Grainger and in the other...

"Oh, *Piers*." The kitten butted against his chin and nestled against the open neck of his shirt. It was *minute*. "Grainger must think it's supper." I half-laughed, with a wobble in my voice. Grainger gave a low growl, which could have meant anything and the kitten shrilled a high-pitched note.

Florrie was jumping up and down on the spot, clapping her

hands. "Can I hold him now, Piers? You promised, when we got home you said...can I?"

Piers casually tipped the kitten into her outstretched hands where it wibbled to gain purchase and let out another *weeeeeee-uuuuuww.* "I kinda thought—if Grainger...y'know—if he—*went...*"

"Yes, I get the picture." I took the basket from Piers, our fingers contacting on the sweaty plastic handle. Piers was looking at me in a way which made me suspect he knew Leo didn't much like cats. "It's very kind of you. Picking up Grainger. I could have done it, you know."

"I don't think Big G is really up for public transport yet." Piers unclipped the door to the plastic cage and Grainger wobbled uncertainly out onto the carpet. "Thought it'd be best. Y'know."

I bent down and put my arms around Grainger. He gave me a brief head-butt, then bit my nose in an experimental way. I hugged him. "Well, it's still kind."

We both stared at the kitten. He was a little ball of honey-coloured fluff, about the size of Grainger's head. "They were going to put him down," Piers said without looking at me. "Just kill him without a thought. He hadn't even had a chance. So I decided, what the hell."

"Piers gave them a hundred pounds," Florence said casually. "To let him take the kitten. I'm going to call him Caspar, cos he's like a little ghost. Aren't you, sweetie?" The kitten looked inscrutable. Piers looked embarrassed. I must have looked horrified because Florrie leaped back in. "You've been saying about getting another cat, Mum, haven't you? Piers asked if I thought you'd mind, and I said you've been on about it for *ages.*"

"Florrie, I've also been saying that I'd like Johnny Depp stripped and posted to me, but you know, sometimes you have to think about these things. Properly." I let Grainger go and he began a shaky stalk around the room, tail waving uncertainly.

"Why don't you take Caspar out the back for a whizz, Flo? Then you can introduce him to Grainger properly." Piers almost shoved Florence out of the door then spun on his heel, collecting another custard cream as he did so. "So, Alys?"

"What on earth possessed you? A hundred pounds? For that little scrap?" I tried to ignore the fact that he looked damn near as appealing as the kitten. "What if I move to Devon?"

He made a dismissive gesture with one hand. "Take it. Call it recompense for screwing up your life."

"But you haven't."

"Telling you about Ma and Alasdair doesn't count?" He lowered his voice. "And you spilling it all to me—tell me that doesn't count as screwing up your life."

I lowered my voice too, although Florence could be heard at a great distance, outside, encouraging the kitten to appreciate the joys of nature in an unnaturally high-pitched voice. "I chose to tell you though. It wasn't your fault."

"Does *he* know? This Leo guy? Does he know about Florence? About all the crap? What you've been through?" I couldn't speak. Shook my head. As gentle as he'd been with the kitten, Piers brushed my hair away from my face and looked into my eyes. "Then I think it kinda counts," he said softly.

"Piers." I stepped away. "Don't be nice to me, I think I might cry."

He smiled. "Just saved one life already tonight, I'm up for another. Bring it on."

To my shame, just for a second, the urge to feel the pressure of his embrace almost overwhelmed me, but I swallowed firmly and the feelings died back. "Thanks, but no. The kitten, I mean, he's lovely and everything—"

Grainger circled back towards us and sniffed the toe of Piers's boot with evident interest. "Just doing what I thought was right, Ally. That's all." Unconcerned now, Piers was munching another biscuit.

"But I can't look after—I mean I'll have to get a litter tray, and special kitten food and—oh bugger, you're going to tell me you've already got them, aren't you?"

"In the hallway." Piers gestured with the edge of the biscuit. "Just call me Mr. Prepared."

Florence re-entered, chirruping and peeping like a massed rank of bats, the kitten perched high on her shoulder, blinking enigmatically. As soon as he saw me, he trod gently down her arm and took a tiny, wobbly leap to land squarely in the middle of my chest with his tiny pin-claws grasping me securely. His miniscule chest throbbed with purrs.

"Isn't love wonderful?" Piers said dryly.

Chapter Twenty-Eight

Grainger gave Caspar a thorough inspection, sniffed him all over including the insides of his ears and sat down to wash his own face whilst watching the kitten out of the corner of his eye with a slightly desperate expression.

"I think Grainger knows the kitten was designed to be a replacement." I ripped into pizza, letting greasy gobbets of cheese ripple down my hand. "He's probably taking it as a portent of his demise, like a kind of cat-banshee. So, are you going out tonight to celebrate your success?"

"Yeah, well. Some of the girls said we might meet up somewhere in town, go round a bit. You know." Florrie avoided looking at me.

"Not drinking, I hope? You're still only sixteen, all of you. I know how much trouble it's possible to get into when you've been drinking. You do things. Things you wouldn't even consider if you were sober."

"Oh, don't worry so much, Mum. I'm not going to get pregnant or anything. I'm not *that* stupid!"

"Thank you."

"I didn't mean that." She seemed to consider stomping out of the room for a moment but relented. "Sorry." Florence had definitely improved beyond measure since she'd come back from London, a few months ago she wouldn't have thought twice about dropping an insult like that, and certainly she wouldn't have apologised. "But, Mum, *were* you drunk when you got pregnant with me?"

Past and present, fact and fiction merged there in my mind for a moment. "Your father and I had really only just started going out when I found out, so I can't be sure."

"You could have had an abortion?"

Being in London had certainly given Florrie a well-rounded view of things. She'd never asked *that* question before. "I didn't want to."

Not wholly true. But I'd thought maybe a baby would be what Flick needed to calm him down. Restrict his wildness a bit. And after I'd found out that curbing his excesses was the *last* thing he had in mind, I'd simply left it too late.

"But why not? You gave up everything, your education. All of it, just to have me."

"I wanted to have you. Your father was, I thought, the love of my life."

Her real father. Flick. Gorgeous bastard that he'd been.

"Where did Piers go?" Florrie was obviously bored with the subject.

"Out to get another pizza, I think."

"Bugger. I was going to ask him to pick me up from town later. Oh well. I'm off to get ready."

Florrie danced out, leaving me with the remnants of our celebratory pizzas and two animals both trying to pretend they were the only cat in the world. I absent-mindedly gave the ring another tug of desperation, this time it slid effortlessly off, lubricated with the sweat of greasy cheese from the pizza. It was about the only thing I hadn't already tried.

As it came off I was overwhelmed with relief, and felt instantly guilty, but not quite guilty enough to put it back on. I laid the ring down on the carpet and looked at it. It had reassumed its air of innocence, no longer weighing on my finger and my mind so heavily. But still. Leo wanted me.

As though he sensed my doubts, Grainger got up and poked me affectionately in the eye with his nose. Then he and Caspar wobbled around each other for a moment before they both sat back down. Honour had evidently been satisfied.

I went to pick the ring up and put it on the table, but it wasn't there. I swivelled around where I'd sat on the floor beside the sofa and peered underneath, into the fluff-encrusted depths. Nothing. With increasing desperation, I crawled around on all fours slapping at the mat like a deranged carpet-fitter, but there was not so much as a glint of sapphire, a hint of diamonds.

"Mum? What *are* you doing?"

"You don't think we could have a poltergeist, do you?" I patted on. "My ring's completely vanished."

Florrie had emerged from her room, wearing a kind of throw-over dress which looked as though her aim hadn't been particularly good. "Even a poltergeist would have better taste than to hang round here. It's probably rolled under the sofa."

"Can you give me a hand to lift it up?"

Florence looked down at herself. "In *this*? Joking, right?" There was a bang at the front door and Piers made another of his decorative entries. Florence positively leaped at him. "Can you pick me up tonight, 'bout elevenish? I'll ring when I'm ready? Pretty please? Oh, and Mum needs a hand with the sofa."

"Jeez, Flo, ever heard of buses? Yeah, okay. Enjoy."

We watched her leave, then Piers turned to me. "Hand with the sofa?"

"To lift it up."

I paused briefly to appreciate his muscles being brought into play, but there was no ring under the sofa. Caspar used the opportunity to dive underneath and chase fluffballs. Grainger was curled on the carpet looking pathetic.

"Do you think he's really better?" I asked. "Maybe it was more than a stroke. Only he looks so thin and scraggy... Maybe he's got a tapeworm."

"Hey, thin and scraggy never did me any harm." Piers raked his hair, stretching out his back, and I fought my eyeballs for control. "Anyway, what *is* tapeworm? Sounds kinda cute."

"Cute? Yuk. What did you take to bed when you were little, a liver fluke?"

"Nah. Weren't allowed toys. I was a weekly boarder. Little school near Boston."

"You hated it that much?"

"It shows, huh?" Piers gathered Caspar up and hauled him onto his lap, his velvet trousers gathered gobbets of pale fur, but he didn't seem to care. "Moving to England was the best thing Ma ever did, far as I was concerned. Okay, I had to go to a prissy school where they made us wear hats, but, hey, I got to go home nights. How 'bout you?"

"Day school. Private though, Dad insisted. He was only something fairly minor in local government, but he and Mum found the money from somewhere. And I had music lessons and dance and tennis coaching."

"You hated it that much?"

"It shows?" I gave him a rueful smile and began stroking Grainger's slightly dull fur. "Dear old Dad had it dead set in his mind that I was going to be something successful. Kind of a good job that they died before I proved them wrong, wasn't it?"

There was a moment of silence. Piers gave my arm a quick rub of sympathy. "Hey, you got Flo, and she's not so bad, is she?"

"I suppose."

"What did *you* want to be?"

"Me?"

"Yeah. When you were a kid?"

I looked at him. "Promise you won't laugh?"

"Hey, you're looking at the guy who wanted to be the first Olympic gold medallist for the Down Stairs Tea Tray slalom. I'm in no *position* to laugh!"

"I wanted—*really?*"

"What can I say? I was a cute kid. Now, you?"

"I wanted to be a writer. Children's books, preferably. Stories about elves and magic and I *knew* you'd laugh."

"I'm not laughing. Trust me. I think it's real sad that you haven't got to do that yet. But you will, one day."

"Yes, one day. Maybe." I sighed. "I don't exactly come across as a dynamic go-getter, do I?"

Piers had an odd look on his face, a kind of inward-seeing expression. "Life's tough, yeah? Have to adjust to not always getting what we want." He came and sat down beside me on the sofa, and leaned over to stroke Grainger, who took this dual approach to cat petting as no more than his proper entitlement. He wasn't going to let us off the hook for sending him into exile any time soon.

"You're well adjusted though, aren't you?"

"On the surface. But inside I'm a mass of torment." He clasped his hands dramatically to his chest and flung his head back. Unfortunately he had misjudged the distance between the sofa and the wall and cracked his skull, giving me the chance to appreciate truly bilingual swearing. Grainger stirred, obviously annoyed.

"D'you reckon he's got it?" Piers eyed the tabby suspiciously, one hand held to the back of his head as though he feared it might come off.

"I'm beginning to. But I daren't pick him up. I've got work in the morning. I don't want to go in looking like something a practising taxidermist has had a go at. Besides, he feels really—"

"Sticky? Mangy?"

"I was going to say fragile."

"Okay." Piers dived on Grainger and lifted him suddenly off the floor. Finding himself with paws dangling Grainger froze for a moment then hung limply like an unconvincing handbag. Exactly where Grainger had been, sat my ring.

"The little bastard." I picked up the ring and resisted any urge to give it a place of safety on my finger again.

"He's got a right to comment, I guess." We stood side by side and looked at the ring twinkling away on my palm. "What are you going to do, Alys? Say yeah to the guy? Or kick free?"

"He says he loves me, Piers. It would give me something beyond this place and work. I mean, I'll miss Jace, and Simon and God help me, I'll even miss *you*. But really why am I staying here?"

Piers looked as though he was about to speak, running both hands through his hair and dropping his gaze from mine. When he brought his fingers forward there was blood on his hand and a bit more multicultural profanity was brought into play.

"Hang on I'll get some Savlon to put on it."

Piers sat heavily next to where Grainger was now coiled, one lip curled in disgust at his recent treatment. "So? What *are* you going to do?" Piers called after me as I went into the kitchen in search of my first aid kit, consisting of a tube of antiseptic cream, two Harry Potter plasters and a bandage, which I suspected had once belonged to Dylan-the-horse.

"I'm going to go down. I think Leo and I need to talk." Slowly, trying to be gentle I tipped my finger with white antiseptic and moved his hair away so that I could see the wound. His hair was silken and there was something very intimate about the whole scene.

"Yeah? That doesn't sound like you're loved-up with the guy. What you going to talk about? Ow. That bloody hurts."

"I need to tell him things. All the stuff about reading his poetry and about Florrie and Alasdair, and yes, maybe even the stuff about Flick." Piers tilted his head back and met my eye. "I owe it to him, Piers. I can't build another relationship on deceit. I won't."

"Well, they say confession is good for the soul." Piers wouldn't let me look away. "Did you feel good when you confessed to me, Ally? Did it make you feel clean and shiny and like it was the right time to start something?"

"Talking to you, it made me realise what I did wasn't so bad. I was only a bit older than Florence is now. He'll understand." I tried not to notice the pleading tone in my voice. "Yes. He'll understand," I said it again, injecting a bit more confidence this time.

I was about to screw the top back on the tube when Piers grabbed my hand and made me jump.

"Do you love him?" His grip was tight, his rings dug into my skin. He stood up and faced me, and for a moment I was slightly afraid. "Well, Alys? Do you?" He was so pale that I wondered if the bash on the head had concussed him. His breathing was rapid and shallow, his eyes dark.

"Are you trying to make me cry again?" I tried to check the catch in my voice. "If you are, please don't."

"*I* don't make you cry, Alys, the *situation* does. I'm just trying to make you see the bigger picture here. Do you love this guy? Honest now, truth or dare."

"Dare, then." I was almost whispering.

"I dare you." Now Piers had lowered his voice too. "I dare you to tell me you love this Leo. Cos, y'see, I don't think you can. I think you're looking at spending the rest of your life with a guy you don't even fucking *like*."

"That's not true."

"Reckon?" He was moving closer. This was no longer my almost-stepson. It was some shadowy stranger, his face virtually touching mine, his hands cupping my shoulders, and I couldn't pull away. "Ally, I don't think you know what love *is*."

"Does it matter?" My voice came out breathy.

"Yeah." His tone matched mine. "I think it does."

I could feel his breath on my lips, his hair drifting against the side of my neck. Couldn't look away, couldn't move. Didn't know what was coming, and a part of me didn't care.

Suddenly a sound came from behind me. A choking, gasping noise that turned out to be the sound of Caspar sicking up a furball down the back of the stereo. The intensity lifted and Piers stepped away.

"Shit, look at the time. I'd better go. Supposed to be tying up with Ma and Alasdair for some kinda family powwow, and I'll have to be back for Flo." Was it my imagination, or was Piers avoiding looking at me? It was rather hard to tell, because I was *definitely* avoiding looking at *him*.

"What happened to going to the cinema with Sarah?" I had a perfect excuse for having my back to him. I was trying to scrape cat sick off my favourite CDs.

"Er, we—we split up today, so."

A warm flood of relief suffused me. He'd split up with Sarah, obviously feeling low. It hadn't been *me* causing all the touchy-feely stuff we'd narrowly avoided, it had been *him*. "Oh, that's a shame."

"Look, umm, gotta go. Catch you later?"

"I'm sure. Oh, and Piers—"

"Yeah?"

"Thanks."

A pause. "Alys." I looked up now, met his gaze. Held it. "Nah. See ya."

I watched him from the window as he strode down the pavement towards the untidily parked Porsche, those red boots making him look like something out of *The Wizard of Oz*. Only someone with a huge amount of style could carry off boots like those, and Piers certainly had a huge amount of style. Huge amount of lots of things evidently.

Chapter Twenty-Nine

I found a taxi driver willing to concede the existence of Charlton Hawsell Stud and arrived just as darkness was beginning to fall. Devon was still baked in the ongoing heat wave, a light toast-brown coloured the whole countryside and the house rose from its seared surroundings in a glorious honey-coloured mound, like a soufflé served on burnt chips.

The encroaching night gave the whole place a slightly sinister air. Walking from the heat outside into the insulated coolness, I felt as though I were walking into a ghost story. I didn't call out but moved through the house in a kind of daze until I came to the kitchen. Leo was in there. I could hear his voice filtered through the solid oak of the panelled door, deep, insistent, but I couldn't hear the words. Slowly I turned the handle and eased the door open, cautious in case his misogynistic terriers were still on the premises. I pushed my face through the opening and looked inside.

There stood the predictable scene of domestic squalor, unwashed plates on the table, a newspaper spread across the worktop, and, at the far side of the room, Leo. He had his back to me, telephone pressed against his ear and was writing furiously on a notepad. I put my overnight bag on the floor out in the passageway and tiptoed across the room. As I got closer to him, my heart began to beat faster. He looked fantastically dishevelled in his navy blue jodhpurs and white shirt, hair awry as though he'd hurried in from the yard. Just as I got close enough to touch him, he gave a final "mmm, call you tomorrow" down the phone and laid it back on the side, turning round to find me pressed almost full length against him.

"Buggering hell." Leo staggered back a step, dislodging a mug half full of tea which had been resting precariously on the top of a chair back, which fell and smashed at our feet. "Alys? What the hell are you doing here?"

"I came to see you," I said, rather downhearted at his less-than effusive greeting, stirring spilled china with my foot. "I thought we needed some time to talk."

Leo stared at me, rather blankly for a moment, then a glorious smile lit his face. "It's wonderful to see you." Back came the clouded expression. "Oh, but tonight's not really a good time. I'm shipping a couple of fillies down to Cornwall, settling them in. We hope one of them's in foal so we don't want her upset if we can help it. Can you stay?"

"My bag." I pointed at the doorway.

"Well, that's fantastic. I'll be back tomorrow, in time for dinner. Can we talk then?"

"Wonderful." I mostly meant it. This dark half-light really suited Leo, carved the planes of his face into sharp angles against his unruly hair and made his eyes behind his glasses shine with a meaningful expression. "I can amuse myself here for a day."

Leo stepped up and enfolded me in an embrace. "No, it's great that you're here. Does this mean you've reached a decision?" He held me away to look into my face. "Is it yes or no, Alys?"

Gently I disentangled him. "That's partly why I came, to help me to decide. I've got a life in York. It's not a great one, but it's mine. I want to make sure that I'm doing all the right things, making the right decisions, do you understand?"

Leo nodded slowly. "I think so. All I can say is if you do say yes, I'll do my very best to make you happy. I'd like everything to be..." He tailed off.

"To be what?" He felt odd against me, somehow foreign, until I realised that I was comparing this hug to being held against Piers in a car park. "What, Leo?"

"To be different," he finished, sadly. "Not like it was with Sabine. None of the lying and avoidance and all that."

"Me too," I said, half under my breath, as Leo collected papers and bags for his trip. "Me too."

Chapter Thirty

The next morning I decided to go for a walk through the fields. Leo had shown me the extent of Charlton Hawsell Stud fields on the big map in the office. He'd also pointed out the neighbouring farm belonging to Isabelle and her husband, so, I put on a white T-shirt and cut-off jeans and set off to explore.

Down the pea-gravelled driveway and over a gate I went, catching vague distant glimpses of girls on ponies in a board-sided school. I walked through a paddock where a bright chestnut mare and foal stood nose to tail reflecting the sunlight, and almost fell over the woman crouched beneath an ash tree.

"Oh!" I clutched at my heart. "I didn't see you down there." I paused to wonder exactly why she was on her knees in a clump of tussocky grass. Surely you didn't have to pray to ponies, did you?

"Look." Her voiced was hushed, wondering. "It's a dragonfly hatching. Isn't it beautiful?" Stuck to one of the longer strands of the grass was the zeppelin-like body of an insect, tugging itself free of a restricting shell and spreading its wings to the sun. It shimmered. "It's like magic, the way they go from this ugly, shrunken thing to this beauty. Don't you think so?" She stood up, shaking her hair back. "You're Alys, aren't you? I'm Jay. Leo hasn't introduced us properly but—well, that's Leo, isn't it?"

"I...hello." I found my hand had been clasped and was

being shaken in a firm grip. "Yes," I finished, feebly. "That's me."

Close up, Jay was pretty. Properly, make-up-free pretty. Her cheeks were rounded and blushed by the sun and outdoor living, her hair glittered a conker-brown and she was shapelier than she'd appeared from the window. She was looking me over in a similar way, though I doubt she'd come to any similar conclusions. Not in this cheap T-shirt, with the draggy-down hem and the uneven cutoffs.

"Leo really thinks a lot about you." Jay had stopped examining my face and was back to staring at the dragonfly emerging from the cocoon. I wondered if there was room in that shrivelled casing for me to crawl inside. At least then I could have avoided the lustre of love that bloomed across her face when she mentioned his name. "He's hoping you're going to marry him." Dark eyes, with a hint of tear-shine, met mine. "Are you?"

Marry him? Right now I could have killed him. How could he not know? How could he not have noticed that this clear-eyed, unencumbered girl loved him so whole-heartedly? He spent *how many* hours a day in her company, yet he'd not picked up on that one?

"I don't know," I answered her honestly. "I just don't know."

A sideways shrug. Not as bad as she'd been expecting. "Oh, okay. Only—"

I half cringed at what I imagined might come next. Was Jay about to confess all to me, her longing and lust for her employer, like some historical novel, which she dare not mention for fear of losing "her position"? What did I say if she did?

"—only I've been offered another job. In Wales. So if you move in you might have to help out in the stud. Just for a while, until Leo can replace me." Her gaze was back on the dragonfly. "Do you have much experience with ponies?" Now she looked up, but it wasn't at me, it was at the mare and foal languidly flicking flies. The expression of love and loss on her face nearly equalled that when she spoke of Leo. "I wouldn't ask, it's just that a few of the mares can be a bit difficult, and handling stallions isn't something you can just pick up in an afternoon."

"Like I said, Jay, I'm still thinking. There's a lot to consider."

The half shrug again. "Okay. Sorry, didn't mean to interfere or anything. Going for a walk? It's lovely down by the river. If you go through that gate, there's a path." She'd turned back to her close examination of the insect, now scaffolded to the grass stem, wings glistening an unnaturally vivid blue.

"Thank you." I didn't just mean for the walker's guide. Jay had purposefully let me see her devotion to Leo. She hadn't even tried to hide how much she cared, and that was courageous, to say the least, when I could have destroyed her dream with just one sentence. But then, she was leaving anyway...

My sandals were soaked by the time I reached the line of trees which marked the edge of the river so I took the shoes off and carried them, enjoying the freedom. It did mean I had to tread more carefully. The grass, which looked so silky-soft and innocent, concealed pockets of thistles and rocks. When I finally attained the bank of the river, I was high-stepping like a chorus girl.

I collapsed in the sandy-floored bower formed by a willow tree stretching its arms towards the water, and stared into the river's rippling shadows. A breeze fingered the back of my neck as I propped myself up on my elbows and a few birds flickered through the air. Flies swarmed above the water. The river's surface moved like lazy cellophane.

"Hey." A shout assailed me from the far side of the river,

the sound snatched at and tossed around by the passing breeze. "Hey. Alys!"

I struggled to sit up, panicked into the here-and-now by the use of my name.

"*Piers?*" Seeing him here, facing me across the narrow band of river, dislocated me. Piers belonged in Yorkshire. Despite the fact that he wore a countrified version of his normal clothes, he still looked out of place. Wrong. "What the hell are you doing here?"

"There was a call. It's bad news, Ally."

Oh God. *Florence. Something's happened to Florence.* Before I was really conscious of my movements, I was wading towards Piers, my shoeless feet nearly numb on the stony-floored bed of the river. When I looked up from my stagger I saw that he too had entered the water and was sluicing his way towards me.

"What's happened?" I gasped.

Piers touched me very lightly on the cheek. "Mrs. Treadgold. She died this morning."

The water reached just over his knees, midthigh on me, tugging gently at our clothes. A cloud of mayflies racketed around our heads in the silence. "She's dead."

"Yeah. You okay?" Piers shifted as stones moved under his feet, some of the dancing insects tangled in his hair and he raised his hand to dash them out.

"I think—I don't know." Another kingpin in my surety of life had been removed. "She'd been ill, Piers, and I didn't even know. I didn't even *notice*." I looked up into his face. "Am I really such a cow? So neglectful? Mrs. T keeps...*kept* giving me advice and I don't even think I took it."

More stones moved, slippery undersides were revealed. I found myself sliding, put out a foot to stabilise myself, and the world turned over.

I grabbed at Piers instinctively, felt his arm go out to catch me and then both of us were down in the water, flailing and gasping at the cold contrast. I resurfaced, arms whirling and grasping, and I found myself with hands full of Piers's T-shirt, gripping on for dear life as I coughed and sucked at the air. His skin was cold where his T-shirt rucked, colder than mine, and I realised this was the first time I'd ever touched him, skin to skin. I didn't let go.

We splashed our way to my bank while he muttered and swore to himself in Spanish. When we finally flopped onto the sandy bank-top, he wrenched off his T-shirt and flung it disgustedly at his feet. "Fifty-three fucking pounds, now it's only good to clean the car." God, but he had a nice torso.

I looked down at my own T-shirt. "Seven fifty, and I reckon it's got a good few years left in it."

Piers stared at me for a second, then shoved wet hair out of his eyes and smiled. "Yeah. Serve me right for being such a poser."

"I didn't say that."

"No. But you think a lot of stuff that you don't say, Alys. You're like—like a kind of book, where the pages are just open enough to read some of the words, but you can't get the whole story. And, by the way, you are not a cow. Or neglectful."

"Mrs. Treadgold was so good to me." Tears felt hot against my chilled skin. "I should have been there for her more. I should have talked to her more."

"Years you've been keeping it all inside, Ally. Years. Years of hiding so that no one would find out what you did or find out how screwed up you'd got over it all."

He'd hunched up, arms around his knees, bare back curved. His backbone protruded through the skin, vanishing up into where his hair fell over his shoulders. I found this oddly affecting. "You need to learn to talk to people."

"Why did you come?" I said abruptly, trying to stop his train of thought. "You didn't need to drive all this way. You could have rung. And anyway, how did you find me?"

"Got the address off the 'net. Went to the house. You weren't there but this woman said you were headed out this way. I guess I picked the wrong side of the river." Piers looked at my still-ringless hand. "You've not told him yet?"

It was either lose my temper or start crying again. I chose anger. "Oh right, so you're here as the front-line deputation of the Alys-mustn't-marry-Leo brigade, are you? I bet Jace put you up to this, did she?"

Piers muttered something.

"What?"

He stood up. I thought for a moment he was going to face me, but he turned his back again and leaned against the tree, staring out over the field, his breathing rapid. I couldn't keep my eyes from the rise and fall of his rib cage. He muttered again.

I gave up. Unfolded my arms and pulled myself upright so that I could stand beside him. "For God's sake, Piers, *what?*"

"I said—" This time he turned round and I nearly stepped back. He looked as though he was about to throw up. His normally pale skin looked grey, his eyes were absolutely huge. "I'm not here for anyone but me. Self-interest kinda thing, y'know?" He took a gulp of air. "*I* don't want you to marry this guy."

I just stared at him.

"Okay, Alys, here's the thing, right?" Another gulp. "I'm in love with you. Can't help it, don't fucking *want* to help it, it's how I feel." Some colour had returned to his face now, faintly brushed across his cheekbones. "That's all. You can throw things and scream now, if you want."

I closed my mouth with a click. Somewhere, deep inside

me, it felt as though someone had wrapped my heart in a warm blanket while somewhere else, somewhere more primeval and certainly farther down, there appeared to be a firework party in progress. My eyes were stapled to his bare chest, the silky coil of hair dead centre which ran down to his belly. And beyond. Oh God, don't let me even *think* about beyond. This wasn't right. I shouldn't be looking at Piers like this.

"Do you think I should?" I stammered. "Scream, I mean?"

"Well." Piers moved closer. "If you did, then I wouldn't be able to do this." His head tilted down, against all probability mine tilted up, and our lips met. There was enough passion, desire and good old down-and-dirty sex there to satisfy any world-stopping criteria, but there was also an underlying softness. If I'd had any of my mental faculties to hand instead of having them flapping around inside my head like a bunch of stoned budgies, I would have said it was a kiss of promise. His mouth tasted sweet, faintly of peaches and there was something succulently alluring about his naked chest pressed against my damp T-shirt.

Eventually, and reluctantly, I pulled away. Piers let the hand he'd had tangled in my hair fall to his side. "I can't do this. It's just too weird. I mean—you and me? What planet did you come from, Piers?"

"Because, why? Why not you and me? Because you've got this Leo sitting on the sidelines, all saddle soap and tight jodhpurs?"

A glance down at Piers's wet jeans, clinging tighter to his thighs than any jodhpurs. My heart was swooping about inside my chest. "I thought—but—you're my *friend.*"

"Four years, Ally. Four years I've wanted you. If friends was all I was going to get then it was still worth it. So, if you're gonna marry your guy, at least I've told you how I feel."

"Have you really thought about this?" I said, quietly. "I

mean, what about your girlfriend? Maybe you're reacting to breaking up with her?"

He let out a hoot of laughter. "Ally, sweetheart, *Sarah didn't exist.* And yeah, I've really thought about this. I've had four years to think about it."

"What do you mean Sarah didn't exist? No one that thin could be a figment of my imagination." I was rather carefully avoiding the issue here.

"I invented her. I gave myself six months, yeah? Six months without a woman, to see if I could either talk myself out of love with you, or find out if you could ever feel anything for me—and you kept on and on about me being with someone. You never took the hint, did you?"

"I didn't know," I exclaimed. "You never did or said anything to make me think that you—"

"Reckon? Anyway, Sarah. I wanted to make you jealous. Thought it might be my last hope. So once I'd pulled her outta the air, I had to find someone."

"So that poor girl, her name wasn't even Sarah?"

"Yeah, it was. She'd been hanging round a while. So I—"

I let out a breath. "So *that's* why you told me she was from Manchester and she said she was from Durham?"

Piers gave me a grin which was manic bordering on the completely insane. "Finding a girl from Manchester called Sarah at short notice. Well, have you ever tried it?"

"Surprisingly enough, no. But all that trouble, just to make me jealous? All those hints that there was someone but it was difficult?"

"That was *you.* And difficult hardly fucking covers it!"

"Oh, Piers," I said helplessly, as ideas and implications as well as memories and feelings all flooded into me together.

"Did it work?" He stood so close that I could feel him

breathing. "Did Sarah make you jealous? Did you think about her with me, that it could have been—*should* have been you?"

I couldn't help myself. Maybe it was shock, maybe it was pleasure, maybe it was the sheer ludicrousness of the situation, but I started to laugh. Proper, head-back, gut-wrenching laughing. "You shit, Piers," I managed to gasp between hoiks of laughter. "You pure, unadulterated *shit.*"

"It did work then." He started laughing as well. "Okay, yeah, I'm a complete bastard, but I had to do *something* or I'd lose you altogether." The laughing stopped. Was replaced by— what? Expectation? The molecules of the air hung heavy between us. It was almost too much of an effort to breathe. "And I couldn't face that. Not losing you to that wanker."

I felt obliged to speak in his defence. "Leo isn't a wanker. He's kind and sweet and..." I was running out of justifications, "...good."

I'd asked for it. I really had. Piers put his head on one side and looked at me out of eyes that burned. "Ah," he said softly. "But I'm not just *good.*" I had nobody else to blame, I really didn't. "I'm a fucking *revelation.*"

He was, too. Tore down all the inhibition borders, shredded away every last self-preserving boundary and quite unashamedly made me surrender my soul to him. There under that willow tree we had sex so hot that I was surprised sheets of molten rock didn't stream from the hills and the river itself didn't catch light and flame like a Sambuca. Piers. My God, *Piers.* It shouldn't be happening, his fingers shouldn't know how to tease me like that. I shouldn't arch under the feel of him sliding inside me, and I *definitely* shouldn't be screaming his name. It felt dangerous, it felt threatening but most of all *it felt right.*

Tongue-to-tongue we lay, a rough description of the explosive sex scribbled in the dusty sand beneath us; the passion and sympathy we'd found in each other had surprised both of us. Eventually Piers raised his head and blew my hair from my cheeks. "This is exactly how I imagined it would be."

"What, the flies and the sand? Do you fantasise about the Foreign Legion?"

Piers just grinned. "You *so* do not want to know about my fantasies. Actually, you probably do. But, I meant this. The losing control and the mind-blowing fucking sweet *awesomeness* of it all." He held out one hand, straggling the rest of his rangy body over mine. "This—*this* is all I've ever wanted."

I reached up from beneath him and ran my hand down his back. "I think," I said slowly, "that one of us could get incredibly hurt."

"You can't get hurt if you don't care." He was responding to my touch, moving restlessly against me, eager once again. "Do you care, Alys?"

"Piers." There was a little sob in my voice, even I didn't know what it meant, but I did know that the heat inside me was crying out for him, for his cool sureness of touch.

Chapter Thirty-One

I walked back to Charlton House on rubber legs and with a slight, but noticeable, flush still staining my skin. I couldn't believe what had just happened. Piers. I mean, *Piers*. Good God, it was almost unthinkable. He was so young. Bloody hell, but he had some experience on him though. So young and so careless. Or should that be *carefree*? He thought he loved me, said he loved me, but where the hell did that leave *me*?

Leo was offering me everything. All those things I'd thought I wanted during the years of loneliness and struggling. Stability, kindness. I looked across the paddock towards the big house which was glowing a pinkish colour as the sun spread its late-afternoon rays across its face, the air dulled with heat. So Leo loved me with all this and with his words, his poetry. Piers loved me with—my legs trembled again—with a passion that registered on the Richter scale. A love that could bend metal.

And the downside? Leo had his horses, his raison d'etre. And the poetry he never let me see. Was he *ashamed*? Of the way he felt or the need to write it down? Piers had his youth, his instinctive spontaneity. Leo was kind, gentle, wanted me to be happy and life to run smoothly. Piers—Piers was just bloody *gorgeous* and who knew what he wanted?

I wanted to think. No. I *needed* to talk.

The Land Rover was drawn up at the front of the house, two-horse trailer still coupled onto the back. There was no sign of the occupants of the trailer nor the car, although the driver and passenger doors were open. It was the Marie Celeste of animal transporters. A faint trail of straw wisps led around to the stable yard. I followed and found Leo inside a stable. He was covered in straw and chatting rather earnestly to Jay.

"Alys!" Leo sounded startled. "I...we...you were out for a walk?"

"Leo. We need to talk."

A rush of emotions made his face go pink as they conflicted, fighting for dominance. "Yes, we do."

Jay and I met one another's eyes. She looked oddly self-assured, but carefully blank-faced, and I wondered if Leo had been telling her his plans for me, for *us*. Something must have shown in my face, because her eyebrows raised.

"It needs to be now." As I spoke I turned. Without even making sure he was behind me, I headed towards the house, back stiff with determination.

Leo followed me into the kitchen, his boots clonking against the old stone floor. "Alys—" he began, but I waved a hand.

"Look, Leo, I—" Then I stammered to a halt. Couldn't think what to say. The pair of us stared, beetroot faced, at each other. "You first."

Leo just shook his head. "I'm not sure how to put it."

I closed my eyes. It was easier when I couldn't see his face, even if it did instantly conjure an image of Piers. He was burned onto my retina.

"Listen to me, Leo. Please." I had to do it. I really did. "I've read your poetry—yes, even the stuff in the drawer in the bedroom. It isn't some psychic tie that we share, it's the fact that I recognised you from your photo in the book Isabelle had printed." I opened my eyes. My face was scalding hot. "And I engineered our meeting. I don't much like horses either. I'm really sorry, but—" I took the ring out of my pocket. "I can't marry you."

Leo stared at the ring. His gaze began to roam around the room as his face flamed again. "I can't marry you," he echoed. He was shifting from foot to foot as though even his boots wanted out.

"Yes. I'm sorry."

"No, I mean, *I* can't marry *you.*"

"What?" I blinked in confusion. "Of course you can't marry me, if I won't marry you."

"No. It...it's complicated." His stare came down off the ceiling and brushed past me on its way to investigate a corner. A shifty little emotion fled through his eyes. "I've only just— things have come home to me that I've been blind to for so long." He went, if it was possible, even redder.

The straw-covered sweater. The expression on Jay's face. "Oh my God. You've screwed Jay."

"She...I...we never...this was the only time." Then, pleadingly, "She was leaving."

"That's one hell of a reinterpreting of the term golden handshake."

"I've just realised what I could have lost. What I've been hiding from myself for all this time. That Jay is the woman for me." A hand reached out. "I'm sorry, Alys. Truly sorry."

"So am I." If I'd been a better person, now would have been the time to confess to the rip-roaring sex with Piers. I couldn't do it. But knowing Leo and I were both guilty made me feel better. I caught his hand, held it loosely. "I think maybe I wanted to be in love a bit more than I was capable of. I tried to fool myself that you could be the one, even when I knew it wouldn't work."

"And I was so bowled over by you, by your interest in me, that I lost sight of what was important to me. The stud, the horses."

"And the poetry?" I met his clear green eyes.

"That's—not important. Not really. Not to me. It's just something I do, it's not who I am."

Therein had lain my problem all along. I'd wanted to fall for a poetic soul and it wasn't Leo's fault that he didn't have one. Just a facility for words and the kind of lonely introspection that made it all come out on paper. Poetry in his heart, perhaps, but not his soul.

Chapter Thirty-Two

Letting myself into the flat, I surprised Florence, who was sitting on the floor in the living room, packing a suitcase. "Mum?"

I didn't answer, barely acknowledged her presence and swept on into my bedroom. The silent sanctuary-ness of it soothed my nerves, although the scarlet throw I'd bought to tempt Leo rankled, until I balled it up and shoved it under the bed.

"Mum?" The door opened quietly. "Are you okay? Is it because of Mrs. Treadgold?"

"I'm feeling fragile," I muttered, muffled by the amount of duvet in my mouth. "Just leave me be, Florrie, please."

Florrie moved closer, sat down beside me and gave my back a tentative pat. "It's all right to feel sad. It's healthy." Another pat. "Piers said you were a bit shaken. Do you want me to call him?"

The mattress barely had time to bounce. I shot to my feet like a reversed film. "No. No, honestly, Florence, I'm okay. Well, I'm sure you can imagine." *Please God, don't let her be able to imagine. In fact never let her feel the way I'm feeling right now.*

"All right then. Just thought. You and he seem so tight these days, and the way he insisted on driving down to tell you—"

"Tell me?" She didn't *know*, did she, what Piers had said?

"About Mrs. Treadgold." Florence stared at her feet. "Did something happen, Mum? With Piers?"

Shock nearly stopped me breathing. "With Piers?" My voice was high with tension. "With *Piers*? Good Lord, Florrie, whatever could happen between me and *Piers*?" I blushed a scalding tide to my hairline, and my hands started to sweat.

"Well, you keep falling out and making up, thought you might have had another bust up. He came by to say you were coming back. Looked completely fucked up."

"Florence." I wasn't so completely appalled by myself that I couldn't spare a bit of appall for her. "Language!"

"Sorry." She cupped her knees up under her chin and fiddled with her toes like a five year old. "Mum—"

Why wouldn't she go away and let me think? "Can this wait Florence? Can't you go out? There's twenty pounds in my bag, go to the pictures or something." Oh, but what if Piers came by to see if I was back yet? Found me sitting in on my own. My mouth was suddenly full of the taste of him, my skin flickering as it had beneath his featherlight touch... "Or rent a film, that's a good idea."

"Something slushy? Romantic? What about *Notting Hill* again?"

"I was thinking more about *Dawn of the Dead* actually. Something violent, lots of limbs hanging off, you know the kind of thing."

Florence stood, then sat again. "I'd really better get this over with." She sounded incredibly adult. "If I stop now I might not have the nerve."

I felt my mouth dry and the blood which had started seeping slowly away from my blush-encrusted cheeks suddenly drained downwards. "What?" I said faintly.

"Mum. Oh shit, there's no easy way to say this, is there? Look, about my A levels... Well. I'm not going to be able to take them. I mean, I'll always have those GCSE results if I want to. But. Not for a while."

"Oh my God." I flopped onto the trunk which served as a bedside table, knocking over a glass of water and a lamp. I didn't even notice. "Oh, *Florrie*."

"In London I met this guy."

"It's all right, darling, I understand... Have you decided what to do yet?" I burbled incoherently for a moment and all I could think of was *like mother, like daughter.* I gave Florence a quick up-and-down look, feeling guilty that I'd not noticed any changes in her. She looked slim in her tiny jeans, no sign of swelling stomach or breasts yet.

Florence was looking at me with pity. Surely that was wrong? Shouldn't it be the other way round? What was I missing? My head felt as though I'd put it on inside out.

"*Mum.* Just listen for a moment. *I'm not pregnant!* Now, will you stop staring at my boobs and just *listen.* When I was in London I met this guy. Keish and I met him actually—well, we didn't exactly *meet* him, more, we went to see him. He's an agent, y'see, and we'd taken our pictures. Proper pictures, like a kind of portfolio thing and he said—he said he'd take me on. He phoned yesterday. Well, he's shown my photos around and, oh, get *this*, Mum, Models Inc. want to have a look at me in person. Apparently they think I've got what it takes! They've got a branch in York, but you have to come with me to sign things and make sure it's all above board and no one's going to sell me into prostitution or anything like that. But if they want me—*if they do*—they want me to go to Paris and do a show with some of the other new girls. Isn't it *fantastic?*"

"You." I needed the whole monologue again, in little bite-sized chunks. "London?"

"Yes, Mum." Florence had started patting me again as if I had Old Lady syndrome. "Keisha and I went to London to see Jamie. That's his name, Jamie Keene. Not *just* to see him of course. We went to see Lex as well and do stuff. We could have sent pictures but we thought it would be better to go in person." She jumped up and executed a stylish pirouette. "To show him how *stunningly amazing* we were. He said that, you know, he called us stunningly amazing."

"Er." I felt not particularly amazed but certainly completely stunned. "You had pictures?"

"Yes. Jack did mine. Came round one afternoon."

And I'd thought they were my birthday present. How stupid had I been? Why had I never asked?

"Well." I breathed in deeply. "Then I guess even more congratulations are in order."

"You're not cross?" Florence put her head on one side. Her white-blonde hair hung down over half her face. She suddenly looked so like her father that my heart burrowed behind my lungs and hid.

"No. Not really. I mean, I wish you'd told me, but, no. Why should I be cross, really? My daughter, my incredibly *intelligent* daughter has officially been recognised as intelligent *and* beautiful."

Florence smiled at me. It was her father's smile too, slightly crooked. I wondered if, should Florence become a successful model, Flick would see her picture and realise who she was. Come crawling out of the Polish woodwork with an Arts Council award on one arm and a beautiful wife on the other to claim his daughter. Then Alasdair would find out—oh God, something *else* to worry about. I was at saturation point. All it needed was a red telephone bill and I would probably go raving insane.

"Thanks, Mum."

I gave her a grin which owed more to my jaw falling beyond

its lowest point than to humour. "Is your father happy about all this?"

"He's being very supportive," Florence said, diplomatically. "Piers has been great though."

"Piers *knew*?" An unwarranted vision of Piers the last time we'd met, cool and damp with river water, my head on his chest, tracing the pattern of hairs which ran down his lean, flat stomach. Against my will my entire body juddered.

"Yeah, I told him when I got back. He thinks it's really cool."

Duty done, Florrie bounded to her feet and sprang from the room to get on with her packing. I lay back down on the bed, not sure whether to be grateful that at least she wasn't pregnant, or angry that, while her father, stepbrother and best friend had all known what was going on, I'd been told at the eleven-and-a-half-th hour. Why—I searched for a scapegoat— why hadn't *Piers* said something? Bastard. I punched the pillow and it made me feel better, so I did it again. Bastard. *Bastard!* Everything had been okay—punch—until he'd appeared. Wading through that river like—punch—like Mr. Darcy, all wet shirt and sex appeal. Had he no consideration for my hormones? Punch.

I woke up in the middle of the night, disorientated. My much-thumped Piers-substitute was clutched to my chest, and I was tangled in the duvet, sweating in the heat of the oppressive darkness and the sexually charged dream I'd been having. I tried to turn over and go back to sleep, but the dream had kicked my brain into action. It was reluctant to relinquish this opportunity for a little undisturbed activity. My life. The middle-class good-girl upbringing. Until. God, I still blushed to think about it. Blushed all over my body, to remember the arousal, the white-heat of desire that had risen in me like steam from a boiling kettle the first time I'd set eyes on Flick, during my first term at university. My first time away from home. So many firsts. God, I'd adored him. I'd thought it was all right if we were in love. It was all *right*. Until it wasn't. Was suddenly real, and frightening and crying in dark rooms. And the start of the lies.

I lay in the darkness with little pinpricks of light behind my eyes swirling and joining like a dot-to-dot puzzle, a picture becoming clearer by the second. I'd married Alasdair without loving him, attempting to make everything right for my baby. Being someone I wasn't? Was that what I'd tried to do with Leo? Make my life normal, stable. Doing the right thing for the wrong reasons? Then, what had I done with Piers?

Shit. Three a.m. philosophy. Dangerous stuff.

Chapter Thirty-Three

Jace's phone rang and rang. There wasn't even the usual recorded message at the other end. "Where *is* she?" I disconnected then redialled, in case by some fluke I'd called the wrong number. "It's her day off."

Florence had her feet up over the back of the sofa and was lying with her head on the floor, tickling Caspar. "Maybe she's gone to the beach or something."

"She never goes anywhere. Except shopping, and I've been ringing her every half hour since I got up, even *Jace* can't do *that* much shopping."

Florrie shrugged and clapped her bare feet together. Grainger, at the far end of the sofa managing to keep one eye on the kitten while he slept, flicked an ear.

"Go round." She flipped herself up the right way. "Her phone might be buggered. Or she might have had an accident." Ghoulish eyes rolled. "Be lying at the bottom of the stairs calling for help."

I shuddered. "I don't think for one minute that's happened, but I might pop into Webbe's for a bit." It would stop me sitting here jumping every time I heard a car pull up outside. "If she's not there, I'll go to her place."

"'Kay."

"Florence..." I had to phrase my words very carefully. A hint of criticism could ruin the new mother/daughter *entente cordiale* which we seemed to be enjoying, "...the whole modelling thing. Why didn't you tell me?"

She looked at me seriously and I found it hard to return her gaze. Guilt, I suppose. "Well, to start with I didn't think it would happen." Eyes dropped, she returned to teasing the kitten. "I thought it would be stupid to get you all wound up over something which could just have been me dreaming. And you've always been so keen for me to get on in life, get qualifications. Mum, I don't even know what I want to *do* yet. I know that really it's only because of what happened to you, and I'm grateful Mum, I really am, that you gave up school and everything to have me, but—"

"But you're not me."

"Um. Yes. I think that's it, really. You're not mad—*angry*, I mean? Truthfully?"

Angry? Me? That my bright, lovely daughter was going into a profession which seemed designed to turn girls into coke-sniffing clones of one another, burnt out by twenty and too thin to stand?

"No. I'm a bit *hurt* that you told Piers before you told me though. And your father," I added hastily. Didn't want her to even suspect that I'd so much as *thought* about Piers in the last twenty-four hours.

"Piers did tell me to tell you. Kind of threatened that he'd do it if I didn't. But he told me to pick the right time and go for it, not to lose my nerve and back out."

"Yes, picking his moment, that's Piers," I said without thinking. Well, without thinking of anything but that moment he'd picked, under the tree, that kiss, with our hair tangling together in the breeze. God, Alys, stop it.

"Er, yes."

We stood silently for a moment. Caspar rubbed his newly

darkening ears against my leg and Grainger wrapped a paw over his own eyes to block out the sight.

"I just want you to be happy," I whispered.

"Aww, *Mum*. Don't get soppy! I am happy. I always do what makes me happy, don't I? And I want *you* to be happy too. Leo seems like a really nice guy, not the kind to sleep his way through your friends or beat you up after a few drinks. You'll make a cool couple."

"I think I need to talk to you about that." I grabbed my bag and headed out to catch the bus to the bookshop. "But it'll have to be later."

Standing at the bus stop, I heard a car come growling past, throaty exhaust rumbling just like the Porsche. Stop it. Now that I'd managed to admit to myself that Leo had been symptomatic of my urge to force my life along unnatural lines, Piers hung heavy in my mind. God, he was gorgeous, fabulous in bed and he said he loved me, but... Hadn't I been here before? Letting one man go and simply moving on to the next?

I wished Mrs. Treadgold was here. This sort of emotional angst would have been right up her alley. I could almost hear her top set clattering with advice.

Webbe's was open. I pushed the door to the tinny clacking of the disabled bell and found Simon himself manning the till, selling a cache of Asimovs to a young man with a guitar strapped on his back.

"Alys." Simon jumped, dropping the young man's change all over the counter. "I thought you were in Devon for the next few days."

"Change of plan. I didn't know you could work the till."

"Sarcasm, Alys." Simon tutted and shook his head. "So, what brings you in here on such a beautiful day?"

"Looking for Jace. Do you know where she is?"

A rather furtive expression crossed Simon's well-formed features. It looked as alien on him as a nylon suit.

I sat down heavily on the stool. "*What* is going on? Am I phasing in and out of existence, or is there some conspiracy deliberately not to tell me things?"

Simon stared at me. The secretive expression was leaving, to be replaced by something which, if he hadn't been so impeccably well brought up, I would have said was shame. "Well...er...I...Jacinta and I...we..."

Behind me the door rattled. I glanced towards it and my heart did a peculiar thing. It felt as though it tried to do the drop of dread, but was counteracted by a desire to become rather unnecessarily floaty and ended up by beating faster. "Great. Hello, Piers. Come and join my set of People Who Like to Keep Things from Me. I've nearly got enough to trade up to Total Paranoia."

"We need to talk."

"As a general premise, yes, we do need to talk. As a specific—too late, Piers. Just too bloody *late*." I collapsed my head into my hands.

I felt an arm come round my shoulders and tried to shrug it off, assuming it was Piers, but it was Simon. "Alys, why don't you go home? You've been under a lot of stress lately. I think I can allow you some compassionate leave."

"Where's Jace?" I raised my head.

"Alys."

Piers again. I glanced up and our eyes met over the top of Simon's head. Piers looked rough, which was unusual. He normally cultivated the appearance of a man who hasn't had time to shave and has been too busy debauching to brush his hair, but managed it whilst looking otherwise impeccable. But now he looked like a man who's been up all night and, if he's slept at all, has done it in the clothes he's currently walking around in.

To Simon's intensely visible relief a customer presented through the door, followed by a family of confused Japanese tourists. Piers and I found ourselves standing outside the door. I felt as though my head had been taken off, rotated three hundred and sixty degrees, and then replaced.

"Where's Jace?" I asked him.

"How the fuck would I know? Look, I don't know anything any more. I'm, like, kinda drifting here. I can't sleep, can't eat. I need to see you."

"Ta da."

"No." Piers caught me by the elbow and propelled me backwards into the alleyway which ran between two buildings and around the back of Webbe's. The street noises died and were replaced by the smell of dustbins and the sound of a lone toilet flushing. "What I said, yesterday. It wasn't a cheap line just to get to you. I love you. Meant it then, mean it now."

"You took advantage of me, Piers. You gave me bad news and then hit me with—with all that stuff."

"I happen to know that Mrs. T would have approved of 'all that stuff' as you put it. And we're not talking about that shit, Alys, we're talking about *us*. About you and me."

He'd got me cornered where two walls met, my back against brickwork and a cheap plastic bin preventing any kind of sideways escape. "Piers—"

"I *know* you, Alys. All the crap, all the shit and I *still* love you. I've been waiting so long. You're thinking this is all to get a fuck, but remember that night? The party? I carried you to the taxi, took you home. I never touched you. I could have done it there, then, on the bed. You were out of it, you wouldn't have known. *But I didn't.* I stayed with you, Alys, watched you all night, never laid a hand on you, because—do you know what?" His face was very close to mine. I could smell the smoke in his

253

hair. I shook my head. "I wanted you to want it too. And yesterday you wanted it. You screamed for me, Alys, and don't try telling me you didn't." He touched my face. "Y'see Alys, what it is."

Now he was almost whispering. I had to bend in closer to hear him. "I don't think you know how love is meant to feel. You don't know it because you never felt it. And now, what you feel for me—sssshhh." He put a finger over my mouth as I opened it to contradict. "It's kinda burning, just here." He laid his other hand over my heart. "That's it. That's love. That wanting, *so bad*, to be touched and kept safe and to lose yourself. *That* is love, Alys, not just liking the way someone is, but *knowing* who they are and not giving a shit." He took his finger away from my mouth. "And this is the part where you kiss me."

"You reckon?"

"Yeah. I reckon."

"You're a cocky bastard, aren't you?"

"Uh huh."

Chapter Thirty-Four

I sat silent next to Piers as he drove towards Thirsk, the big engine making mincemeat of the miles. "You could have told me *earlier* that Alasdair wanted to talk to me," I said, peevishly. "What about? Is it Florrie's going modelling?"

"Dunno. We had a kinda big family-discussion thing. Ma and Alasdair were asking me what my plans were. Was I still looking to move into my own place. They both seem to think it's time I moved on. Guess they're right. I can work anywhere after all."

"Oh yeah. Your translation stuff." Piers had worked for the last three years as a freelance English/Spanish translator. A remarkably respectable job, considering that he looked as though he spent all day wafting about the streets dressed like a breakaway faction from an historical drama. It was a complete waste of those immaculate cheekbones.

His hand brushed mine as he changed gear. "I know you're confused," he said softly. "Trust me, I'm at least *twice* as confused. I kinda thought, y'know, I'd grow out of it. Fantasy older-woman thing, yeah? But it seemed the more I knew you, the closer we got, that everything before was kinda like *practicing*. I talked to Jace a lot too. She reckons you got it bad for me, you just don't see it yet. She thinks we're made for each other. Now, me, I really *know* it."

"But you're too young to have any idea what you want."

"Hey, Alys? I've been having sex since I was fourteen. All kinds of women, old, young, some I paid, some seduced me, some I thought I loved. And I can tell you this. *Not one* of them made me feel the way you do. Yeah, I've had sex that ripped my mind apart, had women I could relate to, feel for. But I've never had both things with one person."

"And you do with me? Really? Sex that ripped your mind apart? With *me*?"

Without taking his eyes off the road, Piers reached over and ran his hand down the side of my face. "Yeah. With you. It was real. Special. Couldn't you tell?"

"I don't know. You always seem pretty ripped to me."

"Ha."

"Ah, Alys. Nice of you to come over." Alasdair met us outside the house in the tarmac-turning circle the size of a tennis court. "Piers, your mother is upstairs resting. Would you go and ask her if she'd like some tea?"

I hadn't seen him for about three years so, as soon as Piers had galloped off up the lengthy flight of stairs, I gave Alasdair a thorough, if covert, examination. If it was possible, he looked even *more* professorial than he ever had. I'd take bets that at least one of his wardrobes now contained a tweed jacket with patched elbows. His thinning sandy hair had thinned even further and was showing a few touches of grey, his six-foot-plus frame was filling out around the middle and he was *wearing slippers*. He looked scarily clichéd, top professor married to American wife. I half expected to see a Stars and Stripes festooning the wall inside the front door, but there was nothing more controversial than family photographs.

"Feel a bit guilty that we haven't had you over for a while," Alasdair was saying, being every inch the good host. "But, you know how things are. Anyway. Thought we ought to have a chat."

The only *possible* reason I could come up with for Alasdair suddenly wanting a face-to-face talk was opposition to Florrie's career decision, which instantly made me want to back her to the hilt. Either that or—I was glad he was leading the way as we walked through the monument to good taste which was their beech-floored, hint-of-grey emulsioned hall, because I flushed at the thought. Maybe he'd found out about Piers and me. Although, how could he? Unless Piers had talked, and I really couldn't envisage Piers saying anything along the lines of "your ex-wife, shags like a stoat, doesn't she?" After all, that really *was* all that had happened, wasn't it? We'd had a damn good session of pure *sex*. I had another one of my sudden visions. Piers naked. His slim body, hair streaming over his shoulders, huge dark eyes nailing me to the earth beneath.

"Are you all right? You look a bit flushed." Alasdair paused in a doorway. "Touch of the sun?"

"Oh yes," I said emphatically, then muttered, "just don't ask *whose*," passing him to enter a room lit by enormous windows hung with floor-length velvet curtains, studded with soft couches and chairs and carpeted a smooth beige. It looked like a tasteful padded cell.

"Sit down. Tea? Coffee?"

"Tea. Thank you." As Alasdair left the room, I wandered around like Goldilocks until I found a chair to sit in. The place was *immaculate*.

"I'm sorry to drag you all the way over here." Alasdair entered by another door, at the far side of the room. "Shouldn't think Piers minded bringing you, did he?"

"What are you getting at?" Defensive again. Guilt did that to me.

"Oh, nothing. He's a good chap. At heart. Bit of a prick sometimes but he's sensible. Mature. Turned out very well."

Absolutely nothing I could say to that. Agreement might confirm suspicions, denial would have been wrong since it all sounded true.

"Anyway." Alasdair poured tea, putting two sugars in mine out of habit. I didn't tell him I hadn't taken sugar for five years. "Thought this was best done face-to-face as it were. A bit sensitive, you see."

Oh God. I felt myself blush again. He did know. He was about to warn me off Piers. Having done the advert for his stepson's charms he was going to tell me that they should be used on someone nearer his own age.

"Thought if *I* told *you* then *you* could pass it on to *Florence*. Sound better coming from you."

"What?"

"Tamar. She—er—*we*, that is, we are expecting a baby. Early days yet, of course, but things are going well, so about February we're told."

My first thought was "you brought me all the way here to tell me *that*?" closely followed by "but that's impossible".

"So if you break it to Florrie. Not that it's going to affect anything of course. Still be welcome here anytime, obviously. But things might be a bit, well, *different*, what with Piers moving out. You look stunned, Alys."

Piers had made it sound as though the results of Alasdair's tests had made him marginally less fertile than Death Valley. "I was thinking. We tried for so long with nothing happening." Couldn't give away the fact that I knew about his infertility, not without some awkward questions. Questions which, if she ever came to international attention, were going to have to be addressed. If Flick ever read anything these days other than *Art House Monthly*.

Alasdair had the grace to look a bit shamefaced. "Promise me this won't go *any* further?" He dropped his voice and raised his eyes as though Tamar might have suspended herself above his head specifically to prevent any such confidences. "*We* tried, Tamar and I, for several years. Eventually, well, they couldn't find anything wrong."

Liar, I thought, and gave an inward grin.

"But we tried a few cycles of IVF, nothing doing. Tamar was getting so het up about it all. Then we had a shot at AIDS, and bingo. So here we are."

"AIDS? That sounds a bit drastic."

"Er, no. It's A.I.D.S. actually. Um." Alasdair was looking extremely uncomfortable, so I just looked at him over the top of my teacup. We might have been apart for a lot of years but I could still tell when he was trying to work up to something. "Artificial Insemination by Donor Sperm," he said eventually, when it became clear that I wasn't going to help him out by asking.

"So *technically* Tamar is carrying someone else's baby?" I gave a cough. "Alasdair." It was no good. I was going to have to tell him. My heart was thrumming like a turbine. There was absolutely *never* going to be another opportunity like this. My head went a bit swimmy as I tried to work out my approach.

"It doesn't matter, not a jot. Not to me, not to her. It's *our* baby, that's what counts, whoever else had input. Like with Florence. I'll be there at the birth, changing nappies, all that kind of thing. The genetic father doesn't count, he's just so much DNA."

I stared at him. "You *knew*?" An enormous gulp of tea, which I'd been unable to stop halfway down my throat, sidelonged itself into my windpipe and I choked. Tea came out of my nose and my eyes streamed, but it was a useful diversion, stopped me having to look at Alasdair's face.

"Knew?" His face swam into focus gradually as my eyes settled down. Very blue eyes Alasdair had, with such fair lashes that they were almost indiscernible, giving him the startled, bald look of a new baby. "About Florence? Oh yes, Alys, of course I knew." Gently he patted me on the back until I could take a gasp of air. "You weren't invisible, you know. You and that arty chap." Reassured that I wasn't going to cause a permanent stain on the noncommittal flooring, he stopped patting and sat down again. "When Florrie was born, well, then I *knew*. Didn't know if you did though, oddly enough. You always seemed so certain that she was mine."

Miserably I looked down into my tea.

"Time she got to be about oh, two or three I should think, she looked so much like him. All that blonde hair. Sam used to fancy him terribly, remember?"

Sam was Alasdair's best friend. I'd always liked him. "How *is* Sam these days?" I tried to change the subject.

"Fine. Looking forward to being a godfather."

"He *does* know that godfathers are supposed to be upright, moral citizens?" Sam, who had about as many morals as the average ten-men-in-a-bed participant.

"He's doing his best."

My hands were shaking.

"I know this wasn't a good time to spring it on you but...I thought it would be best if we cleared things up between us. Florrie might not be my natural daughter, but I was there, wasn't I, when you were sick every morning for the first four months, when you had those cramps, when you couldn't face anything but raspberries for weeks? I was there when she was born. Just as I'm going to be this time. So, what I wanted to say was—I don't mind if you never tell her the truth. As far as I'm concerned, I'm her father."

I had a sudden memory of Flick, standing at the doorway to his van, holding it shut behind him so that I couldn't see past, while I tried to tell him I was having his baby. What would I have seen if I'd been able to? Another half-finished canvas dripping paint in the weak March sun? Or another woman, sprawled across his divan, awaiting his attentions? He'd been irresistible, Flick, and I'd not been the only person to find him so.

"As far as I'm concerned, you are too. Oh, and congratulations." I meant it.

"Thank you."

"How's Tamar?"

"Not too bad. Still a bit sickly. Otherwise she's blooming. It's Piers we're most worried about. He's been a bit—"

"Hard." Whoops. "I mean, he must be taking it hard. Moving out and all that." I think I got away with it, because Alasdair never even flinched.

"Oh, he's decided to go back to the Argentine, work out there for a bit. He's got dual nationality so there's nothing to stop him. He's been so terribly restless these last few days. Wondered if you might have a word with him. His mother will miss him if he goes."

"Me?" I squeaked. "Why should he listen to *me?*"

"Oh, come on, Alys. You can't tell me you've never noticed that Piers has the most almighty crush on you! If you told him to go and live in the Sahara, he'd buy a camel tomorrow."

"Crush? Has he?" My voice had gone very small. How did I feel about the prospect of him leaving the country?

"Good Lord, yes. Has done for years. No wonder he's confused with the girls he goes out with. Maybe you could have a quiet word with him about that too. You know, point him in the right direction?"

"I'm not sure he needs any help with that," I muttered weakly. "I'll go and find him, shall I?"

"Oh, no need, he'll have gone up to his flat. You know the

way, I believe? Oh, and Alys—"

"Mmmmm?" I was thinking, *Please don't make me go into his flat. Please. Things might happen. You know, things... Things I had determined to myself would never happen again. Couldn't. Shouldn't. Ought not to—*

"I admire you. Turning down the money that I offered. I realise now that you were doing it from the most honourable of reasons. I had thought that you were being typically stubborn, all that 'I can do it alone' sort of thing, which is why I used to overindulge Florrie a little. But now I see it was because you *did* know and I think it was jolly decent of you. Misguided, but decent."

"And you're not worried about her modelling?"

"Goodness, no. What is it Piers says? Ah yes, 'If you've got it, flaunt it.' I am certainly prepared to give her the help she needs to get her career underway, and if it fails...at least she'll have stories to tell her grandchildren."

Well. Marriage to Tamar had certainly loosened Alasdair up a bit. In fact, he was so loose he was nearly unravelled. I made my way up the stairs which led to Piers's flat, thinking that if Florence carried on modelling wearing the tiny little clothes she had been, she'd probably have grandchildren before she was thirty.

Chapter Thirty-Five

On reaching his front door, I found myself physically incapable of knocking. Only Alasdair standing behind me stopped me from running. I couldn't do this. Piers deserved— Piers *needed* someone, someone better than me, someone who wanted him, loved him for himself. Not as a rebound.

When he opened the door at Alasdair's knock, I nearly turned and flung myself down the stairs. "Go on, Alys. Piers won't mind you going in," Alasdair encouraged.

I followed Piers inside, not knowing what to say. He draped himself over a chair and waved an arm to indicate that I should do the same, but I didn't have half his style and settled for perching rather awkwardly, hands between knees, searching for a conversational topic that wouldn't *and couldn't* be thought of as sexual. "I wonder where Jace is."

"Maybe it's something, y' know, private."

"If you mention the words 'women's trouble', I swear I'll swing for you." God, I needed a drink. There were far too many unspoken emotions around in this room.

"Hey, I'm a New Man, just had twenty minutes of Ma telling me how her boobs are too big to let her get into a size eight. You want vodka?" The grin he slid my way was as warm and crisp as new toast. "Or are we still pretending that yesterday didn't happen?"

"I don't want a drink. When I drink with you I end up with a killer hangover."

"Yeah. Ever wonder why that is?" Piers hauled himself up, flipping to his feet with a twang of muscle tone. "D'you reckon it's because the only time you can really relax, really let yourself go, is with me?"

"I reckon," I called after him as he went into the see-through kitchen and fetched drinks from the walk-in chiller cabinet with the transparent door and mirrored back, "that it's because you don't know when to stop and you drag me down with you."

"That's not dragging, that's pulling." He came back carrying a tray of assorted alcohol in bottles, little pearls of condensation beading the sides like 1920's cocktail dresses. My mouth watered as he handed me a frosted glass filled with liquid and lemon slices. "Consider yourself pulled."

"Cheesy, Piers, very cheesy." But it tasted good and the relaxation was welcome. "Do they teach you chat-up lines like that at those expensive schools you went to?"

"All my own work, Ally, all my own work."

Dusk came slanting down across the gardens. The phone rang and Piers answered it, while I suppressed a smile at the thought of the damage a toddler would do to those beautifully coiffed acres. Well, I wouldn't have been human if I couldn't have indulged in a few moments of Schadenfreude on behalf of Alasdair and Tamar. A perfect couple with a perfect lifestyle which cried out for an injection of chaos. I stared at Piers while he chatted, draping himself ornamentally against the worktop. I didn't know what was going to happen. I didn't even know what I wanted to happen.

"Fuck." Piers hung up the phone. "Work. Sorry, Ally. Didn't mean to ignore you."

"Don't worry about it." I helped myself to another tumbler

of the slightly yellow alcohol. Didn't know what it was, it tasted of melons and grapes, passion fruit and papaya. Surely anything with that much fruit in it *had* to be good for me?

"It's an on-site translation job, some contacts of Alasdair's, wanting me up in Aberdeen for a coupla days. Got some guys from Barcelona coming by." Piers rotated his shoulders backwards, easing cramped muscles and causing more than a little fluttering in my stomach, although I was carefully keeping at least a hand-knotted Kilim rug's distance between us. "Sorry. Won't bore you with it any more..."

"It's okay." My tongue seemed too big for my mouth.

"Nah. Rather talk to you, yeah?" And then, there he was, standing beside me as the room grew darker, neither of us making a move to switch on any lights as though anything which happened in the shadows didn't really count. "Ally."

"Don't. Piers, it's not fair. You and me."

"What's this 'not fair'? Huh, Ally? We're made for each other, babe."

"I can't do it. Don't you see, Piers, I'm just repeating what happened before, with Flick and Alasdair—one guy out, one guy in."

Piers looked at me long and steady. "You've given the guy the push? Leo? Whoa, Ally, this is serious stuff. Why didn't you tell me?"

"Because you're involved. Things were so much easier when we were just friends. Then I could offload onto you, tell you my problems without worrying that you'd—" I stopped myself.

"That I'd? Oh, I get it. You reckon I'd take advantage? Hey, sweetie—" Piers came closer, brushed a fingertip over the tears that fell. "Love doesn't take advantage."

"Piers—" I put one hand on his shoulder, pushed slightly so that he stepped back. "I've lost Mrs. Treadgold. Now I've lost you. I need a friend right now, that's all. I don't want to do it

265

again, jump from one guy to another, even when—"

He smiled. His eyes possessed my face, absorbed me. "Even when you know you want to?" he asked, gently. "Even when you want more?" His tongue moved on the side of my neck, rippled its way down as his hands travelled up under my shirt. "When this is the grand passion you've always wanted, and you're going to turn it away because you reckon you're on the rebound?" The silver on his fingers rolled against my skin, cool on my nipples. "You are so fucking screwed-up, Ally."

I gave a sigh, my body hanging in his hands. "Tonight, because I want—I want to feel. And then—then it's over."

Piers bent over me. Dark hair tingled on my flesh, his mouth dipping, licking. "You can say that now, Alys," he whispered, accent much more pronounced when he spoke softly. "But feeling isn't *here*," and a light finger traced down over my stomach, "it's in *here*." The gentlest of touches on my forehead. "It doesn't stop just because you think it should."

Well, what can I say? It was a night of all the most delicious things in life rolled into one glorious, duvet-twisting, sweat-sliding, panting, wanton lubriciousness. It was black velvet, silk lace, cream, chocolate, strawberries, sunshine, dead of night, summer rain and blasting thunderstorms. It was—oh, add your own ideas of pure, ecstatic abandonment. It was all that. And then he brought out the big guns, fired the twin barrels of tenderness and concern to hit me direct in the heart. Whispered beauty, romance and love to me in the dark as we lay drying our heat in the cool night air, arms, bodies, mouths entwined.

"Just tonight, Piers"—I found myself repeating like a mantra which would save my soul—"just tonight."

"Don't cry, Ally."

"Just tonight."

"Yeah."

Chapter Thirty-Six

I lay on my bed, alone in my flat. Alasdair had taken Florrie shopping for the new wardrobe she'd need to rise like a sun into her future while I lay with my head under a pillow and a cat purring behind my knees, listening to the phone ring.

Was this madness? I felt heavy, so terribly heavy. My whole body wanted to sink right down through the mattress, through the flat below and on down into the earth. The effort of breathing, of raising and lowering my rib cage was so taxing that I wanted it to stop.

The pain was sharp. Focussed under my chest but above my stomach, like an ulcer, like some internal parasitic thing gnawing away at me. A nasty alien feeling which stopped me from thinking, simply absorbed me into the hugeness of itself. The phone rang. Stopped. Rang again. I didn't care.

I must have slept. When I opened my eyes, the sun had dropped away from my window, Caspar had moved from my legs and was curled with his tail over his nose. Grainger was crouching beside my head like a malignant Florence Nightingale with a personal hygiene problem, staring at me as though my face had become char-grilled tuna. "Wha'?" I muttered, and the whole of last night crept up and hit me round the head. "Oh. Shit."

Grainger continued the cat hypnotism. Caspar stretched out his dark socks and arched his back but didn't wake. Taking to my bed in the throes of misery was all very well, but it wasn't terribly practical. At least with sleep the sore feeling around my heart had been anaesthetised to a dull ache. I could almost forget about it. I tried to hasten the healing by not letting myself even attempt to pick at the scab. Instead I got on a bus and headed for work.

"Alys." Simon was outside, kicking next-door's pavement sign unobtrusively until it was level with their window rather than ours. "I wasn't expecting—"

"Ah, no one expects the Spanish Inquisition." I slid past him and in through the door.

"I'm not saying any more about Jacinta." Simon followed me, already on the defensive.

"It's a quote, Simon. *Monty Python.* Surreal humour. You know what humour is, don't you?"

Simon eyed me askance. "Yes. It's the third section down over there, under ghost stories."

"Hurrah. Another expensive education that wasn't wasted. What *are* you doing?"

Simon was sidling along in front of me now, looking furtive in a gangling, upper-class way. "Er. Nothing. No, nothing. Umm. Alys, could you pop out and get me a sandwich please?"

"Pop *out*? I've only just got here. And it's hardly 'popping' distance, is it? The nearest sandwich shop is in the middle of town, a good twenty minute round walk given the crowds."

"Thank you. Chicken salad, if you would." Simon shoved a fiver into my hand and rushed behind the till, leaving me standing in the shop doorway fondling his money and feeling bewildered. What the *hell* was going on?

As luck would have it, at least on my part, a travelling sandwich vendor had set up shop at the end of the road, and I was able to buy a surprisingly fresh-looking chicken sandwich and be back at the shop within ten minutes. No one appeared to be behind the counter.

I heard Simon's shout of "just a minute" come from behind the curtain and, presuming he was deep in accounts, wandered to the back of the shop, sandwich held out like a peace offering.

"I've got your..." I flung back the curtain and caught Jacinta and Simon frozen into almost-cartoon attitudes of shock. "I...oh gosh...I..." Hastily I wheeled the curtain closed again, leaning against the counter and clutching the sandwiches to my chest rather tighter than they could accommodate. There were sounds of flusterment in the cubbyhole, then Jacinta appeared from the neck up.

"We are sorry, Alys. We did not wish you to find out this way."

Well, it explained a lot. It explained almost *everything.* "But why the secrecy?" I stammered. "It's not something to be ashamed of, is it?"

More of Jacinta appeared. She'd removed the wig but still had on the jacket and trousers, and the makeup made her eyes slant and difficult to read. "Well."

Now Simon's head joined hers. He too had removed his wig. "Not everyone understands you see, Alys. That's why we have to be so circumspect. And we hadn't had chance to talk to you about it."

The curtain was now pulled back totally. I swallowed. It was tough enough to accept that my coworkers were dressed up as members of the *Star Trek* crew. The fact that *she* was dressed as Mr. Spock and *he* as Lieutenant Uhura made it harder still. "Everyone needs a hobby," I said weakly, mayonnaise dripping down my bosom. "Do you go out dressed like this?"

"Weekends there are conventions. There is one next weekend, in Whitby," Jacinta explained. "We are trying new costumes. This is why we must be here."

"And when you'd vanished?" Now I knew what had been in the squashy parcel. I tried not to think of the ears.

"I was at a conference in Hull. We—Simon and I—wish to start our own convention. We are thinking here, at the shop."

Although I tried to avert my eyes, I couldn't help but glance at Simon, his real hair held back in a net, his miniskirt and tights. "Lovely," I said. "You look very nice."

Simon smoothed his skirt down. "Do you think so? I do feel a bit strange. I must admit, I'm not usually Uhura but these were the only costumes left this time." I breathed out a tiny puff of relief. "No, I'm usually Counsellor Troi."

"Why don't you go over to Jace's, perfect your outfits, and I'll mind the shop? You've got a ladder in your tights, by the way."

I was sure one of them said, "Beam me up, Scotty," but thankfully I couldn't tell which one.

The rest of the day passed in speculation and the occasional sale, then I travelled home, cooked myself something from my enormous freezer collection of loose unidentifiable objects frozen into frostbitten fists and checked my phone messages.

"Hey." My stomach clenched then relaxed to the point where I feared for my bowels. "I don't really know what to say here. Guess it's better this way, leaving a message than talking to you direct—shit." The message was abruptly severed then restarted as a new one. "Alys. Look. This is the thing here, right? I know you think you don't want this, me, that you think it's a better thing to be alone than repeat past mistakes, that you reckon I—shit, I don't know *what* you think of me! Stupid, huh? And, yeah, okay, I'm just this crazy young guy with more money than sense and no fashion, but—look—I love you. I want you. I know I can make it right."

The message reached the end of its available length, but

immediately started again. "Yeah, I *know* I can. *We* can make it work. So. Look. I'm going to the Argentine, day after tomorrow, flying out at three. Decided to see if I can live out there again. I've got to tie up a bit of business, work for some of Alasdair's people, but. Yeah. I'll come by before I fly out. Morning, 'bout ten. I'd really like you to come with. Meet my pa, he'll think you're cute, have a couple weeks lying in the sun, chilling. Us, together. Take it from there. Maybe you could finally get to write that book you were talking about. But, hey, no commitment. See, I *know* it's more than just the sex with us." There was a broken quality to his voice, as though he either was, or had been, crying. "I've got your ticket. Grab your passport, take care of the cats. We can sort everything else when we get there. If you come. I'll..."

"You have no more messages."

I listened twice more, with my heart almost drowning out the sound of his voice. Piers had always had a nice voice, the way his vowels dropped occasionally from mid-Atlantic to pure, rounded full-on American; his phraseology which always sounded as though it had been lifted wholesale from a Douglas Coupland novel. And his body—lean and tight, as though his bones were shrink-wrapped in his flesh. And the way he held me, just *so*, as though I was precious and wonderful...

I sliced a few tears away from my cheeks and sniffed heartily. Yes, it was great, yes it was wonderful, but it didn't get toilets scrubbed, did it? I turned the radio up loud to drown out my thoughts and, accompanied by both the cats who clearly thought I'd gone mad, I began to clean the bathroom.

Chapter Thirty-Seven

Next morning I was up before Florence had even begun her morning closed-eye moan routine. She'd come in last night laden with shopping and informed me that the York Models Inc. wanted to see her "the day after tomorrow, nine o' clock sharp. Bet they're testing to make sure I can be out of bed at that time, don't you reckon? We can be there by nine easy, can't we? Mum?"

Oh yes, I'd assured her. We could be there by nine.

And Piers was coming by at ten.

Leaving at three.

So of course I couldn't see him. Could I. Florence came first.

Didn't she.

I looked around the shop as I unlocked the door. Simon and Jace, obviously glad that their secret was now out, had left me a message—they'd gone to see someone about possibly using the shop as a Sci-Fi convention point, and were sure I wouldn't mind. Mind? Me? I looked around Webbe's, which had the approximate internal floor space of a cheap fridge and wondered where everyone would fit if they had meetings here. The last time we'd had a visiting author, we'd had people sitting in the yard. Oh well, they'd obviously thought about it. As long as no one came dressed as Godzilla, we'd probably get by.

Then I sat by the phone. So. How did I do this? How did I play it? Cool—all yeah it was great but it's over, get a life? Emotional—I really care about you, but, well, the age gap? Or truthful—I just want to see you one last time to say goodbye?

There was only one person in, an elderly man in a damp raincoat, flipping through some old maps, and when he left, I rushed over to the door, locked it and put the closed sign up. Some things shouldn't be interrupted. Dialled his mobile. No pickup, but thank God for voicemail.

"Piers, hi. It's me. Alys. Well, you knew that but. Anyway. It's me. Um." So far, so good. Now, what was it I wanted to say? Oh yes, that no way would I be going to Argentina with him. Have a nice life without me. Catch you on the flip side. And other such jocular, disposable remarks. I cleared my throat. "Look, I can't..." Then my voice kind of took on a life of its own, one I swear my brain had nothing to do with. "It's not fair. How can you ask me to go away with you like that? You *know* how it is for me, and you make me feel—something, I don't know—and I wanted—and I still want... But you—you—anyway, I'd miss the funeral."

Bugger. That hadn't gone as well as I'd hoped. Perhaps I could erase the message? I dialled Piers's mobile again and was horrified when this time it was answered on the third ring.

"Hi there." Didn't sound at all like Piers. Sounded, in fact, *female.*

"Tamar?" Oh God, my voice sounded horribly weak. "Is that you?"

"Alys?" There were so many unspoken questions hanging in her voice that I was surprised her voice box didn't break down. "Why?"

"Oh, Florence asked me to ring to ask Piers if he'd seen her white shoes." Pathetic, Alys, just pathetic. "How are you?"

"Puking like a goddamn dog," she answered, most

273

unTamarlike. "Feel like shit. And Piers goes to Aberdeen and leaves his phone behind. Don't know what he was thinking, I reminded him. D'you know what he said? He said that anything anyone wanted to say, could wait until he saw them. Well, that's just great, there he is in Bonny Scotland, and his phone keeps ringing while I'm chucking."

"You could always turn it off. Oh, ginger biscuits always worked for me when I was throwing up."

"Ginger..." Her voice trailed away and the phone went dead. I smiled down the receiver, ashamed of myself for the tingle of glee I felt at perfect, impeccable Tamar being continually overcome with the urge to vomit. But bloody, *bloody* Piers leaving his phone when I needed, wanted, *ought* to get in touch.

I piled back home to the cold shoulder from Grainger and a trail of clothes which led from Florrie's room to the door and meant she'd probably gone out for the evening to spread the good news about her modelling among her friends. Knowing the friendship levels of teenage girls, I hoped she wasn't expecting them to be delighted for her.

I slouched around, picked myself an outfit to wear to the model agency tomorrow, something which made me look reasonable and would not provoke people into asking where I thought Florrie got her looks from. It was ten o'clock now. Twelve hours until Piers came floating by expecting...what? Me to go with him? Seriously, would he expect that? Or would he be realistic, hoping for a peck on the cheek and no hard feelings? How would he feel when I wasn't even here?

Was it too late for Florence to cancel her meeting? Tell them someone—some*thing* had come up for her mother? But that wouldn't exactly give them the impression that she was a committed career girl, would it? Oh God. Seventeen hours until he left the country. And I couldn't even reach him to explain. And Florence needed me.

Chapter Thirty-Eight

Twenty to ten. Florence and I were still sitting outside an office. She was reading *Vogue* and I was visibly twitching. Not that I was going back of course. Piers could leave without seeing me. *Twenty minutes and he'd be gone.*

"Mum." Florrie laid *Vogue* down, reverentially. "You know Tamar and Dad? And the baby?"

"Yes," I said cautiously. Florrie had taken the news suspiciously quietly. "What about it?"

"I've been thinking. I mean, I love Piers and everything, but he's not my real brother, thank God. Jeez, the way he's been lately, I'd hate to be related—"

I restrained myself from snapping "what do you mean" only by biting my lip. I'd not even considered how Florrie would have reacted to Piers and I. Not that I needed to worry about that. Now it was over.

"I think it'll be really great to have a proper brother or a sister." She looked at me shrewdly. "One that doesn't fancy my mother."

I developed a sudden, and incredibly intense, interest in the magazines.

Ten minutes.

The door opened at last and a pretty dark-haired girl and over-made-up mother were ushered out. Florrie and I looked at one another, raised our eyebrows and entered. Sat on plush chairs. Florrie and the woman behind the desk talked. I fidgeted.

At five to ten, I snapped. "Look, can I just sign the papers please?" Florence and the woman stared at me. "You like Florence, she likes you, you're obviously not recruiting for the white-slave trade or child-labour market. Can I sign what I have to and go?"

More staring, then the immaculate woman with her shiny hair and taut face smiled. "I admire that," she said. I looked down at myself in case she was talking about my skirt or bag. "No, I really admire your forthrightness. It's refreshing. Most parents are so obsequious, so, like, please take our daughter on, have our house, we'll sell you our kids, just let our daughter be a model."

"Can I sign then?" *Four minutes.*

Leaving an astonished Florence and an admiring agent, I fled through the front doors into a taxi and snapped out my address. It might work. Piers might have got held up in the traffic. He might have been late getting back. *Why* was I so desperate to see him this one last time?

We arrived at the flat and I propelled myself out onto the kerb, hearing, as the taxi pulled away, the unmistakeable sound of the Porsche's big growly engine changing down to hit the main road at the other end of the street.

"Piers!" I screamed at the top of my voice, pointlessly I knew, and set off at Olympic standard down the road. "Piers, wait!" I reached the junction just in time to see the yellow car make the tight turn at the lights and disappear off into the thinning traffic under the walls, exhaust blarting and engine shrieking. I could make out Piers, hair flung back by the wind, wraparound shades on as I panted to a stop outside the newsagents.

There was absolutely nothing I could do. I limped back indoors and stood at the window. Maybe I should phone him? And say what? Sorry I missed you. Goodbye? If he'd picked up my voicemail, he'd assume I didn't want to see him again anyway. Wouldn't he? I mean, the message had been clear enough if a little rambling, hadn't it?

Oh bugger it. Bugger everything. Bugger, bugger, bugger.

Surely it was just frustration which brought the tears to my eyes. Only the irony of the situation which made me snatch up Caspar from his comfortable position in front of the food bowls. Merely anger at my own weakness which sent me into the quietest room in the house to sit on the toilet seat, weeping from somewhere deep inside my chest and hiding my face in the soft kitten fur.

I felt ragged inside. As though some vital, elemental part of myself had been dragged out through my chest and left me with a gaping hole where something had been. The feeling was familiar. The last night with Piers. I'd cried like this, then. The same feeling of loss, when I'd told him that I couldn't see him again, that we could never love like this again. Only that time, he'd been there holding me. I could pretend that the words meant nothing. Even as I said them he'd kissed them away.

I'd lost him. Lost the feeling that he gave me, the feeling that I could stretch up and touch the sky, grab great handfuls of it. I wanted that feeling again. Not to be tied into a life which was stable and safe, but to be free to have a life which was scary and edgy and risky and might just make me happier than I'd known I could be. Who cared about the mistakes of the past? That was then. This, very painfully, was now.

Piers. It was real. What I thought I'd felt for him but not dared to admit even to myself. Was real. Had been real.

I loved him.

I wiped my eyes on the cat again. Caspar squeaked once in

protest but seemed to sense that I needed something warm to hold onto and butted his little nose into my face, clinging to me with his claws. I welcomed the tiny painful sharpnesses into my flesh. I deserved the pain. I'd sent away the man who understood, who cared. Piers, whose presence had finally filled that emptiness inside me which had been there forever. And now I was realising all this—it was too late.

What had I always said to Florence? Make sure you find a man who wants to be your friend first? And what had I done? Found that very man, then let him get away. What the hell had I been *thinking?*

Ring Piers. I should have rung him. He'd probably have his phone off now, on the road, then he'd be at the airport, then he'd be in the air and then—a deep shudder inside. I could barely get my head around the thought. He'd be gone for good. And besides—the sound now piercing my self-created isolation chamber—somebody was ringing *me.*

Should I answer?

"Hello." My voice sounded heavy, unlike me.

"Hey, Ally."

"Piers!" The rush was incredible, sudden sweetness pouring in, like a vein full of sugar. "I..."

"What happened? I came by. Assume you're not coming."

"Piers, I love you. I've been bloody stupid."

"Yeah, I know. Shit, woman, are you going to open this door or not?"

"What?"

A deep sigh at the other end of the phone. "I'm standing on the fucking doorstep now. You gonna open?"

I carried on talking as, dazed, I made my way to the door. "I saw you leave, I missed you—ran after the car." Even after I'd opened the door I carried on speaking into the phone, watching him answering me with his own phone held to his ear. "I thought you'd gone without me."

"Nearly did. But then I thought. That voicemail wasn't exactly one hundred percent clear, y'know? Never believe anyone telling me to fuck off until I can look in their eyes while they say it."

"Do you know something?" I was just about whispering into the receiver. "You are *such* a poser."

Carefully, gently, Piers reached out and pressed the button to disconnect the call. "Yeah."

We missed the flight. And the next one. Piers eventually got us booked on a flight which left from Heathrow and would take us via New York ("Some real cool clothes in NY. Bought this jacket there." "Really? I assumed you'd mugged a pimp. Ow!") which gave me time to arrange that Jace—over the sound of her smugness—would take the cats to live with her for the meantime.

And to attend Mrs. Treadgold's funeral.

As I cried, winding my fingers through Piers's at the graveside, Mrs. Treadgold's words came back to me. *With your true love, you feel that you don't have to hide.* And through my tears came a quiet smile at her surety that Piers and I had been a couple. The knowledge that the love that she'd seen in my eyes had been for him, not as I'd thought for Leo. That Mrs. Treadgold, Jacinta and even Piers had known me better than I'd known myself. Because I'd been so scared of repeating past mistakes.

"I'm not hiding any more," I whispered, dropping a small wreath onto the surprisingly tiny coffin. In deference to Mrs. Treadgold's obsession, the wreath had been worked into the shape of a basket of kittens. "I think I'm found." Then I looked at Piers, modestly dressed in a black leather jacket and jeans, hair respectfully tied back and my heart began to pound. "Or, at least, I'm completely lost in the right way."

Postscript

A year later

I lay on a reclining chair, stretched out beneath the Argentinian sun. Florence, visiting from Italy, lay beside me and a small table between us held tall glasses of chilled water. Ice cubes clinked, but apart from that the only sound was the filter on the swimming pool humming gently to itself, and the cats purring under my chair.

A shadow fell, cooling my skin. "Hey, Ally. How're you doing?"

I struggled to sit up. "Piers, you're back!" Shading my eyes against the sun, I could see him if I squinted, tall and sun-tinted with fair highlights coming out in his hair. He leaned over me and his lips brushed my rounded stomach.

"What, stay away from my girls for longer than I have to? Nah." Then his voice lowered, words for me alone. "Can't be away from you, Ally. Love kinda does that to you."

I laughed, rubbing a hand over the itchy, taut skin. "Yes, and love does this to you as well. Come on, baby, give your daddy a damn good kicking, show him how much you appreciate him being away."

Our unborn daughter rolled lazily beneath my hand and gave her father a leisurely boot. Florence opened her eyes and regarded us from a prone position. "God, you're disgusting, you two. Can't you keep your hands off each other?"

I pointed at my six-month pregnancy. "Evidently not," and Piers grinned.

"You're just jealous, Florrie. Don't worry. Any day now the boys will come knocking."

Florence gave her stepbrother the contemptuous look he deserved and flopped back down onto her sunlounger, adjusting her sunglasses for optimum coverage.

Piers perched alongside me, stretching his long legs out and arching his face up towards the sun. Without looking he reached out and grasped my hand, weaving his fingers through mine. His touch pressed the ruby ring against my palm and I glanced at it.

"What you grinning at, Ally?"

"Nothing." The smile took over my face, my voice. Even the baby seemed to be absorbed in it. "Just life."

And suddenly everything seemed so simple.

About the Author

In a now discredited experiment, Jane was raised as a human being. She lives in the North of Britain with her semi-nomadic family of singers, dancers and mathematicians, and is believed to be the first person to need inoculations and a visa to enter her own house.

She has a patient fiancé, a love of books and sanity that is no longer visible with the naked eye.

To learn more about Jane Lovering, please visit www.JaneLovering.co.uk. It's largely bonkers, but the pictures are lovely. Send an email to mail@JaneLovering.co.uk or join her Yahoo! group to get the latest news on Jane's books, win stuff and chat with other readers.

It's all happening at:

http://groups.yahoo.com/group/janelovering.

There's also www.myspace.com/janelovering. But, you know, save it until you're feeling strong.

Life, love and unlikely legacies.

Reversing Over Liberace
© *2007 Jane Lovering*

Willow runs into Luke, the university lust-of-her-life, ten years on and this time around he's interested—she's lost twenty pounds and found fashion. But their meeting turns out to be no accident. What is Luke *really* after, Willow or her new inheritance?

Her best mate Cal is gorgeous and...well...*gay.* Then reveals himself to be more than a mild, unassuming computer geek and she is no longer sure exactly *who* is telling the truth or who to trust.

Is anyone in her life what they seem to be?

Add to the romantic confusion, twelve pairs of rubber boots, two elderly spaniels, a pregnant sister and the unexpected contents of a matchbox and you get a funny, touching story of a woman in search of revenge and getting what she needs, rather than what she thinks she wants.

Available now in ebook and print from Samhain Publishing.

'Tis the season to get deadly...

Still Waters
© 2008 Kate Johnson

It's a week before Christmas. Sophie is out of work, out of love and out of her depth—literally. Stuck in Cornwall on the holiday from hell with her ex-boyfriend, her boyfriend's ex, and two intimidating colleagues. If that's not enough, Sophie's got her hands full trying to prevent her best friend's perfect engagement from blowing up in her face.

When a corpse turns up in the local harbor it's the perfect distraction...at least until someone tries to add Sophie to the body count.

Tangled love, tangled lives, tangled clues. Now there's a holiday menu Sophie can't resist.

Warning: This title contains bad language, bad behavior and bad puns. There are scenes of violence, gore, and unashamed sentimentality.

Available now in ebook and print from Samhain Publishing.

hot stuff

Discover Samhain!

THE HOTTEST NEW PUBLISHER ON THE PLANET

Romance, fantasy, mystery, thriller, mainstream and
more—Samhain has more selection, hotter authors, and
everything's available in both ebook and print.

Pick your favorite, sit back, and enjoy the ride!
Hot stuff indeed.

WWW.SAMHAINPUBLISHING.COM

GET IT NOW

MyBookStoreAndMore.com
GREAT EBOOKS, GREAT DEALS . . . AND MORE!

Don't wait to run to the bookstore down the street, or
waste time shopping online at one of the "big boys." Now,
all your favorite Samhain authors are all in one place—at
MyBookStoreAndMore.com. Stop by today and discover
great deals on Samhain—and a whole lot more!

WWW.SAMHAINPUBLISHING.COM

GREAT cheap FUN

Discover eBooks!

THE FASTEST WAY TO GET THE HOTTEST NAMES

Get your favorite authors on your favorite reader, long before they're out in print! Ebooks from Samhain go wherever you go, and work with whatever you carry—Palm, PDF, Mobi, and more.

Samhain
puDlishing
Ltd

WWW.SAMHAINPUBLISHING.COM

CPSIA information can be obtained at www.ICGtesting.com
Printed in the USA
LVOW052009050313

322843LV00001B/109/P

9 781605 043098